Sign up for our newsletter to hear
about new and upcoming releases.

www.ylva-publishing.com

# Other Books by Jae

Happily Ever After

**Standalone Romances:**
Wrong Number, Right Woman
The Roommate Arrangement
Paper Love
Just for Show
Falling Hard
Heart Trouble
Under a Falling Star
Something in the Wine
Shaken to the Core

**Fair Oaks Series:**
Perfect Rhythm
Not the Marrying Kind

**The Hollywood Series:**
Departure from the Script
Damage Control
Just Physical
The Hollywood Collection (box set)

**Portland Police Bureau Series:**
Conflict of Interest
Next of Kin

**The Vampire Diet Series:**
Good Enough to Eat

**The Oregon Series:**
Backwards to Oregon
Beyond the Trail
Hidden Truths
The Complete Oregon series (box set)

**The Shape-Shifter Series:**
Second Nature
Natural Family Disasters
Manhattan Moon
True Nature

# Chemistry Lessons

Jae

# Acknowledgments

Like Regan and Kylie, the characters you are about to meet, I'm blessed with a wonderful group of friends and family—by blood and by choice—who support me and have my eternal gratitude.

Many of my readers and beta readers feel like part of that circle too. A big thank-you in particular to Melanie, Trish, Chris Zett, Erin, and Laure for beta reading; to Anne-France for making sure I portrayed Regan's teaching background accurately; to A.C. for providing inside knowledge about Portland; to Mari for double-checking the chemistry (the one between the characters and the one in test tubes!); and to Carmen for her insights on working in a school cafeteria. Kylie was relieved to hear she could ditch the hairnet!

Thanks also to my editors, Helen and Claire, and to my proofreaders, Maggie, Julie, and Louisa.

The awesome members of my Facebook group for readers provided me with help and motivation along the way, and two of them—Mindy M. and Meredith S.—picked Regan's and Lilia's names respectively. You chose well!

Last but never least, I'm grateful to every single reader who keeps reading my books, writing reviews, and letting me know how much they enjoy my work. Keep reading, and I'll keep writing!

# Chapter 1

Where on earth was Regan? A surprise party was hard to pull off when the unsuspecting guest of honor was late.

Kylie paced her room and checked the messaging app on her phone for the fifth time.

Still not a peep from her best friend.

Before she could text her again, her phone rang with the *Rizzoli and Isles* theme tune. "Regan! Finally! Where are you?"

"Whoa, hold your horses. I'm on my way." Traffic sounds indicated that Regan was in the car and had her phone connected to Bluetooth. "Since when are you so eager to get to Home Depot?"

They weren't going to Home Depot; that was only the excuse Ky had used so she could lure Regan to their favorite neighborhood restaurant, where their friends were waiting. "What can I say? It's a lesbian thing."

Regan chuckled. "Sorry to make you wait for your happy place. It really wasn't my fault. Mrs. Kallmaker wanted to have a talk just as I was getting ready to leave."

"You got called into the principal's office?" Laughter bubbled up from deep in Ky's chest, and every bit of tension fled her body. "Some things never change."

"I have no idea what you're talking about," Regan said but didn't manage to sound very innocent at all.

"Oh yeah? Let's see… There was the time you talked me into replacing all the markers from the whiteboard with tampons, the time when you thought TP-ing the gym was a bright idea, and I lost track of all the times we ended up in detention for being late or passing notes in class."

Regan laughed. "Okay, okay, I might have gotten in trouble a time or two."

"A time or two?" Ky echoed. "Ha! The only reason you weren't in trouble every single day as a kid was because you fooled everyone with those big, brown eyes, cute nose, and perfect-angel curls of yours! I still can't believe you became a teacher, much less our district's Teacher of the Year!"

"What can I say? Must be my big, brown eyes."

Even without seeing her, Ky knew Regan was batting her eyelashes in an exaggerated fashion.

Truth be told, in Ky's admittedly biased opinion, no one deserved that award more than Regan. She was an amazing teacher who cared deeply for her students and always went the extra mile for them. Maybe if Ky had had a teacher like that, she wouldn't have almost dropped out of high school.

"You okay?" Regan asked.

Ky cleared her throat. "Yeah." She left her room to grab her jacket. Since she lived only half a mile from Hamilton High School, Regan should be pulling up any second. Her roommate was lounging on the couch, headphones on, so Ky merely waved as she passed her. "So, what did Mrs. Kallmaker want? You aren't really in trouble, are you?"

"Define trouble."

Ky grinned. "What did you do?"

"Nothing. I just gave an interview to our school newspaper, and apparently, someone's mom didn't like my answer to one of the questions."

"Oh, let me guess." Ky left their ground-floor apartment to wait for Regan outside. "The article's dramatic headline was 'Popular chemistry teacher Ms. Romano is having a sordid fling with Kylie Wells, the irresistible lunch lady.'"

Regan's booming laugh blasted through the phone.

Even after twenty-five years, it still amazed Ky that a laugh like that could come out of such a tiny person.

"No," Regan said once her laughter had softened to a light giggle. "It's been a couple of years since the school tabloid last wrote about our imaginary affair. Apparently, we're old news."

A honk sounded, and Regan's Toyota Yaris pulled into the parking lot.

Ky trotted over, swung open the passenger-side door, and dropped onto the seat. She put the phone away and reached for the seat belt. "So if it wasn't that, what got the mom's panties in a twist?"

Regan pulled back onto Division and gave Ky a quick sidelong glance. Her dark, curly hair was even more tousled than usual, springing in every direction. "The students asked me how I got into chemistry."

"Oh no. You told them about helping *Unonn* make his homemade wine as a kid, didn't you?" Regan's Italian grandfather had been a man of few words, but he'd made the best red wine Ky had ever tasted.

"I was talking about how much fun it was to figure out the right ratio of sugar and yeast for the fermenting process. Apparently, that's promoting the abuse of alcohol among minors." Regan threw up one hand and gestured wildly.

Ky nervously eyed the steering wheel, half expecting her to let go with the other hand too. "So are you in hot water with your boss now?"

"No. Luckily, she backed me up. I just wish some parents would pay as much attention to their kids' behavior as they obviously do mine."

"Don't I know it. Remember the dad of the freshman with the dairy allergy from last week?"

Regan winced. "Yeah, that was bad. Miranda was on lunchroom duty that day. She said she could hear him shout at you from across the room, accusing you of contaminating the non-dairy area during lunch prep."

Ky leaned forward in her seat so she could rotate her tense shoulders. "Guess what? Today, I caught Junior with a bag of cheddar chips on his tray."

Regan let out a loud *tsk*. "Are you sure you want the promotion they offered you? As an assistant cafeteria manager, you'll probably have to deal with parents on a regular basis."

If Ky was honest with herself, she wasn't sure at all. But now wasn't the time to discuss it. This was Regan's special evening, so Ky shrugged and focused on pulling off her surprise.

When they approached Washington Street, where Regan would have to turn right to take them to Home Depot, sweat broke out along Ky's back. Of course she'd prepared an excuse to lure Regan to Stark Street instead, but could she manage a casual delivery? That was the one disadvantage of having the same best friend since kindergarten: Regan knew all her lying tells.

Just as Ky opened her mouth to suggest a quick stop at the Bipartisan Café for Regan's favorite cookies, Regan pointed up ahead toward the next intersection. "Do you mind if we stop at the sewing center for a second? Denny asked if I could pick her up some sewing machine oil since we would be in the neighborhood."

Wow, that worked out great! If Ky remembered correctly, the sewing center wasn't far from the restaurant. She reined in a grin. "Oh, sure, yeah. No problem." She snapped her mouth shut before she could give herself away.

"Ooh, a parking spot!" Regan pumped her fist and made a quick left turn into SE Stark.

Um, wasn't the sewing center to the right? But Ky wasn't about to say anything because the parking spot Regan pulled into was directly in front of The Observatory. She couldn't believe her luck.

When Regan rounded the car to join Ky on the sidewalk, they were in the perfect position to spring the surprise on her friend, only two steps from the restaurant's front door. God, this was going almost too well.

"Surprise!" Ky yelled.

"Surprise!" Regan's louder shout nearly drowned out Ky's voice. "We're not going to Home Depot!"

They stared at each other.

What the hell was going on? Ky squinted down at her best friend. "We're not? I mean, I know we're not, but…how do you know?" If one of their friends had given it away, she'd kill them.

"What? Of course I know. It was my idea."

Ky shook her head, but that didn't help her see the situation more clearly. "What are you talking about?"

A mischievous twinkle entered Regan's eyes as she tilted her head and grinned. "I planned a surprise dinner to celebrate your promotion!" She swept her arm in a wide gesture toward the restaurant. "Ta-da!"

Ky gaped at her. No, that wasn't possible, was it? What were the chances of them planning a surprise party for each other—at the same time and day, at the same restaurant?

Regan nudged her shoulder. "You didn't suspect a thing, did you?"

"Hell, no! I thought I'd lured you here for a surprise dinner to celebrate your Teacher of the Year award."

"Oh my God!" Regan burst out laughing, making the people at the sidewalk tables look over. "That's why our friends gave me these weird looks when I told them to meet us here."

They doubled over laughing and clutched each other's arms until the glass door swung open and Eliza stepped outside in her trademark yellow sneakers. "Double surprise! I take it you realized you both had the same idea?"

Still breathless with laughter, Ky just nodded.

"Are you coming in, or are we throwing the confetti and putting on the party hats right here?" Eliza asked.

Ky glowered at her. "I said no confetti, no party hats, no balloons. Just food and conversation. You stuck to that promise, didn't you?"

Eliza grinned and held the door open more widely. "Come in and find out."

When the waitress slid the plate with the chicken curry salad wrap in front of her, Regan barely kept herself from salivating. "That looks great, thanks."

The young woman leaned across the wood table toward Ky, who had claimed her customary seat next to Regan in the window booth. She placed the pulled-pork sandwich in front of Ky and gave her a smile. "Cool eyebrow slit." She tapped her own brow next to the piercing she wore.

"Thanks." Ky didn't return the smile or tell her the gap in her eyebrow wasn't a fashion statement. The scar bisecting her left eyebrow was a reminder of their childhood, when Ky had face-planted into the wooden top rung of the rope ladder leading up to the tree house Regan's mom had built for them. Regan still felt guilty because she'd been daring Ky to climb faster.

Ky tugged the sideswept bangs of her otherwise short, brown hair over her eyebrow and brushed her shoulder against Regan's as if sensing her moment of guilt. She gave the waitress a fleeting nod without making eye contact.

Regan bit back a smile. Her friend could be a tough nut to crack and showed her more goofy side mostly when it was just the two of them. She likely hadn't even noticed the waitress's subtle flirting.

A mouth-watering scent rose up when Ky cut the ciabatta bun, piled high with pulled pork and coleslaw, in half.

*Yum.* Good thing Regan didn't have to decide between her two favorite dishes on the happy hour menu.

Without a word, she and Ky started their usual exchange. Regan deposited half her wrap on Ky's plate while Ky slid the slightly bigger part of the sandwich over to her.

Heather stared at them with her fork hovering over her sesame chili chicken salad and gave them a slow shake of her head. "God, that's so gay." She glanced around the table, first at Denny and Eliza, who were sharing the last piece of oregano fry bread they'd ordered as a starter, then at Miranda. "Do straight people do that too?"

Regan's colleague, the only straight person at the table, looked up from her veggie burger. "Do what?"

Heather waved her fork toward Regan and Ky. "Share food with their significant other."

Ky had been just about to take a bite from her half of the sandwich. Now she snapped her mouth shut with an audible *clack*.

Regan exchanged a look with her. *There we go again.* For some reason, their friends loved making remarks like that.

"She's not my significant other," they said in unison.

"Of course straight people do that. At least some of them." Miranda laughed. "Not me, though. If I tried to take half of my husband's food, he'd stab me with his fork!"

Had Miranda and the rest of the gang even heard their protest? Admittedly, with The Observatory's casual, lively atmosphere and every table filled, the restaurant was a little noisy.

Regan straightened her five-foot-two frame to catch her friends' attention. "She's not my significant other," she repeated. Then she grinned over at Ky and caught her familiar eyes. Their color defied description, especially in the fading light that filtered in through the skylight and the low glow of the star-shaped lamp above the booth. "I mean, this one's pretty significant to me"—she nudged Ky's solid thigh with her own—"but we're not an item."

Miranda shrugged. "Oh, whatever you want to label it. I might be straight, but I'm not narrow."

Regan glanced toward the long bar and the bottles lined up behind it. Christ, she needed a drink—something stronger than the house red she'd ordered. Miranda had joined Hamilton High School as a social studies teacher in September, and they'd become fast friends. Had she assumed she and Ky were together the entire time?

"No, that's not what I..." Regan sent Ky an imploring look. "Feel free to jump in any time."

"She's right," Ky said. "We're just friends."

Regan scrunched up her nose. *Ugh.* She hated that phrase with the fiery intensity of a thousand supernovas. To her, friendships were as important as romantic relationships.

"Not *just*," Ky quickly added before Regan could say anything. "I know you hate that phrase. I meant, we're friends. Best friends."

"Friends who tease, bicker, and share food like an old, married couple," Eliza threw in with a smile.

Ky glared at her. With her serious exterior and her bold features, which were striking rather than traditionally beautiful, she could intimidate even the unruliest teenager, but Eliza's grin didn't waver as she leaned into Denny's shoulder.

"Wait!" Miranda waved a parmesan-sprinkled garlic fry back and forth between Regan and Ky. "You mean you two are really not...?"

"No."

"Oh." Miranda actually looked disappointed.

Eliza reached across the table and patted her arm. "Don't feel bad. I assumed the same when Heather introduced us last summer. It took Denny and me until Christmas to figure out they're not an item."

Seriously? Regan gaped at her. Granted, they had all known each other for less than a year. Heather had started working in the cafeteria for a couple of hours in between her runs as a school bus driver last May. As different as they were, Ky and Heather had instantly hit it off, and when they had introduced their friends to each other, it quickly felt as if they had all known each other forever. But maybe the gang didn't know them as well as Regan had assumed. "Why does everyone keep thinking we're together? Why can't two queer women be friends without everyone assuming they're—"

Several people at surrounding tables looked over.

Damn. Had she been that loud? Regan bit her lip.

"Knocking boots," Heather suggested when Regan didn't continue.

"Making whoopie," Eliza added.

Miranda grinned. "Sharing a carnal embrace."

They all looked at Denny, the shyest person in their friend group, as if waiting for her to contribute something.

Regan used the moment to reach over and try to steal the pickle garnish from Ky's plate.

Without even glancing at her, Ky batted her fingers away but then relented and handed it over.

Denny's cheeks reddened, but she gamely added, "Doing the no-pants dance."

Regan and Ky shared a why-are-we-friends-with-them-again look.

"We're not doing any of that with each other." Regan spoke slowly, as if explaining thermodynamics to the kids in the last row.

"Or anyone else," Heather said. "It's been ages since either of you went on a date. You even take Kylie as a plus-one to all of your family events and don't even try to get an actual date."

"So what? My family loves Ky. They would disinherit me if I didn't bring her. That doesn't mean we're a couple. Why does everyone keep thinking we are?" Regan shoved most of the pickle into her mouth and chewed vigorously.

"Oh, I don't know." Eliza pointed at the pickle Regan was munching on. "Maybe because of the way you're taking food off each other's plates."

"But—" Regan struggled to speak around the mouthful of pickle.

"—that's what friends do," Ky said for her.

"Or the way you finish each other's sentences," Heather added with a smirk.

Denny took a swig of her beer. "Or those book club meetings you had last year."

"Why can't two friends have a book club?" Ky asked.

"It's not the fact that you had a book club. It's that it was a two-person book club. It never occurred to you to invite anyone else to join you."

*Oops.* Regan rubbed her earlobe. She looked at Ky, and they both shrugged.

When they'd been kids, her parents used to worry about them barely having any other close friends and playing only with each other, but Regan had never felt as if she was missing out. And now that she was an adult, she had made this wonderful group of friends—even if they wouldn't let go of this ridiculous idea of her and Ky as a couple.

"It's not because Ky and I wanted to be alone so we could whisper sweet nothings to each other or anything," Regan told them. "It's just that…" How could she explain it? Why did she even *have to* explain it?

Ky threw the French fry she'd been about to eat back onto her plate. "We—are—not—a—couple. Period."

"Too bad," Eliza said quietly. "You would be perfect for each other."

"Come on!" Regan gestured at Eliza and Denny. "Just because you two lovebirds are the poster children for a deliriously happy relationship doesn't mean everyone else has to pair up. Ky and I are great as friends, but we have no chemistry. None. Zero. Zip. Zilch."

"How can you be so sure if you've never tried it?" Miranda asked. "Um, I mean, gone on a date. Not…"

"A carnal embrace," Heather supplied.

Ky shook her head at them. "You're asking Regan of all people if she's sure about a chemistry thing? Of course she is. If anyone knows about chemistry, it's her. She teaches chemistry after all and has just won an award for it." Her fierce look softened into a proud smile. She lifted her wineglass. "Let's drink to that and stop this fruitless discussion."

As they clinked glasses, their gazes met over the rims.

"To you and your award," Ky said. "I'm so proud of you."

The look in Ky's eyes filled Regan with warmth. "Not half as proud as I am of you, Ms. Assistant Cafeteria Manager."

Ky lowered her head. "Um, about that… I—"

Heather reached across the table and nudged her. "That's our Ky! Modest as always."

Ky looked up. "Kylie," she said firmly.

"But *she* calls you Ky all the time." Heather pointed her fork at Regan.

"Yeah. I don't know why, but that's different. It feels wrong if anyone else calls me that."

Heather shook her head. "And you wonder why everyone keeps thinking the two of you are a couple…or should be one?"

"New rule, everyone!" Regan used her teacher voice to get their attention. "The next person to bring it up pays tonight's bill."

As they all hastily found other things to discuss, Regan gave Ky a satisfied nod. It wasn't that she minded being mistaken for Ky's girlfriend. In her opinion, the woman who finally took Ky off the market for good should consider herself lucky. But it wouldn't be her. She and Ky were like two substances that didn't react with each other, at least not in a romantic way. You could mix them together, but there would be no chemical reaction whatsoever.

Now the question was just: How could she teach their stubborn friends this simple chemistry lesson?

# Chapter 2

*Shit, shit, shit.* Regan's flats squeaked on the linoleum floor as she rushed down the hallway connecting the school's main building and the west wing, where her chemistry classroom was located.

God, she hated mornings—especially Monday mornings. Not the best trait for a teacher to have, but even after teaching for six years, she hadn't learned to embrace getting up at five thirty. Once she got to school, she was fine. Preparing for the day ahead and seeing the kids come in always gave her a jolt of energy.

Usually, she arrived at school at least an hour before the students did so she could get the materials together for class, but today, she had hit the snooze button one too many times. Okay, a few too many times.

Now she didn't even have time to stop at the teachers' lounge for a cup of coffee.

She skidded into her classroom. The bright fluorescent lights flared on as she hit the switch in passing. She didn't take the time to nod a good morning to Marie, Alice, Rosalind, and the other famous female chemists whose posters hung on the walls.

She forced herself to slow down as she gathered up the equipment—beakers, test tubes, and microspatulas—and then got the chemicals she would need for today's lessons from the locked cabinets in the prep room.

It only took her a few minutes to set up five stations in the lab area of the classroom.

A grin tugged on her lips as she cut a section of magnesium ribbon into pieces. She couldn't wait to see the kids' faces when the magnesium reacted with the hydrochloric acid.

They loved that kind of hands-on chemistry. Of course, their enthusiasm would fade quickly once they began the daunting task of writing down the chemical equations for the reactions they had observed. Regan chuckled.

Her stomach gave a loud growl as she set down packages of sugar on the last lab station. She'd rushed out of the house without breakfast. *It's not a snack,* she told her digestive system. Dissolving sugar in water was the experiment she used to show her students that not every two substances you put together had a chemical reaction.

*Kinda like Ky and me.*

If only there was an experiment as simple as the one she would show her students today that would convince their friends there really was no chemistry between them.

Regan finished her lab prep with five minutes to spare. *Damn. Not enough time to get a coffee.*

She walked over to her desk to turn on her laptop—then paused mid-step.

A gleaming silver travel mug sat in the middle of her desk, next to a cinnamon almond granola bar and a note.

Regan knew without reading it who'd left her this emergency breakfast. *Aww.* Ky was the best. She always had Regan's back, even if it meant she had to get to school earlier than her six-thirty start time.

With a groan of appreciation, Regan perched on her desk and reached for the note.

*You stayed up too late and overslept, didn't you?* it said in Ky's messy handwriting that only she could read.

Even though Ky couldn't see it, Regan nodded ruefully. She'd been up late, putting together a practice exam for her AP students and tweaking the worksheets for today's labs in an attempt to make the lesson more interesting for the kids. Over the past few years, she'd gotten better about carving out time for herself and not letting her job take over her life, but it still happened every now and then, and Ky seemed to have a sixth sense for when she needed coffee or a snack.

On paper, the rule about not eating in the chemistry classroom was pretty strict, and Regan always avoided doing it near her desk, which doubled as a demonstration table, so she took her bounty over to the bookshelf.

Eagerly, she ripped open the wrapper, devoured the granola bar in three bites, and washed it down with a big gulp of coffee. *Yum.* Ky had made the coffee exactly the way Regan liked it, strong and sweet.

Another sip of the lifesaving beverage, then she put it on the bookshelf and pulled her laptop and the stack of worksheets from her briefcase.

The top sheet fluttered to the floor.

As she bent and picked it up, her gaze landed on one of the questions the kids would need to answer.

*Is there any evidence that indicates a chemical reaction?*

Hmm. Evidence. Maybe that—or rather the lack thereof—was what their friends needed to finally believe there was no chemistry between her and Ky.

Grinning, she opened her laptop just as the first students filed into the room.

Yep. A little experiment might be in order…even though the results would be much less spectacular than those of today's lab experiments.

Steam rose as Ky stirred the marinara sauce in the forty-gallon tilt skillet with a huge stainless-steel paddle. She lifted her nose and deeply inhaled the aroma of tomatoes and basil.

Pasta day in the school cafeteria always took her back to her childhood, when she had spent more time at Regan's house than her own, fleeing her parents' constant arguing. Every Sunday, she had helped *Anonn* and later Regan's father prepare Neapolitan *ragù*.

Of course, the simple pasta dishes on the school's menu couldn't compare to the wonderful recipes Regan's grandmother had brought with her from Italy.

Ky often wondered what *Anonn* would think of her job as a cafeteria worker. Would she have been proud, or would she have crossed herself and been horrified at the paint-by-numbers cooking?

For sure she would have declared the canned tomato purée and the dried spices a heresy.

District, state, and federal rules and regulations limited what ingredients Ky could use, and she certainly didn't have the time to let the sauce simmer for six hours, as *Anonn*'s recipe called for. But at least Hamilton High

School's cafeteria made some of their dishes from scratch or semi-scratch instead of just reheating pre-cooked frozen meals, like many other school cafeterias.

Ky dipped a spoon into the sauce to try it. The sweet-and-sour flavors mingled on her tongue, making her hum.

While being on the cafeteria staff wasn't her dream job, it was decent work, and the team was great. Dream jobs were overrated anyway. Her father had constantly strived for more money, more accolades, more luxuries, and in the end, it had cost him everything. Ky wouldn't make the same mistake.

Fran, the cafeteria manager, squeezed past her with a baking sheet of hot rolls, startling Ky out of her thoughts. "Is the sauce ready to go on the line?"

"Yeah." Ky held out a clean spoon. "Do you want to taste it?"

"No. You haven't poisoned anyone yet. Get it out there."

That was the biggest compliment she'd get from her no-nonsense boss. Ky checked the sauce's temperature, then turned the skillet off and hit the tilt button.

The back of the rectangular skillet lifted up toward her, emptying the sauce into a large container Ky had placed beneath it.

Lilia Fernandez, her roommate and colleague, came over with the pasta, and they mixed it with the sauce in several big hotel pans, then put the lids on. Together, they slid the pans into the serving counter.

Moments later, the lunch bell rang. The cafeteria's double doors crashed open, and a wave of chatter, shouts, and laughter swept over them.

Ky straightened her apron and school polo. "Here they come." She took her position at the serving station and braced for the onslaught of hungry teenagers.

Her lunch lady autopilot kicked in as she dished pasta onto trays, urged the kids to take some steamed veggies or a fruit cup, and kept an eye on the students with known allergies.

As one teen paused before her, trying to decide whether a scoop of broccoli would kill him, something made Ky look up and toward the end of the line, where Regan was just picking up a tray.

She was one of few teachers who occasionally braved the lunchroom, while most of her colleagues preferred to eat in their classrooms or the teachers' lounge. Ky couldn't blame them. Chairs scraped the floor, trays clattered onto tables, and the kids created a noise level that rivaled an airplane during takeoff.

Having Regan come through her line was always special. If it had been up to Ky, she would have gotten to cook for her every day.

Regan laughed at something the kid ahead of her said. Her signature laugh boomed through the cafeteria, making Ky smile. She wasn't wearing anything special, just a pair of olive skinny jeans with her long-sleeved *Let's get chemical* T-shirt and what Ky called her teacher cardigan draped across her shoulders. The students surrounding her topped her height, but somehow, Regan still stood out.

When they made eye contact, a big grin spread across Regan's face. She mimed drinking, then bowed as if worshipping a goddess and mouthed, "Thank you."

"You're welcome," Ky mouthed back. When they'd exchanged a few texts last night, Regan had still been up to her neck in lessons prep, so Ky had known she would stay up late, oversleep, and rush to school without having time for coffee.

The teenager in front of Ky cleared his throat. "Apple?" He drew out the word slowly, as if she otherwise wouldn't grasp its meaning—probably because he'd repeated it several times already.

*Oops.* Ky quickly put one of the shiny apples on his tray and returned her attention to the lunch line. While she served pasta and sauce, Regan's laughter drifted over a couple of times as she chatted with students.

Finally, Regan reached her station. "Has anyone ever told you you're a lifesaver?"

"Yeah, I think the quarterback mumbled something like that." Ky pointed a gloved finger at one of the round tables in the middle of the lunchroom, where some players of the high school's football team sat.

"Oh, did he get coffee and a granola bar delivered to his classroom too?"

"Nope. We reserve that kind of service for our Teacher of the Year."

"We, huh?" Regan's snub nose scrunched up as she grinned, making the smattering of freckles across it stand out even more. "Does that mean Lilia is going to start bringing me coffee too?"

"Only if you pay me," Lilia called from where she was refilling the fruit cups.

The kids in line behind Regan began to shuffle their feet and inch their trays forward.

*Damn.* Time to move on. "So, pasta?"

"What else?" Regan held out her tray, and Ky deposited a generous serving of spaghetti and sauce onto it, then spooned parmesan on top.

"Roll?" She held out one of the dinner rolls with a pair of tongs.

"Of course." Regan gave her a playful wink and leaned across the counter to whisper, "You know I can never resist your buns."

*Jesus.* Heat rose up Ky's chest. Why did her best friend have to be such a flirt? The kids couldn't know she was only joking around and had managed to resist Ky's "buns" just fine all these years. She tugged on the collar of her school polo and peered at the students, who, luckily, were engrossed in their phone screens. As a punishment, she heaped green beans onto Regan's tray, knowing she hated them, and handed it back with a grin. "Enjoy your meal."

Regan wrinkled her nose. "Thanks. See you tonight."

"Oh?" Monday wasn't their Netflix night, and neither was it their usual time to play *The Last of Us*.

"Yeah," Regan said while already walking away. "You're coming over so I can make you dinner and tell you about an idea I had."

A groan escaped Ky. She wasn't sure what was more dangerous: Regan making dinner or having one of her infamous ideas.

Regan's unruly locks bounced with every step as she marched toward the checkout, practically vibrating with excitement. Once she had punched her four-digit number into the keypad, she threw one last glance back at Ky and flashed her familiar troublemaker grin—the one that had gotten Ky grounded a time or two as a kid.

*Oh shit.* Ky had a feeling Regan's idea would turn out to be more dangerous than her cooking.

If only dating had been more like hanging out with her best friend, Regan might have done it more often. There was no panicked last-minute cleaning and no need to dress up when Ky came over. They could just sprawl on the couch side by side like two sloths, sometimes even in baggy sweatpants and no bras. Plus she didn't have to try to impress Ky by preparing a lavish meal.

Her movements had none of Ky's practiced elegance as she sliced the tomatoes, but thankfully, Ky never tried to chef-splain. After being on her feet all day, Ky seemed content to crash on the couch and wiggle her feet on the coffee table.

Regan peeked around the fridge and stuck her head out of her small kitchen so she could get a glimpse of her in the living area. The sight of Ky made her smile. She was the only person Regan knew who still wore boot-cut jeans, but she had to admit Ky wore them well. They emphasized her slim waist, broad hips, and sturdy thighs.

"What?" Ky asked without opening her eyes. "Want me to help?"

"No, I've got it." Regan slathered red pepper spread on two ciabatta buns and piled slices of ham on top. "I might not have inherited my family's cooking gene, but I can make sandwiches with the best of them."

Ky let out a grunt of agreement. "True. I never got why you can be a chemistry genius but have no talent for cooking. Our jobs are not that different from each other, you know?"

Regan chuckled and peered past the fridge again. "You mean they both pay like shit?"

Ky's angular face softened as she laughed. "That too. But I meant mixing chemicals together is a lot like following the steps of a recipe, right?"

"Kind of, but when you're doing a lab, you'd better not..."

"...lick the spoon," they finished the sentence together.

An easy silence fell, interrupted only by the hum of the oven. That was another advantage of hanging out with her best friend: Regan never felt as if she had to make conversation, which was a wonderful change of pace after having to talk all day.

"Oh, I nearly forgot." Ky padded to the door, where she'd left her backpack. "I brought the salami you like. Want to put some on your sandwich?" She appeared in the U-shaped kitchen area and held up her offering.

"Where did you get it? It looks like the soppressata my parents buy for the restaurant." Regan took the salami, sliced off a bit, and popped it into her mouth. "Mmm. Tastes like it too."

Ky chuckled. "That's because it is. Your parents sent me a package of goodies last week."

Regan leaned against one of the honey-colored kitchen cabinets and stuck out her bottom lip in a pretend pout. "Why are they sending you all my favorite food stuff?"

"Probably because they know I'm the cook in the family." Ky paused and swiped her bangs from her wide forehead with the back of her hand while lowering her gaze to the tiles. "Uh, I mean…"

"Hey." Regan put the knife and the salami down and gently bumped her with one hip, but since Ky was taller and heavier, she didn't manage to move her even an inch. "Of course you're family."

Ky was like a sister.

She considered it for a moment. No, that wasn't quite true. Their relationship was different from the one she had with Mackenzie or Robbie, her older siblings, although Regan couldn't explain what made it different. It just…was.

Regan wrapped one arm around Ky and leaned against her. Pain and longing radiated off Ky like heat from a pizza oven. She returned the half-embrace more tightly than she probably realized. Regan cradled her carefully and tried not to stiffen up as she gritted her teeth. She could have killed Ky's parents for doing this to her.

*Ugh.* Good thing she hadn't said that out loud. It would have only reminded Ky that her mother was dead…and her father might as well be. Ky had barely spoken to him since he'd gone to prison when she'd been sixteen, not even after he'd been released.

Softly, she squeezed Ky's shoulder. "You know my parents consider you the daughter they never had, right?"

Ky peered up from the floor. "They have two daughters."

"They have three. And some days, I think you're their favorite."

"Am not," Ky grumbled, but a hint of a smile played around her lips.

"Are too, and you know it. Come on. Help me get these sandwiches into the oven, or I'll never get around to telling you about my brilliant idea."

Preparing food always seemed to cheer Ky up, and Regan hoped it would work this time too.

Ky squeezed back, then let go.

They worked together, shredding lettuce and slicing mozzarella and soppressata without getting in each other's way, even though the kitchen in Regan's apartment was tiny.

Maybe Ky had been right. Cooking could be just as much fun as chemistry—at least with the right lab partner.

By the time they settled down on the couch with their sandwiches, Ky had nearly forgotten her moment of weakness. With anyone else, she would have been embarrassed, but Regan had lived through all of the low points of her life with her. She'd been there when Ky's father had been caught embezzling money their junior year of high school, when Ky's mom had filed for a divorce shortly after and moved them halfway across the state, and when her mother had overdosed on Xanax and alcohol the day before Ky's twenty-first birthday.

Not once had Regan's support wavered, not even during the years they'd spent apart, with them finishing high school in different places, then Regan going to college while Ky had worked in fast-food joints and stocked shelves in supermarkets. She had always found a way to be there for Ky.

Regan bounced up and down on the couch next to her as if to jostle Ky out of her contemplative mood. "Stop thinking broody thoughts and eat. Your sandwich's getting cold."

"How do you know I'm thinking broody thoughts?"

"You get this deep wrinkle right here." Regan tapped Ky's forehead right above her eyebrow scar.

Ky reached up and touched the spot. She had a wrinkle there? "Really?"

Regan grinned and took a bite of her sandwich. "No," she said after barely having swallowed. "I just...know. Now eat, or I'll steal your sandwich as soon as I finish mine."

Ky knew it wasn't an empty threat. Regan might not have inherited her grandmother's or her father's cooking skills, but she definitely had their appetite. Ky held on to her sandwich more firmly and lifted it to her mouth. The melted cheese, the crispy bread, and the spicy pepper spread harmonized into a perfect symphony of flavors and textures on her tongue. "Oh my God." She let her head fall back against the couch and moaned.

"Forget what I said about you not knowing how to cook. I'd choose this over dinner at a Michelin-star-worthy restaurant any time."

Regan swallowed another bite of her own sandwich. "I bet you say that to all the women who cook for you."

"Women? What women? It's been ages since I went on a date." She had Regan, so her life felt complete, even without her dating.

"Um, yeah, that's kinda what I wanted to talk to you about." Regan put her ciabatta bun down and wiped her hands on a napkin. "I hate to admit it, but Heather was right about what she said."

Ky paused with her sandwich hovering in front of her lips and squinted over at Regan. She couldn't possibly mean…? Did Regan honestly think there could be any chemistry between them? Despite the warm sandwich in her hands, cold crept through her body, forming a lump of ice in her belly. Regan couldn't suspect that once, many years ago, Ky had had a bit of a crush on her…could she?

Regan laughed. "Now you've really got a wrinkle there." She rubbed at it with her index finger.

*Phew.* Ky slowly exhaled and batted her hand away. She was imagining things. Regan didn't know. There *was* nothing to know. It had been just a silly teenage thing, and clueless adolescent fantasies aside, she had never seriously considered acting on it. Back then, she hadn't even known Regan liked girls as well as boys. Hell, Regan hadn't figured it out either.

And then Ky's father had been arrested, and her whole world had collapsed, with only one constant remaining: Regan and her family.

Thank God she had been clever enough, even at sixteen, to never blurt out her feelings and risk her sanctuary.

Now that childish infatuation no longer mattered. She had gotten over it many years ago.

"I don't have any wrinkles." Scowling, she tugged her bangs down over her forehead.

"Well, you're older than me, so…"

Ky snorted. "By one month and sixteen days." She took a bite of her sandwich to settle her queasy stomach. "So," she finally said, "what is it that you think Heather was right about?"

"It's been longer than I care to admit since I…both of us…have been in a relationship."

As far as Ky was concerned, relationships were overrated. None of them had ever lived up to her expectations—and she certainly never seemed to live up to her girlfriends' expectations either. "And that's a problem why?" At least while they were both single, there was no one to nag them about how much time they spent with each other.

"It's not," Regan said. "Other than it's making our friends think we should go out with each other."

Ky stared at her across the length of her sandwich. "You want to get involved with someone just so they finally shut up about us?"

Regan jabbed her with her shoulder. "God, no. But when I set up the lab for my kids this morning, I had an idea."

"Does it involve poison ivy?"

Regan flicked a bit of bread at her. "You'll never let me live that one down, will you?"

"Nope." Ky popped the piece of ciabatta into her mouth. "After all, I had a rash for weeks. Fran had to put me on bread duty, telling me to stay in the back, so the kids would stop staring."

"It's not like that this time. This idea really is brilliant. I think I know how we can get everyone to shut up about us once and for all."

"All right, let's hear it."

Instead of blurting it out, Regan stuffed the remainder of her sandwich into her mouth and chewed it thoroughly.

What was going on? Regan wasn't normally one to hold back. Ky waited none too patiently.

"You know what we do in science to prove that two substances don't react with each other?"

"You're asking me?" Ky tapped her chest. "I barely managed a passing grade in chemistry, despite all your tutoring."

"Okay, I'll tell you. We conduct an experiment."

Ky nearly choked on her last bite of sandwich. What on earth was Regan suggesting?

Regan's booming laughter filled the one-bedroom apartment. "Get your mind out of the gutter, Kylie Wells. Not that kind of experiment. In my chem class, we put two substances together and watch for indications of a chemical reaction. If there's no heat, odor, gas bubbles, or any other sign, we conclude that there's—"

"No chemistry," Ky finished for her.

"Exactly. So if you and I go on a date and there's no—"

"Odor or gas?" Ky threw in with a grin.

Regan glared, but with her pink cheeks, cute nose, and petite frame, she was the least intimidating person Ky knew. "If there's no heat or any other changes…" She swept her arm as if presenting a magic trick.

Ky dabbed at a splash of pepper spread on her empty plate while she thought about it. Somehow, it didn't sound like a brilliant idea. If something went wrong, it would burn much more than the poison ivy rash. "I don't know, Regan."

"Why not? The results of that experiment are totally predictable. We've had more sleepovers than I can count. We've bathed together naked several times."

"In an inflatable pool when we were five!"

Regan waved her protest aside. "Hell, we even kissed!"

They both wrinkled their noses.

Okay, that one definitely wasn't going down in history as the world's hottest kiss. Mostly, it had been sticky, awkward, and kinda cute. "What did you expect? We were in first grade."

"My point is that there's never been any chemistry between us before. Why would that suddenly change just because we share a candlelight dinner or something?"

Yeah, why would that change? An unrequited crush that had long ago faded didn't mean a thing. Ky was probably worrying about nothing.

Regan turned on the couch to face her more fully and studied her closely. "Unless you think it's—"

"No, it's fine. We've gone out to dinner a thousand times before. Nothing to it, right?"

"Right."

It wouldn't be a real date. They were only doing this to get their friends to shut up about them. It would simply be a pleasant evening with her best friend. Regan had seen her at her worst. Ky could relax and just be herself, not the carefully presented version she showed her regular dates. No airs. No pretense.

"So, we're going to do it?" Regan asked.

Ky grimaced. "Yes, we'll do it. Although that might not be the best choice of words."

"Haha. I'll have you know I'm not that easy." Regan lifted her chin and playfully brushed her shoulder-length locks back over her shoulder. "It takes more than a little wining and dining to seduce me."

With any other woman, Ky would have taken it as a challenge, but Regan wasn't just any woman. Besides, she was only joking around. "Well, *you*'ll be wining and dining *me* anyway."

"Oh, I am?"

"*You* asked *me* out, remember?" God. Of all the words she'd been sure she would never say, these topped the list.

Regan tapped one finger to the elegant Cupid's bow of her upper lip—the one Ky had been fascinated with as a teen. "Hmm, you did say you prefer my sandwiches to a Michelin-star-worthy restaurant."

"No, no, no. You think I'm that easy? Nope. You're going to take me to a proper restaurant with a table that I didn't help you put together after the longest, most embarrassing trip to Ikea in the history of womankind."

Regan let out a groan. "You're never going to let me live that down either, are you?"

"Nope. Never," Ky said cheerfully. "So you'd better make sure you don't do anything embarrassing during our no-chemistry date that I'd have to add to the already long list of stories I'm going to tell your kids one day."

"Me?" Regan batted her big, brown eyes. "Don't worry. It's going to be the most uneventful date ever."

Right. Completely uneventful. Nothing to break out into a sweat about. Ky wiped her brow. "So, *Rizzoli and Isles*?"

Regan reached for the remote and swung her feet up onto Ky's lap. "I thought you'd never ask."

# Chapter 3

"Oh my God, that's so cute!" Regan lifted the polymer clay charm off the table to study it. The tiny pizza looked amazingly lifelike, and the scent from a nearby food cart drifted over, adding to the illusion. "This is perfect for my dad's birthday. How much do you want for it?"

Eliza took the charm from her and wrapped it in a piece of tissue paper. "I'll give it to you at mate's rates. Which means you get it for free."

"No, no, no. Art shouldn't be free. Even you and Denny can't just live off love and air." Regan looked around until she spotted a sign in the back of Eliza's Saturday Market booth, saying *Small figurines and charms: $5*. She pulled a five-dollar bill from her wallet, but her friend refused to take it.

"Why don't you and Kylie come over tonight and bring a bottle of red, and we'll call it even?"

Regan opened her mouth to agree, but then she remembered their plans for tonight. "Uh…" She glanced at Ky, who was at the other end of the stall with Denny, holding up a pair of Real Pockets jeans. "Actually, we've already got plans."

"Book club?" Eliza asked.

"No. We, um…" Regan gave herself a mental kick. Why was she suddenly reluctant to admit it, as if it were a private thing she needed to protect? They were doing this to get their friends off their backs, so telling the gang was essential. "We're going on a date."

"I knew it!" Eliza threw her girlfriend a triumphant look. "Didn't I tell you that waitress was flirting with Kylie?"

"Uh, no… I mean, yes, she was totally flirting, but that's not what I'm trying to say."

Eliza probably hadn't even heard her since she'd been busy grinning at Denny and getting lost in her eyes. Now she tore herself away and turned back toward Regan.

"Ky and I..." Regan tightened her grip on the tissue-wrapped pizza charm. "We're going on a date."

Even the hustle and bustle of the busy market around them seemed to fade away, and silence descended on them.

Then Eliza laughed. "Jeez, for a moment, I thought you meant you two were dating. Each other." She held up her hands. "I know, I know. You've told us a thousand times. No chemistry. So, you're talking about going on a double date, right?"

"Oh God, no," Regan and Ky said at the same time. "It's not a double date."

"There's nothing wrong with double dates," Eliza said. "Denny and I go out with her sister and Matt all the time."

Regan scrunched up her nose. "No, thanks. No double dates for us. I'm still not over our one and only triple D."

"Triple D?" Eliza asked.

"Double date disaster," Regan and Ky answered in unison.

Ky groaned. "My date went on and on about her root canal for at least an hour."

"And the weirdest thing was that my date seemed totally interested. He hung on her every word. They ended up ditching us before dessert and left together." Regan laughed. "They're probably married and have three kids by now."

"Maybe we should do that as a side gig during summer break: the DDD Matchmaking Agency," Ky said.

They looked at each other, then shook their heads. "Nah."

"So you're going on separate dates?" Eliza asked. "Who are you going out with, Regan? Let me guess...the PE teacher at your school?"

"No." Regan grinned at Ky. "My date is way hotter."

A sound halfway between a laugh, a cough, and strangled choking escaped Ky. The pants she had held up against her hips slid from her grasp and would have ended up on the ground if not for Denny's quick reaction. "You're such a bullshitter, Regan Romano," Ky finally gasped out. "I've met the PE teacher, remember? I bet she even has a six-pack, while I've got more of a keg!"

Regan reached over and playfully backhanded her across the belly. In her job, Ky had to lift thirty-pound cases of French fries and giant cans of beans all the time, so Regan encountered exactly what she'd known she would: a firm core under just the right amount of cuddly softness. "Nonsense. You look great. Besides, she's got more like a four-pack."

"She showed you her abs?" Ky let out a whistle. "The teachers' lounge is a lot more interesting than the cafeteria. The only four-packs my colleagues are flashing at me are packages of—"

"Wait!" Eliza thrust out one hand so forcefully that even the woman selling sea glass jewelry in the stall next to theirs looked over. "Are you saying…? You two are going on a date…with each other?"

"Don't look so baffled. You're the one who suggested it."

"I did? I mean, right. I did. I just didn't think you were listening." A pleased smile spread over Eliza's face. She let out a cheer and leaned across the table to high-five Denny. "Hey, maybe *we* should open a matchmaking agency! We've got our first successful match right here."

"Whoa!" Regan held up a hand. "You might not want to print your business cards yet. I said we're going on one date, not renting a U-Haul. Think of it as a science experiment. We're doing it to prove that there's no potential for a chemical reaction between us."

Eliza's smile turned into a frown. "Science experiment? Jesus, only a chemistry teacher would ever approach dating like that!" She raised her finger at them. "You'd better give this a real shot, or we'll keep badgering you for the next fifty years."

"Okay, okay," Ky said. "We'll even do the candlelight thing. Happy now?"

"Depends." Eliza sent Regan a questioning look. "Where are you taking Kylie?"

Apparently, Regan had been chosen as the head of Operation No-Chemistry Date. But it had been some time since she'd last wined and dined someone, and The Country Cat—the restaurant where their triple D had taken place—hadn't fared any better than that date and had closed a couple of years ago. "I don't know. I thought we'd have dinner at The Observatory."

"For a date?" Eliza shook her head. "The food is great, but it's too noisy for intimate convos."

The thought of Ky gazing deeply into her eyes while she whispered words of adoration caused a strange, unsettling feeling in the pit of Regan's stomach. Only because it was so absurd, right?

A wrinkle formed above Ky's eyebrow. Finally, it smoothed out, and she shrugged. "We'll play it by ear. The setting doesn't matter; the person you're with does." She made it sound like a teasing remark, but the look in her eyes was sincere.

"True," Regan said. Their last few nights out had been get-togethers with the entire gang, and while she always enjoyed those, she was looking forward to spending tonight with just Ky.

Two women strolled up to the booth. One of them pointed at the banner hanging over Denny's side of the stall. "Holy denim! Women's pants with real pockets? Where do I sign up?"

Denny's cheeks turned crimson, but she smiled at the enthusiastic reaction. "Right here."

Regan slid her arm through Ky's. "Come on. Let's give the paying customers some space and go get some empanadas to tide us over until tonight."

As they walked away, waving to their friends, Ky exhaled. "Phew. Saved by the customer." She tugged Regan toward the line in front of PDX Empanadas. "You know you don't really have to take me anywhere tonight, right? I mean, it's not like either of us makes a lot of money. We can order pizza and—"

"No, no, no. We're going to dinner, my treat." As Regan slid the pizza charm into her pocket, an idea for the perfect dinner spot came to her. "You know what? Let's drive down to Lake O. I know this lovely little Italian restaurant right on the lake."

"Ha! Your treat, my ass!" Ky gave her a playful bump with her shoulder. "Your parents own the place, and they act like we're insulting them any time one of us tries to pay."

Regan stepped slightly out of line so she could study Ky's face. "I'm not just being cheap. We haven't seen them in a while, and Mom has started a campaign in our WhatsApp family group to get me to bring you down for a visit."

"I know. She added me to the group, in case you forgot. I'm just wise enough to rarely speak up so no one remembers my presence."

"Oh, we remember, believe me. We just let you think you're flying under the radar so we can gang up on you when you least expect it." Regan let her grin fade away. "If you'd rather go somewhere else…"

"No," Ky said immediately. "I'd love to see them. I kinda miss, uh, your dad's pizza." She regarded Regan with a straight face.

That serious demeanor might trick anyone else, but Regan knew a softie hid beneath Ky's tough exterior. She dug her fingers into Ky's sides, making her let out a startled squeak. "The pizza. That's what you miss. Sure."

"What can I say? It's really, really good pizza."

It was. For the first time in ages, Regan was looking forward to a date—even if the only chemistry happening would be the yeast in the pizza dough breaking down the sugar into carbon dioxide and ethanol.

# Chapter 4

"This is not a date," Regan told her reflection in the mirror. "Not a real one at least. This is just Ky."

There was nothing different about tonight at all. She was going to visit her parents and enjoy great food with her best friend, as they had a thousand times before.

Ky had seen her in the threadbare T-shirt that she'd owned since high school, in her *I get paid to be a nerd* shirt, and in the pair of jeans that was slowly coming apart at the seams. There was absolutely no need to dress up or take any extra time with her hair—and it definitely wasn't necessary to pull her sexiest bra from its hiding place in her dresser and make sure her panties matched.

But that left the question: What did you wear for a not-really-a-date date with your best friend?

Regan tapped her fingers against her chin as she stared into her closet.

She should at least make an effort, right? After all, that was what they'd promised their friends. She also couldn't very well show up at her parents' restaurant in her oldest pair of jeans. While La Casa Nostra had a relaxed vibe and was far from being posh, its prime location at the lake put it into a different category than the small family restaurant her parents had run when she'd been a kid.

Besides, Ky could still appreciate her taking the time to look good—in a completely platonic way, of course.

Not allowing herself to hesitate, she reached for a black knitted dress she hadn't worn in ages. As she slipped it on, she prayed it would still fit, despite all the yummy treats Ky regularly left on her desk.

It did. She studied herself in the mirrored sliding door, trailed one hand over the curve of her hip, and peeked at the hint of cleavage the dress revealed. Doubts gnawed at her. Would Ky think it was too much?

She closed the top button of the V-neck front. But now she looked as if she were going to a PTA meeting. She popped the button back open.

The dress's long sleeves and below-the-knee hemline should balance out the fairly deep cut of the front, right?

*Jesus, Regan Romano!* She had spent less time picking an outfit for an actual date. *Must be why I'm single.*

With a wry grin, she turned away from her reflection and slid the closet door shut.

She slipped on her ankle boots with a low heel—not because she knew they made her calves look good or anything but because she wore only comfy footwear at school so she was overdue for a change of pace.

When she hung out with Ky, she never bothered with makeup, but the dress called for at least some eyeliner, didn't it?

*Do it, but pronto.* If she was late to their one and only date, Ky would never let her live it down.

Finally, with only a minute to spare, she parked her car in front of Ky's apartment complex at the southern end of the Mount Tabor neighborhood. As she walked toward the two-story building, she automatically searched for the right key on her key ring.

But when she reached the door to Ky's ground-floor apartment, she paused. Using her key didn't feel right. If she were a stranger Ky was going out with, she wouldn't let herself in.

*Yeah, but you're not. It's not a real date,* she repeated her new mantra. It wouldn't be going anywhere. *Don't be weird. Just use the damn key.*

Before she could talk herself into it, the front door swung open. Ky's roommate, Lilia, stood in the doorway, her hands raised at chest level. Foam dripped off the pink rubber gloves she was wearing. "I saw you from the sink. Did you forget your key?"

"Um, something like that. Thanks, Lil." Regan followed her in. Her heels sank into the ugliest brown carpet in Portland—heck, probably the entire West Coast. The weird triangular patterns didn't help.

"Kylie will be out in a minute. She's still getting dressed." Lilia pointed at the open doorway leading to their bedrooms and the tiny bathroom, where the salmon-colored tub and tiles gave the carpet a run for its money when it came to ugliness.

Lilia stepped back into the galley kitchen.

Regan didn't join her. Instead, she took a seat on the nearby couch. The kitchen was so claustrophobically small that you had to press your back against the stove on the other side so you could open the fridge.

No wonder Ky spent more time at Regan's place than her own. Regan hated that cafeteria workers were paid so badly, making it impossible for Ky to afford a better apartment. A few times over the last six years they'd both lived in Portland, she had thought about suggesting they move in together, but one of them had always gotten involved with someone else before she could actually do it. At least this apartment was within walking distance of Hamilton High School so Ky didn't need a car.

Lilia placed a huge pot on the dish rack. "So, you and my roomie have finally realized the obvious."

"That pizza is the most genius invention ever?"

"Please. We both know that's tacos." Lilia waved a gloved hand before Regan could defend the honor of Italian cuisine against dishes from Lil's native country. "Besides, I'm talking about you and Kylie finally realizing how great you'd be together."

A groan escaped Regan. Why did everyone think they knew more about their friendship than she and Ky did? "Not you too, Brutus."

"Give it a rest, okay?" Ky said from the doorway. "I told you it's not like that."

Regan looked up. If Lilia countered something, she missed whatever it was.

Clearly, Ky had decided to put some effort into her appearance too. Regan was used to seeing her in faded jeans and a worn T-shirt or, at work, in her school polo, apron, and a baseball cap with the school's logo. Tonight, she looked a far cry from a lunch lady.

The charcoal chinos fit her to a T—probably because Denny had custom-tailored them for her, making her sturdy legs look longer. Her white, short-sleeved sweater with the polo neck showed off her athletic arms and the light tan she somehow managed to keep year-round. She had carefully swept her bangs to one side instead of letting them fall however they wanted, and the result reminded Regan of the haircut Charlize Theron had sported in *The Old Guard*.

Regan's mouth went dry. *What's wrong with you? Stop staring! She's not Charlize!*

Ky reached for the fleece-lined plum-colored corduroy jacket Regan had talked her into buying a few years back and turned her attention from her roommate to Regan.

The jacket tumbled to the floor. The familiar wrinkle formed on Ky's brow as she stared at her.

"What?" Regan peeked down at the knitted dress. "Too much?"

Ky bent to pick up the jacket, delaying her answer for a moment.

Regan fidgeted with the top button. Should she close it after all?

But when Ky straightened, a teasing smile crept onto her face, and they seemed to be back on more familiar ground. "Oh yeah. Go home and change into something less—"

"Hot," Lilia threw in.

Ky snapped the jacket in her direction. "Elegant. Seriously." She let her gaze trail down the dress without lingering anywhere. "You look, um, great."

"So do you." She really did. Regan hadn't been as blown away by how Ky looked since prom night, when Ky had picked her up in a tux. But then again, Ky wasn't one for dressing up, so it was just the newness of it that had thrown her off balance.

Lilia shook her head at them. "*Por Dios*, you two."

Ky shot her a look. "Come on," she said to Regan. "Let's go. Your dad's pizza is waiting."

"I won't wait up," Lilia called after them.

Driving south on Highway 43 toward Lake Oswego felt like going back in time. Her senior year of high school, Ky had made the trip as often as her mother would allow.

The tiny, conservative town where they had moved after losing the house in Lake O had felt suffocating, and so had her grandparents' admonishing glances at her short hair, baggy jeans, and the rainbow bracelet Regan had made for her when Ky had come out to her at sixteen.

Regan and her accepting family had been her safe haven that she fled to whenever she could, even if it meant braving the hateful looks of her former classmates after her dad had been caught stealing from their families.

Now they were once again living in the same city, going home together. Ky grinned. Amazing how life worked out sometimes—at least for her. It hadn't worked out for her mom. Her smile fell.

"What?" Regan asked from the driver's seat.

It was the first thing either of them had said since crossing the Ross Island Bridge. Neither of them had felt the need to talk, so they had enjoyed the sun shining through the trees to their right and the glimpses of the Willamette to their left in silence.

"Just thinking."

"About?"

"Life."

"Your mom," Regan said quietly.

Ky sighed. "Yeah, her too."

Without taking her gaze off the road ahead, Regan reached over and put her hand on Ky's thigh. The warmth of her palm filtered through Ky's chinos.

A lump formed in Ky's throat. "Hey, you'd better not try any funny business on our first date."

Regan gave her a sidelong glance. "And you'd better not try to laugh it off and pretend going home doesn't bring up a lot of memories."

Damn, Regan knew her too well. No use in pretending. "It does. But most of them are good. At least the ones B.E."

Before embezzlement. Thankfully, there was no need to spell it out for Regan, who gave a soft squeeze before returning her hand to the steering wheel.

At least memories of the past kept Ky from thinking too much about the present—and about the way her best friend looked in her dress. It clung to curves Ky had always tried not to notice.

Earlier, she had nearly swallowed her tongue at the sight of Regan.

A stab of guilt pierced her chest. She knew Regan probably wouldn't mind her admiring the way she looked—and that was all it was, right? Just honest admiration. Okay, *mostly* honest admiration. As much as she tried to deny it, she wasn't completely immune to how Regan looked in her sexy dating outfits.

No woman who loved women would be. It didn't mean anything. Usually, it was only a fleeting blip on her attraction radar, something she could brush off easily to focus on what really mattered: their friendship.

But normally, Regan put on her sexy outfits for other people. She had never dressed this way for *her*, and it threw Ky off balance in a way she hadn't expected.

She didn't know where to look, so she kept her gaze trained on the upscale boutiques and cute, chalet-style buildings with their gabled roofs and hanging flower baskets as Regan made a right onto A Avenue, then turned left onto First Street.

They found a free space in the parking garage that was part of Lake View Village, the shopping center in the heart of downtown Lake Oswego.

A light Oregon drizzle had fallen earlier, so Ky slowed her steps to avoid Regan slipping on the wet cobblestones.

Not that it was actually necessary to adjust her stride to Regan's. Despite Ky's seven-inch advantage, Regan always kept pace because Ky's height was mostly in her torso, whereas Regan had amazingly long legs for such a short person.

While they strolled toward Millennium Plaza Park, sidestepping a duck that had made its way up the street from the nearby lake, their arms brushed every now and then.

Ky hadn't put on her jacket so she could enjoy the last rays of the setting sun on her skin, and now a prickle of awareness ran through her body.

She dug her teeth into her bottom lip and ignored the sensation. Where the hell was this coming from?

It was the dress. This damn dress with its buttons down the front. She had rarely seen Regan in something like this; that was all.

In a minute, she'd get used to it, and until then, she'd just have to remind herself that Regan was the girl she'd watched stick French fries up her nose while ignoring the fact that she was also the girl she'd had her first crush on.

Completely in step, they walked toward the plaza where the restaurant was located. The familiar sight of Fortuna greeted them. The seven-foot bronze sculpture, with water cascading from a stone bowl balanced on its head, rose up from a rock pedestal in the middle of a small roundabout.

Beyond was the area where the farmers market was held every Saturday morning. Going to the market with Regan and her dad to pick out fresh produce for the restaurant had been one of the highlights of Ky's week growing up.

"I've nearly forgotten how nice it is." Regan gestured to the reflecting pool on the other side of the roundabout and the view of Lakewood Bay and the mansions at its shore. "Isn't it strange how we couldn't wait to escape this little bubble when we were teens, and now it's starting to look kind of appealing?"

"Yeah, it is." Ky shrugged. "Guess it means we're settled down and boring now."

"Ha! Speak for yourself. I'm still wild and adventurous." Regan raised her arms high above her head and twirled.

Ky watched with an indulgent grin—until Regan's dainty ankle boots lost traction on the wet cobblestones and her feet slipped out from under her.

*Shit!* Ky dropped her jacket and caught Regan with both hands on her hips. Her heart pounded a rapid staccato...from the near fall, not from holding Regan tightly against her, of course.

Everything had happened so fast that Regan's arms were still half-raised. Now she lowered them and took hold of Ky's sides to steady herself. Her fingers curled into the fabric of Ky's sweater. "Phew!" Her long, shaky exhale tickled the skin left bare by Ky's polo neck. "Thanks for the save."

Ky opened her mouth. At the last moment, she held back a slightly cheesy reply such as, "Always." Instead, she said, "Let's not get too wild, okay? Your parents would have my head if I didn't keep you from breaking a leg just a few steps from their restaurant."

"Yeah." Regan chuckled, still sounding breathless from the scare. "That would be bad for business."

A snort escaped Ky. "As if they would care about that." Regan's parents had never put their business, as successful as it was, above family—unlike Ky's own. Her father had always focused on his career as a lawyer and barely paid her any attention, while her mother had been busy trying to fill up the holes in her unhappy life by popping pills and spending all the money he made on things they didn't need.

Regan put her hands on Ky's and rubbed them as if sensing where her thoughts had gone. "Come on. Pizza's waiting." She picked up Ky's jacket and tugged her past the French bakery to La Casa Nostra.

The red chairs and the small, square tables on the patio were beaded with drops of water, and the temperature had fallen now that the sun was setting, so dining outside was not an option. Ky pulled open the door and let Regan enter ahead of her.

The scent of tomato sauce and melting cheese wafted out even before Ky got one foot inside. Warmth from the wood-fire oven engulfed her...or maybe the warmth was from the rustic yet cozy atmosphere. The Romanos' restaurant had always felt like home.

They hadn't even made it two steps in when Regan's dad caught sight of them. He was behind the counter that formed a semi-circle around the beautiful, blue-tiled pizza oven that was his pride and joy. Without a second's hesitation, he plopped down the dough he was kneading and rushed toward them.

Several guests looked up from their dinner, but he paid them no attention as he engulfed both of them in a group hug.

"Tammy!" he boomed. "They're here!"

His wife burst from the office in the back, from where she ran the business end of the restaurant.

Within seconds, Ky found herself in the middle of a Romano family hug. Forget pizza. This was what she was really here for. She returned the embrace with equal enthusiasm, not caring if she got flour from Joe's apron all over her clothes.

"Come on. Let the girls get a table," Joe finally said to his wife, as if she had been the only one refusing to let go of them. "I bet they're starving." He marched behind the counter and began calling out orders for a pizza margherita and a white pizza with garlic cream sauce.

"Um, don't we get a menu?" Regan brushed flour off her dress. "What if we wanted to order something else?"

Her mother waved her hand. "When did you ever do that?"

"I had the bucatini with meatballs once," Ky said.

Tammy ushered them to their favorite booth in the corner, where two wooden pizza peels decorated the wall. "When you had your wisdom teeth out and couldn't chew the pizza crust."

Wow. She actually remembered that!

Tammy squeezed into the booth next to her daughter and studied Ky across the table.

Good thing their friends couldn't see them. So much for their intimate dinner for two. But Ky didn't mind...quite the opposite. Tammy's presence made her forget about the dangerous direction her thoughts had strayed in earlier. Ky returned the appraisal.

Tammy's straight, blonde hair—so unlike her daughter's dark curls—held a few more silver strands, and the laugh lines around her eyes had deepened, but otherwise, she was still the same woman who had built them the coolest tree house ever.

Finally, Tammy finished her scrutiny and leaned back in the booth. "I was worried when you didn't visit for spring break, but you look great. You both do. I think the last time I saw you two so dressed up was when Regan insisted on you going to prom with her. Is there some special occasion I've missed, or are you—? Wait!" She clutched her chest and looked as if she'd been surprised with the world's biggest gift basket. "Oh my God! Are you two finally dating?"

Regan let out a string of Neapolitan curses—pretty much the only Italian she spoke. "Not you too! For the last time, Mom, we are not dating!"

The guests at the table next to theirs looked over.

"Well, not really," Regan added more quietly.

"What's that supposed to mean?" her mother asked. "Call me old-fashioned, but isn't dating like being pregnant—you either are or you aren't?"

"We aren't," Ky said, as much to remind herself as to clarify for Tammy.

Tammy leaned forward, eyes twinkling. "Pregnant or dating?"

"Both. Neither." Ky's head started buzzing. Sometimes, she felt as if she was too slow and could barely keep up with the way the Romano brains worked.

"Our friends keep pointing out how great we'd be as a couple, so we finally agreed to go on one date to prove that there's nothing there," Regan said.

Tammy gave them the same look she had directed at them when Regan, at nine, had begged her parents to buy her a set of walkie-talkies, insisting they needed them so they could chat with each other about homework. "Clearly. Nothing there at all." She got up from the booth. "What can I get you to drink? We've got a case of Gran Passione Rosso that I think you'd like."

"Just water for me," Regan said. "I'm driving."

"For me too, please."

Regan cocked her head at her. "I don't mind if you have a glass."

"Nah, that's fine." Ky already felt a little light-headed any time she looked at Regan in that dress for too long; she didn't need red wine to add to that—especially not a wine called *great passion*.

Tammy got them their water, then pulled a lighter from her pocket and lit the candle on the table between them before walking away with a promise to talk later.

*Candlelight. Great. Thanks, Tammy. Just what we needed.* Ky took a sip of water and watched Joe toss the pizza dough in the air to stretch it as their conversation echoed through her mind. "For the last time," she repeated.

"Hmm?" Regan had watched her father too. Now she looked at Ky. The glow of the candle flickered across her face, making her big, brown eyes appear even darker.

"You said, 'For the last time, we're not dating.' Like you had to tell her that before."

Regan's lips quirked into a smile. "Did I ever tell you what my parents said when I came out to them?"

"Yeah, of course."

There wasn't much they hadn't told each other over the years. Ky had been the first person Regan had come out to as bisexual when she'd been a sophomore at UO, and she'd been the first person Regan had called after telling her parents.

"They told you they'll always love you, just the way you are."

"No."

"No?"

"Yeah, that's what they said, but the first words out of Mom's mouth were actually, 'We know.'"

Ky clutched the edge of the table. "They knew? But...how? Even I had no clue! You could have knocked me over with a feather when you confessed your crush on what's-her-name."

"Her name's Melissa; you know that."

"Yeah, yeah. Can we focus on what's important here? How the hell did your parents find out before me?" Ky had always thought she knew Regan better than anyone else did, including her own family.

"To quote what my dad said back then: 'Are we supposed to pretend we didn't know you and Kylie are a couple?'"

Despite her white-knuckled grip on the table, Ky nearly slid down the booth. "They did not say that!"

Regan laughed. "I swear."

Ky pried her fingers from the table and took a gulp of water, now half wishing she'd accepted Tammy's offer to get her a glass of wine. "They really thought we...?" Her head was spinning. She wasn't sure she wanted to know what Tammy and Joe had thought was going on behind Regan's closed bedroom door. Christ. It was a wonder they had even allowed them to close the door!

"Don't worry. I set them straight. So to speak." Regan reached across the table and patted her arm.

Ky stared at the hand lingering on her forearm. It was probably things like this that made everyone assume they were together. She leaned heavily against the back of the booth. So much for knowing everything there was to know about Regan. Why had Regan never told her? She opened her mouth to ask.

Two steaming pizzas being slid onto the table interrupted whatever Ky had been about to say.

When Regan looked up, her dad stood next to them, beaming as if he were single-handedly saving them from sure starvation. Knowing him, he was probably about to remind them that his ancestors had invented pizza. She made eye contact with Ky above the flickering candle, and they mouthed together, "Three, two, one..."

"Did I ever tell you that pizza was invented in Napule?" Her father nodded gravely. "Right where your grandparents grew up."

"Only about a million times, Dad."

"The espresso machine too," Ky said. "At least that's what I read somewhere."

"Suck-up," Regan mouthed across the table, but Ky just flashed her a grin.

Her father gave Ky's shoulder a hearty pat. "At least someone appreciates our rich cultural heritage."

Regan pretended to roll her eyes, but truth be told, the way her parents treated Ky—as if she was truly part of the family—melted her heart. Ky deserved it. She also needed it, even if she would never admit it.

Her father lingered next to the table, watching them dig in.

Regan barely waited for the fresh-from-the-oven pizza to cool down a little before taking a huge bite. The garlic cream sauce, the ricotta, and the mozzarella blended together into melt-in-your-mouth perfection, while the pesto, the soppressata, and the chili flakes added a kick to make it more interesting.

"Did your mother tell you about the teaching job?"

Not about to interrupt the pizza-gasm going on in her mouth, Regan only shook her head.

"Lake Grove Elementary is looking for a new third-grade teacher."

Regan sighed. Their attempts to talk her into teaching in Lake Oswego were as old as her father's claims that pretty much every culinary feat of importance had been invented in Naples.

"You know we've got the best schools in Oregon, and only the best is good enough for my daughter," he added when Regan didn't say anything.

"Dad, I teach high school, not elementary, and I don't want to change that. I love working with teenagers."

Her father shook his head and pointed at the gray parts in his salt-and-pepper hair. "God knows why. I barely survived your teenage years."

Regan tsked. "Teenagers are fun. Their emotions…everything is bigger than life. Things never get boring. I love that."

Her dad sighed. "All right. We'll keep an eye out for any positions opening up at a high school. I think your old chemistry teacher is approaching retirement age."

The thought of moving back to her hometown, closer to her family, was more appealing than Regan would have thought possible a few years ago.

But there were things—and, more importantly, people—she wasn't ready to leave behind. She popped a piece of soppressata into her mouth and peeked over at Ky while she chewed. "It's not just that. My life is in Portland, Dad."

"What about you?" Her father focused on Ky now. That, too, was the same procedure as every visit. He was like a German shepherd who tried to keep his flock close to home. "When will you finally come work for us? Now that we'll open a second location in Vancouver next month, we could use someone to run things here."

Ky's water glass wobbled precariously as she set it down with a shaky hand. "R-run things?"

That part of the offer was new. Usually, Regan's father just tried to talk her into working at the restaurant.

Regan wasn't sure how she felt about that. On the one hand, she knew her parents could use the extra help. Her sister, Mackenzie, would be the manager at the new place, while their cousin Vanessa would run the kitchen, but with both of them being new at their jobs, her parents spent a lot of time making the half-hour trip to Vancouver, Washington, to offer guidance. She could easily imagine Ky stepping in for them, running La Casa Nostra.

On the other hand, if Ky moved to Lake Oswego, that would probably make hanging out on weeknights a thing of the past, and Regan wasn't ready to give up Netflix night, book club meetings, and spontaneous walks up Mount Tabor.

"Why not? Since Robbie and this one"—her father nudged Regan's shoulder—"want nothing to do with the food service industry; Mackenzie is only interested in the business side of it, and their cousin will be the head chef of the new location, we need someone to run the kitchen here. So, what do you say?"

Ky stared at her pizza instead of looking at him. "I don't know, Joe. I'm honored, but it's not like I'm a real chef."

"Not a real chef?" Regan's dad repeated. "You cook for hundreds of kids every day!"

"Cafeteria food isn't exactly fine dining." Ky still hadn't looked up from her plate.

"And this is? It's pizza, Ky, nothing fancy." With a glance at her father, Regan quickly added, "Even if it's the best pizza in the world."

"Still," Ky said. "I don't have the skills for a place like this. Making one simple dish in bulk is very different from cooking a dozen individual dishes from scratch."

What was this all about? Regan tried to read the emotions on Ky's lowered face. Ky had helped to cook most of the dishes on the menu before she'd been able to spell them. Did she really think she lacked the skills, or was this an attempt to let him down easy? Maybe she was as reluctant to leave Portland and their life together as Regan was.

Her father opened his mouth, no doubt to convince Ky otherwise.

Since this was clearly making Ky uncomfortable, Regan decided to come to her rescue. "Maybe Ky likes working with teenagers too and isn't ready to give up her job. Besides, she was just offered a—"

Ky kicked her foot beneath the table.

Pain flared through her toes. "Ouch! What the hell, Ky?"

Ky quietly shook her head.

"She was just offered…what?" Regan's father asked.

"Dessert," Regan said, still studying Ky. "Mom offered her a plate of cannoli."

The exhale from across the table was audible.

What on earth was going on with Ky? Why didn't she want Regan's dad to know about the promotion? When they'd been kids, she had always rushed over to share her accomplishments with Regan and her family because Ky's parents had been too self-involved to ooh and aah over them.

"Of course there'll be dessert," her father said. "But you'll have to finish your pizza first."

"We would, but someone keeps talking to us." Regan gave him a pointed look.

Laughing, he held up both hands. "All right. I'm going back to work. *Buon appetito.*"

As soon as he walked away, Ky dug into her pizza as if she hadn't eaten all week, but Regan had a feeling she wanted to avoid having to talk.

*Nope. Not happening, Kylie Wells.* "What's going on?"

"Hmm?" Ky gave her an I-have-no-clue-what-you-mean look.

"Come on, Ky. That look might work on someone who hasn't been your best friend since puking on you the first day of kindergarten, after I ate that family-size pack of M&Ms. This is me. What's up?"

Sighing, Ky put down a piece of pizza crust. "I haven't accepted the promotion yet, and I'm not sure I'm going to."

Regan stared, for a second sure she had misheard. "What? Why not? Why didn't you tell me? We tell each other everything!"

"We do. I do...usually. But..." Ky pinched the bridge of her nose.

"But what? Jesus, Ky, I threw you a surprise party to celebrate your promotion!"

Ky hung her head. "I know. I'm sorry. You seemed so happy when I told you, and I didn't want to spoil that before I'd made up my mind."

"I was happy because *you* seemed happy!"

"I was," Ky said. "I swear I wasn't lying or consciously trying to keep this from you. At first, I really thought I'd say yes. I was pretty flattered Fran thought I could do it. And making more money would be nice."

"Then why are you hesitating now?"

"The more I think about it, the less sure I am. The promotion wouldn't just mean more money. It would also mean more paperwork. As Fran's assistant, I would spend more time filling out lunch count and order forms than doing food prep, and you know I've always been shit at math."

"So use a calculator," Regan shot back.

"It's not that easy." Ky painted circles in the condensation on the outside of her water glass.

Regan pushed her shock and anger aside, along with her plate and the candle between them. She reached across the table and put her hand over Ky's. Her stomach knotted. How had she not known something was going on with her best friend? "Talk to me. Please."

Finally, Ky looked up. "I'm good at what I do right now—being a lunch lady. Lil and the rest of the team are great, and even the kids seem to like me."

"Are you kidding?" Regan blurted out before she could stop herself. "They love you. Especially on pizza day. Which is why I think Dad is right. You'd be great at this too." She waved her hand, indicating the restaurant. "Or at being the assistant cafeteria manager. Whatever you choose to do."

Ky shrugged. It was the kind of awkward, insecure shrug Regan hadn't seen from her since she had convinced her not to drop out of high school. "Maybe. But this is the first time I've ever had it all. A job I'm good at. A team I like and that likes me back. A roommate who doesn't drive me up the wall."

"I get that." Regan had witnessed her jump from one minimum-wage job to the next, from waitressing at a kids' restaurant to working the grill at greasy burger joints. She had actually outlasted most of the other employees, so making friends had never been an option.

"I think I'm better off appreciating the job I have instead of risking it all if it turns out I'm not good enough," Ky said quietly.

The last piece of the puzzle fell into place, completing the picture. Of course! Keeping her job, as lousy as it paid, was the safe bet, and Ky hated gambling. Her father had gambled on being able to pull off his clever embezzlement scheme, and he had lost it all. *Ky* had lost it all—her father and later her mother, her classmates' respect, the house she'd grown up in. No wonder she wasn't willing to risk losing anything else and would rather settle for what she had.

"I'm really sorry I didn't tell you sooner."

Regan sighed. She still didn't like it, but at least now she understood why. "It's okay."

"And I'm sorry for spoiling this evening. I'm a terrible date." Ky chuckled, but it sounded forced. "Good thing we weren't planning on a second date anyway."

Regan put her other hand around Ky's too, now cradling it in both of hers. "Listen to me, Kylie Rose Wells."

The use of her full name made Ky shudder, and they both had to grin, which lightened the mood.

"You are not a terrible date, and you are good enough." Regan emphasized every word, as if she were teaching her students the name of a complex chemical, and firmly squeezed her hand. She held Ky's gaze, willing her to read the truth in her eyes. "You're good enough to be an assistant cafeteria manager, a restaurant manager, or a chef. But if you don't want to be any of these things, you'll still be good enough."

The fingers beneath hers tightened around the glass they still held. Ky searched her face with almost desperate urgency. "Good enough…" Her voice came out in a husky rasp, so she cleared her throat before she continued. "For what?"

"Anything you want," Regan said without hesitation.

"What if I still don't know what that is?" Ky rubbed at her eyebrow scar with her free hand. "Damn. I'm thirty. I'm supposed to have things figured out, but here I am..."

"Here you are," Regan repeated but in a much more positive tone, "in the best restaurant in town." She flicked a glance at the counter, where her father was watching them with a concerned expression. "In the world. Having the best pizza in the world, with the best friend in the world."

"In the universe." Ky's lips curled up into a smile, but her eyes were serious.

"Well, I was trying to be modest, but if you insist..."

They grinned at each other.

"Seriously, Ky, who says you've got to have it all figured out just because you're a certain age?"

"Growing up, we thought we would long before reaching thirty."

Regan snorted. "We also thought it was a good idea to drink an entire bottle of cough syrup to see if we would get drunk."

"*You* thought it was a good idea."

"Yeah, yeah. I never claimed to have anything figured out. It's not a requirement. As long as you stay true to yourself and make the most of every moment, that's all that counts."

Ky joined her left hand to the tangle of their fingers around the glass. "Thank you. I know you're right. It's just... Sometimes..." She growled as if the right words to explain escaped her.

But Regan didn't need them. "I get it."

"Yeah. You really do."

Regan looked into Ky's grayish-green eyes that seemed to glow with gratefulness and affection, even though it was probably at least in part due to the flickering candlelight. When the intimacy of their eye contact became too much, she pulled the glass from Ky's grasp and signaled the waiter. "You need new water. We warmed this up to bath temperature."

"And the pizza has gone cold. I'm sorry."

"No need to be sorry. That's the great thing about pizza: it tastes just as good cold as it does hot." Regan took a hearty bite and let out a hum.

A slow smile spread over Ky's face. "So you still think this isn't a terrible date?"

Regan made a show of thinking about it while she chewed. "Well, we haven't made it to the glorious culmination of the date yet, so I'm reserving judgment."

Ky froze with a slice of pizza halfway to her mouth. "Glorious culmination? You don't expect me to kiss you good night, do you?"

Laughter bubbled up from deep in Regan's belly. "You think a kiss from you would be glorious? And people tell me I lack modesty! I'm talking about Dad's cannoli."

"Oh. Of course. I mean, it's not like I'd kiss you, with your garlic breath and all. Um…or even without it."

Regan lifted another slice of pizza to her mouth to hide her grin. A stammering Ky was the cutest thing ever. But, of course, she was right. Garlic breath or not, the night wouldn't end with a kiss. The only thing that would touch her lips tonight was her dad's yummy Italian food.

An hour later, Regan ducked into the back room, where her mother was working on the computer. "Hey, Mom. We're heading out now. Are you sure you're not going to let us pay?"

"You know the answer to that." Her mother peered past Regan. "Where's Kylie?"

Regan laughed. "In the kitchen with Dad, getting loaded down with enough food to last us a week."

"Is she okay?"

"Yeah." Regan stepped farther into the room and lowered her voice. "It's just… Everything she's been through over the years left its mark. But she'll be fine."

"Of course. She's got you after all." Her mother smiled, but the worry lines on her forehead didn't completely smooth out. "Let us know if she needs anything."

For the millionth time in her life, Regan thanked her good fortune for her family. "Will do."

"Oh, before you leave, what do you think? Kinkie, Lover Bunny, or Majestic Romance?" Her mother gestured at her computer screen.

Regan stared at her. Kinkie? Lover Bunny? What the hell? She was almost afraid to peek at the computer.

Her mother laughed. "What? You think I've got time to shop for sex toys a month before the restaurant in Vancouver opens?"

Regan covered her ears with her hands. "Lalalala, I can't hear you."

Chuckling, her mother walked over and pulled Regan's hands down. "I'm talking about the font for the headings on our menu. Would it look better in Kinkie, Lover Bunny, or Majestic Romance?"

"Majestic Romance," Regan answered without even looking at the different fonts because thanks to her mother's comment, the two others now evoked images of sex toys.

"Good choice. Speaking of romance..." Her mother pointed at the restaurant's main room. "Are you sure you're only going out with Kylie to prove that there's nothing there—or because, deep down, you know there is?"

Anger boiled up inside Regan like a volcano ready to erupt. "Would everyone please stop that and let Ky and me decide what our relationship is and what it isn't? It's getting really old, you know?"

Her mother sank onto her desk chair. "I'm sorry. You're right. I just want you to have someone who's always there for you, the way your dad and I have each other."

The fiery lava in Regan's belly instantly cooled. She perched on the edge of the desk, the way she'd done as a child. "I do have someone." They both glanced toward the kitchen. "We don't need to be a couple to be each other's support system."

"I know. I just want you to have everything—friendship, romance, love, sex. You and Kylie are so good for each other, but sometimes, I'm afraid you're keeping each other from having it all."

The lava bubbled up again.

"Hear me out," her mother said before Regan could interrupt. "You and Kylie spend pretty much all of your spare time together."

"What's wrong with that?"

"Nothing. Except...how is a partner going to compete with that and with all the history you two share? Would they even have a place in your life? Even the spot next to your toothbrush is already taken up by Kylie's. How do you explain that to your dates when you decide to take someone home with you?"

"Why do I have to explain anything?" Regan paced away from the desk. "Besides, for the most part, I don't take anyone home."

"That's my point, sweetie."

Just when Regan felt she'd reached her boiling point, a short knock announced Ky's arrival. She looked from Regan to her mother and instantly seemed to sense the tension because she lingered in the doorway instead of coming in. "Uh-oh. Am I interrupting something?"

Her presence was like a valve that released some of the steam that had built up inside Regan. "No. Mom was—"

"Making an ass out of myself." Her mother sighed. "I'm sorry. I didn't mean to make you feel like I'm criticizing the way you live your life. I got enough of that from your grandpa when I married your dad, and I swore I'd never do that to any of my kids."

"You don't...usually," Regan added. Now that the pit of lava in her belly had cooled off, she managed a teasing grin.

Ky gave her a questioning look but remained where she was.

"Come here," Regan's mom said. "Both of you."

When they did, she pulled them into a tight embrace, ignoring the bags of food in Ky's hands. "I'm sorry," she whispered into Regan's ear.

"It's fine," Regan answered. "I get it." And if she was honest, her mother wasn't completely wrong...at least not about everything. Ky's toothbrush in the cup holder next to hers had led to a misunderstanding or two in the past.

Her mom gave her an extra squeeze before letting go.

"What was that all about?" Ky asked as they walked to the car.

"Your toothbrush."

"Um, what?" Ky switched a bag of food to her other hand so she could breathe on her palm and then sniffed it as if she was afraid she might have bad breath.

Regan couldn't help laughing. "Just Mom being her overprotective self, worried that we'll miss out on love."

Ky shrugged. "Love is overrated."

"Exactly." Regan took one of the bags from her and slid her arm through Ky's. "Who needs love if they can have cannoli?"

# Chapter 5

Dark clouds hung low over the green trusses of the Hawthorne Bridge, but for once, it wasn't raining, so Ky had bundled up in her windbreaker and met Regan, Denny, and Eliza for a Sunday afternoon walk at the waterfront.

A colorful dragon boat glided past them on its way upriver, and the April breeze ruffled Regan's curly hair, making it appear even messier than usual.

Ky stuffed her hands into her jacket pockets to keep from reaching over to swipe an errant strand from her face. At least with Regan's jacket zipped up to her neck, Ky's thoughts weren't veering into dangerous territory, as they had last night.

"So?" Eliza tugged Denny closer to Ky and Regan by their joined hands. "Don't make us wait for the big news."

Regan flashed her innocent grin—the one that had always convinced people Ky was the troublemaker and she had only been along for the ride. "Big news? Oh, wait, I know! La Casa Nostra now offers the option to add a light drizzle of honey to your white pizza."

"Aaaand?" Eliza drew out the word.

"And it's surprisingly yummy."

Ky bit down on the inside of her cheek to hold back a chuckle.

"I meant your date, you goof! How was it?" Eliza looked from Regan to Ky. "Any sparks?"

"No, of course not," Ky said quickly. So what if she'd been overly aware of how wonderful Regan had looked in that clingy button-down dress? That hadn't been a spark. More of a fluke, because she hadn't been with anyone since the Stone Age. And that intimate moment, with Regan cradling her hand and the candle throwing flickering shadows across her face, had probably just felt so emotional because she was PMSing or something.

Thankfully, Regan had been clueless. She had never once thought of Ky in a romantic way, and Ky would never risk the most important friendship in her life by trying to turn it into something more.

Now, with the date experiment safely behind them, they could go back to hanging out in sweatpants, and soon, she would forget that damn dress.

Eliza squinted at them. "What aren't you telling us?"

Ky stared ahead to the Hawthorne Bridge and watched as the lift span was slowly being raised, allowing the *Portland Spirit*, its deck full of tourists, to pass underneath.

"Nothing," Regan said. "We had a wonderful evening, but—"

"Wait!" Denny stopped walking, drawing them all to a halt. "Did you say La Casa Nostra earlier? Isn't that the restaurant your folks own?"

"It is. I wouldn't subject my lovely date to anything but the very best." Regan beamed proudly and wrapped one arm around Ky.

Even through her windbreaker, Ky was very aware of where Regan's fingers rested on her hip. Maybe she wasn't quite over that damn dress yet.

"You didn't!" Eliza shook her head at them. "Regan, that's not a date; that's a family reunion."

"Nonsense. It's not like my parents sat at the table with us…um, at least not most of the time."

"If it had been anyone but Kylie, you wouldn't have taken them to meet your parents on the very first date, would you?"

Regan laughed. "Hell, no!"

"Then why take Kylie there for your date?" Eliza shook her head at Regan.

Ky's protective hackles rose. "There's nothing wrong with taking me to La Casa Nostra. We had a very nice—"

"But we don't want *nice*. We want sparks," Eliza said. "Or at least a fair chance of seeing if there could be any between the two of you, and that's not going to happen with Regan's parents right there, watching your every move. You'll have to conduct part two of your little chemistry experiment under more realistic conditions."

"Part two?" Ky and Regan echoed.

"I insist on a second date." Eliza paused. "Actually, make it *two* more dates."

"Two?"

*Oh. My. God.* Ky wanted to sink to her knees on the dirt path. She would not survive that.

Eliza nodded firmly. "Repeatable results. That's what you science geeks are after, right?"

Regan nibbled her lip. "Right." She sounded less than enthusiastic.

"Look at it this way: You two could really use a refresher when it comes to dating, so at the very least, this will be good practice. Do we have a deal?"

Regan and Ky looked at each other.

"Deal," Regan finally said. "As long as you agree that after two more dates, you'll shut up about it forever."

Ky barely heard her words over the buzzing in her ears. She was too busy praying that no other sexy dresses lurked in the back of Regan's closet.

# Chapter 6

Regan was having a déjà vu moment. When she went to pick up Ky, her roommate Lilia opened the door again and studied Regan with the exact same smirk as last Saturday. "So, second date, huh?"

"Well, kinda...not really."

"Not really?" Lilia wrinkled her nose as if smelling a heap of shit. "You seriously want me to believe this is your Netflix night outfit?" She waved her hand at the long-sleeved black bodysuit and the hip-hugging pair of jeans Regan wore.

Regan tugged on her sweetheart neckline. "What? It's comfortable."

"Yeah. Right. Comfort. That's why my roomie is taking a suspiciously long time to get ready—because she can't find a comfortable thing to wear in her closet."

Regan peeked toward the closed bathroom door. At least she wasn't the only one, but that didn't mean what Lilia thought it meant. "We're just putting in extra effort because our friends didn't think the setting of our first date was romantic enough."

"Why? Where did you take her?"

"My parents' restaurant," Regan said.

Lilia laughed. "If your family is anything like mine, that would definitely kill the mood."

"For crying out loud, there was no mood to begin with! At least not a romantic one."

"No, of course, none at all," Lilia replied with a fake straight face. "So where are you going tonight?"

For once in her life, Regan had gone with the safe bet: they had decided on the classic date activity so their friends couldn't possibly find anything wrong with date number two. "Dinner and a movie."

The bathroom door swung open. "Hey, Lil, is this too tight?" Ky stepped into the living room in a navy-blue sweater that molded to her every curve, accentuating the elegant lines of her torso and her marvelous shoulders. It was tucked into a pair of light blue jeans, with a broad leather belt.

"No." Lilia chuckled. "Judging by the look on Regan's face, it's just fine."

Regan glared at her. She did *not* have a look on her face, other than friendly approval of Ky's wardrobe choices. Just because she was her best friend didn't mean Regan couldn't notice when Ky looked especially good.

"Oh. Hi. You're here already." Ky stopped running her hands over the front of her sweater and shoved them into her jeans pockets. "I seem to have, um…"

"Completely lost track of time while you were busy throwing on something comfortable," Lilia finished the sentence with a smirk.

Regan chose to ignore her. "Ready to go?"

"Ready." Ky slid her wallet into her back pocket.

When they walked to the door together, Regan caught a whiff of Ky's perfume—fresh but not overpowering. She deeply inhaled the clean, compelling scent. She had always loved it because it reminded her of hiding out in their tree house, surrounded by pines and firs, but today, there seemed to be a new note to it…something almost sultry. "That's not new, is it?"

"Hmm?" Ky paused and held open the door for her.

"The perfume."

"No. Same as always."

Regan took another whiff as she stepped past her. Strange. Why did it suddenly seem so different?

*Oh, come on. You know why, Ms. Chemistry Teacher.* Of course there was a scientific explanation for it. Over time, exposure to heat or light would break down the bonds between molecules in the fragrance, changing its chemical composition and therefore its scent. She unlocked her car with a satisfied grin. There. Chemistry could explain everything.

When Ky got in next to her and reached for the seat belt, her sweater tightened across her breasts and shoulders.

Regan quickly looked away and started the car. "What on earth is wrong with you?" she said to herself. She shouldn't notice things like that, no matter how perfectly that sweater molded to Ky's torso.

Ky sent her a baffled look. "What? I didn't do anything."

*Oh shit.* Had she said that out loud? This dating experiment was really messing with her head. "Um, I wasn't talking to you. I meant…" Her cheeks burned as she darted her gaze around, searching for an explanation, then vaguely gestured at the car's loudspeakers, where soft music had started to play.

"I thought you loved Jenna Blake," Ky said. "Don't tell me that changed."

"Oh, no, no. I still love her music. I'm just, um, getting hangry."

Ky widened her eyes comically. "Uh-oh! National emergency! Clear the streets and alert the restaurant!"

Both chuckled, and part of the tension coiling in the pit of Regan's belly eased. They would have dinner at their favorite neighborhood restaurant—which, as Eliza had pointed out, was too noisy for an intimate atmosphere—and Ky would playfully bat her hand away but still allow her to steal half the fries on her plate.

Only dinner with her best friend.

Nothing to it. Right?

Every time the waitress stopped by their table to ask if they—or rather Ky—needed anything else, Regan mentally deducted two dollars from her tip. Three if she "accidentally" brushed Ky's shoulder or touched her arm while refilling her water.

By the time they asked for the check, Blondie owed her fifteen dollars.

*Eighteen,* she corrected as the waitress put the leather-bound folder with the check on the table, again managing to brush Ky's arm. She nearly toppled over the half-full glass since she was busy staring into Ky's eyes.

Granted, Ky's eyes were beautiful. According to her ID, they were blue, but Regan had always thought they were gray with hints of green. But no matter how interesting they were, that was no reason to dreamily stare into them.

It wasn't that Regan was jealous. Of course she wasn't. But what if they really were on a date—one where they both had romantic intentions? Blondie couldn't know they were only humoring their friends.

Flirting with Ky right under her nose was beyond rude, and Regan would not stand for that kind of disrespect. She snatched the leather-bound folder with the check off the table. "I'm paying," she told the waitress with her sweetest smile. "After all, I asked her out."

Blondie paled. "Oh. I didn't... Um, let me double-check that. I think I made a mistake with the drinks." She tried to take back the folder.

Regan held it out of reach and peeked inside.

That was bold. Blondie had written her phone number across the top of the check.

Regan ungritted her teeth to confirm that she had indeed made a mistake—not with the drinks, but by flirting with Ky. But then she stopped herself. *What are you doing? You and Ky have no chemistry, remember?* Apparently, Blondie was convinced there was plenty of potential for a chemical reaction between her and Ky, though. If Ky thought the same, Regan couldn't stand in the way.

She closed the folder with a loud slapping sound and held it out to Ky. "You know what? The check is yours tonight."

They always argued over who got to pay, so Ky stared at her for a moment before taking it. "Oh, sure." She pulled her credit card from her wallet and opened the folder. Her gaze went from the check to Blondie. Finally, she handed the folder back to Regan. "Actually, why don't you pay tonight, and I'll cover the next date?"

Regan reached out to take it but forced herself to ask, "Are you sure?"

"Yes," Ky said firmly. "I've got something special planned."

The waitress rushed off with Regan's credit card as soon as she had handed it over.

*Shit.* Now Regan almost felt sorry for her.

Ky stared at her retreating back. "Was she trying to ask me out, or was that phone number for you?"

"For me? Yeah, right! Didn't you notice how she kept brushing your arm or leaning against you when she refilled your water and brought your food?"

"Oh. I thought she was just being clumsy."

Regan burst out laughing. "God, Ky. You're so oblivious." It was kind of adorable. "She's been flirting with you for weeks. So if you are interested, it would really be okay if you—"

"Nah. I'm not into blondes."

Regan snorted. "Most of your exes were blonde!"

"Maybe I changed my type and prefer brunettes now."

Regan had reached up to run her fingers through her dark locks. Now she snatched her hand away.

They stared at each other with the echo of Ky's words hanging between them.

Then Ky looked away to slide her credit card back into her wallet, and Regan exhaled the air caught in her lungs.

*Jeez, calm down. She didn't mean it like that. This is Ky, remember?*

Good thing they were going to the movies next. They would sit in the dark, without having to talk or look at each other, and by the time the flick ended, they would be past this weird awkwardness and back in friend territory.

What was it with flirty food people today?

The guy behind the concession stand at the Academy Theater was clearly chatting Regan up.

Ky loved the historic movie theater with its 1940s charm and its very affordable ticket prices, but Mr. Chatty was starting to piss her off. How long could it take to prepare an order of popcorn and two sodas? Was he trying to draw it out so he could enjoy Regan's presence a bit longer?

Not that Ky could blame him. Regan was dressed to kill…and Mr. Chatty wasn't her only casualty. Ky really shouldn't notice how the bodysuit outlined Regan's subtle curves or how its neckline, square on the back, dipped low and didn't reveal any straps, making her wonder if Regan was even wearing a bra.

She had thought it was only the damn dress from last week, but apparently, every single item from the back of Regan's closet now had this effect on her.

Or maybe it wasn't the clothing. Maybe she had been deluding herself and wasn't as over her childhood crush on her best friend as she had assumed.

The thought zinged through her brain like an electric shock, leaving her weak-kneed.

She grabbed on to the water fountain along the back wall with both hands and held on until the room stopped spinning around her.

Bullshit. She'd just gotten caught up in this chemistry experiment. So what if she wasn't completely oblivious to how great Regan looked? And even if it was a flare-up of her old crush, she had gotten over it before, so she could do it again. She would be fine as long as she didn't do something rash—like put her hand on that exposed piece of bare skin on Regan's upper back to guide her to the theater.

She splashed cold water onto her overheated cheeks.

Of course, Regan chose that moment to finally return from the concession stand. "Popcorn!" she cheered, then paused and studied Ky. "What's up with you?"

*Shit.* Regan knew her too well. She could read Ky's body language with her eyes closed. "Nothing. I was just beginning to wonder if that guy was having to harvest the corn for our popcorn first." God, she hated lying to Regan. But what was she supposed to do? She wasn't about to risk their friendship.

Regan's dark eyes remained trained on her face, probing. Finally, her intense expression eased into a grin, and she thrust the tray with their sodas at Ky. "Come on. Let's grab seats before the best ones are gone."

They picked two seats in the last row, as they had done as teenagers.

"Or is this too far back for you to ogle Grace Durand?" Regan asked as she sank into the seat next to Ky. "I heard she even dyed her hair because you're no longer into blondes."

Damn, she should never have said that. "Yeah, sure."

"No, she really did. Well, probably not for you, but she's playing a brunette."

Truth be told, Ky didn't know much about the characters Grace Durand and her co-star portrayed. Her favorite actress playing a lesbian was pretty much all she needed to know. Besides, what little she'd read about the movie seemed perfect for them: the romance should make Regan, ever the hopeless romantic, happy, while the supernatural twist would keep Ky entertained.

It wasn't long before the lights dimmed, and the red velvet curtains slid back to reveal the big screen.

The Academy never showed a lot of commercials, so only a few minutes later, a preview for a romantic comedy appeared on the screen.

"Ooh, that one looks good too," Regan whispered. "Will you go see it with me?"

"Yeah, of course. It's in the best-friend contract after all." Without looking away from the screen, Ky reached into the bucket of popcorn Regan had wedged between her thigh and the armrest.

Her fingers brushed Regan's, who had grabbed a handful of popcorn at the same moment.

A tingle ran up Ky's arm.

Popcorn went flying as she jerked her hand back. No, no, no. She shouldn't be tingling. Their hands had brushed like this hundreds of times, and there hadn't been any tingling since she'd grown out of that silly crush.

Regan let out a muffled squeak. "What was that?"

"Um, one of the kernels was still pretty hot." Ky rubbed her hand as if she had burned herself. Maybe she had, but not on the popcorn. She could still feel Regan's touch.

Regan pulled the front of her bodysuit away from her chest and reached inside.

*What the…?* Ky looked away before Regan could catch her staring.

Regan fished a piece of popcorn from her cleavage, slid it into her mouth, and licked her buttery fingers.

*Jesus Christ.* That so wasn't fair! What had she done to the universe to deserve that kind of torture? Ky's face burned, along with the rest of her body.

Why had she ever thought the movie theater was the perfect location for their second no-chemistry date? For the third one, she definitely needed a place where no finger-licking and no cleavage-flashing could happen. She chucked down half of her soda with big gulps.

"Whoa, slow down." Regan leaned closer to study her in the semi-darkness.

"Guess I was more thirsty than I—" An unexpected spasm interrupted her. *Hic!* Ky groaned. *No! Not that too.*

The opening scene of the movie flashed across the screen, and Ky tried to focus on it, hoping it would distract her and stop her case of cleavage-induced hiccups. Surely the first glimpse of Grace Durand—in blue scrubs no less and with dark, sexy-messy hair—would make it happ—

*Hic!*

The hiccups continued, unimpressed by the drama unfolding on the screen as Grace's character shouted orders and shocked her female patient, only to be zapped herself.

Ky tried everything she could think of to get rid of them. She recited the alphabet backward and held her breath until she had to gasp for air.

*Hic!*

A quieter scene now played across the screen—the ER doctor talking to the young woman whose life she'd saved—so the loud hiccuping seemed to echo through the entire theater.

Several people in the row in front of them turned.

Regan leaned across the armrest. Her breath washed over Ky's ear, making her shiver. "Have you tried holding your breath?"

"Yes. Every trick in the—*hic*—book."

"*Anonn* always gave me a spoonful of vinegar when I had the hiccups."

Ky patted her pockets. "I'm all out of vinegar. Any other ideas?"

"There's only two I can think of." Regan's teeth flashed in the darkness as she grinned at her. "A nice, long..."

"Bath? Sorry. Don't have a—*hic*—tub with me either."

"No." Regan cleared her throat. "I'm talking about a nice, long, passionate...kiss."

She was so close that Ky thought she would make good on her suggestion and lean in to kiss her. Her heart thudded against her ribs.

"Ky?" Regan whispered. "Are you breathing?"

"Uh. Yeah. No. Just holding my breath to get rid of the hiccups."

"Hey, I think it worked."

Ky paused and pressed her hand to her diaphragm, waiting for another spasm. Nothing came. *What do you know?* The thought of Regan kissing her had cured her hiccups. "Wow. I guess—"

A woman in the row ahead of them turned. "Would you mind taking your conversation—? Oh! Kylie? Is that you?"

Ky froze. It was official now: she was in hell. "Uh, hi, Lindsey." Of all the people in Portland, she had to run into her ex!

*Hic!*

Groaning, Ky let her head fall back against her seat.

Sometimes, Portland really was a small town. But, of course, every women-loving woman in the city would want to see Grace Durand in the sapphic movie of the year, so maybe running into Ky's ex at the Academy wasn't much of a coincidence.

Her attitude toward Regan hadn't changed in the two years since she and Ky had broken up. When Lindsey caught sight of her sitting next to Ky, she huffed, muttered something, and turned back around.

"Nice to see you too," Regan mumbled.

Another hiccup, even louder than before, came from Ky. "I'll be right—*hic*—back." Before Regan could answer, Ky got up and squeezed past the two people at the end of their row.

Regan stared after her. It wasn't only the hiccups that had made her flee the theater; she could sense that. Was this about Lindsey, or was something else going on with Ky?

Things had felt off all night, and she wasn't sure if it was Ky or her or both of them or this weird situation.

She was still having fun, as she always did whenever she spent time with Ky, but it wasn't the casual night out they had shared in the past. Whenever their arms brushed on the armrest, a shiver of awareness rushed through her. Had Ky felt it too?

Nah. Regan had never been Ky's type. She had never *wanted* to be Ky's type, and things like that didn't suddenly change after twenty-five years of friendship. That was why she'd do what she had always done: make sure her friend was okay.

She slid past the two grumbling people in their row and made her way down the steps to the exit. When the heavy door swung closed behind her, shutting out the sounds of Grace Durand playing squash with her love interest to test their mysterious connection, Regan squinted into the sudden brightness.

There was no sign of Ky at the water fountain. Had she gone to the restroom?

Regan nudged the door open with her elbow and peeked inside.

*Phew.* There she was.

Ky stood at the sink, with the water running, but she wasn't washing her hands. She was staring into the mirror as if she were trying to make it explode into a thousand little pieces by the sheer intensity of her glare. Water dampened her sideswept bangs and glittered on her flushed cheeks.

Regan's heart did a quick double beat. "Ky?" she said, but for once in her life, her voice was too quiet—so soft that Ky probably couldn't hear it over the gurgling of the water.

Ky looked up anyway, as if sensing her presence.

Their gazes met across the otherwise empty restroom. The entire situation felt surreal, as if they were caught in Grace Durand's movie.

Oh God, that would be bad. If there really were some kind of telepathic connection between them, Ky would be able to sense what strange thoughts she'd been having. Luckily, things like that didn't exist in real life.

"You okay?" Regan finally took a step into the room.

Ky interrupted their eye contact to shut off the water. "I'm fine. I think I got it to—*hic*! Damn. I thought it had stopped."

"Remember when *Unonn* had the hiccups for two full days? If they hadn't already been married for forty years, I swear he would have proposed on the spot when *Anonn* got them to stop."

"How did she manage that?" Ky waved one hand in a gimme-gimme motion.

When Regan cleared her throat, the sound echoed through the restroom. "Um, that's where the trick about the kiss came from."

"Oh." Ky chuckled nervously. "Now I'm almost afraid to ask about—*hic*—the second remedy you mentioned earlier."

"That one's completely PG-rated." Thank God. "It's just pressure points."

"Cool." Ky slid up the sleeves of her sweater, revealing her strong forearms. "So where do I tap? Here?" She drummed her index finger against the bend of her elbow.

"Um, no. And you don't tap; you…" It was easier to demonstrate than to explain, so Regan stepped closer, right into Ky's personal space.

Ky's eyes widened, and she went completely still as Regan placed one fingertip in the small indent below her earlobe.

Along the length of her finger, she could feel the thud of Ky's pulse. Her own heart sped up too, as if trying to match it. "You press down very, very gently." Why was she whispering? There was no one else in the restroom, so she wasn't bothering anyone. Regan cleared her throat and moved her finger to the second pressure point, right above Ky's upper lip.

The skin there was soft—so incredibly soft—and the almost microscopic hairs seemed to vibrate beneath her fingertip.

Ky's breath washed over her knuckles, and Regan's own breathing stuttered in response. She fought against the urge to trail her finger along the curve of Ky's mouth.

What the heck was she doing? This suddenly no longer felt PG-rated at all. Quickly, she snatched her finger away, but the third and last pressure point wasn't any better—quite the opposite.

"Um, can you…take your sweater off? I have to…" She gestured at Ky's upper chest.

Was it just Regan's imagination, or did Ky's already flushed cheeks turn an even more intense shade of scarlet? But she gamely whipped the sweater up over her head, tousling her hair, until she was standing there in a white tank top.

Regan had seen her like that—and in much less—a hundred times before. Totally old hat. Or at least it should have been. But today, everything about Ky seemed to register in a new, very confusing way.

*Focus and get this over with.* She traced one finger down the center of Ky's throat until she reached the hollow at the base, where she placed the tips of both index fingers.

Ky's heart thudded along with her own as Regan slid her fingers down an inch, then to the sides, along the edge of her tank top. Goose bumps sprang up beneath her touch. Ky's chest heaved as she sucked in a breath. She covered Regan's fingers with her own, either to press them closer or to keep them from moving. "I think you can stop. They're gone."

"Gone?" Oh, right. The hiccups. "I mean, great. I—"

The door swept open, and heels clacked on the tiles.

Regan looked up and was faced with Lindsey's cool gaze, which seemed to heat up when she took in Regan's hands on Ky's chest, Ky's tousled hair, and the sweater, which had somehow ended up on the floor.

Cheeks burning, Regan slid her hands out from under Ky's.

"Oh, yeah, nothing going on, right? Just two gal pals hanging out. And to think I almost believed you!" Lindsey whirled around on her heel and stormed out.

"Lindsey!" Ky called after her. "It's not what you think!"

Regan grimaced. That sounded like a total cliché. Worse, Lindsey wasn't the only one who'd gotten the wrong idea. Regan's body seemed to have misinterpreted the situation too.

Ky picked up her sweater and pulled it on as if needing the layer of protection. "I don't know why I even bother," she muttered. "I should know by now she won't believe me."

Regan turned toward her.

Ky didn't seem upset or even surprised. Apparently, this kind of accusation wasn't new to her.

"Is that why she always hated me when you were together?" Regan asked. "Because she thought there was something going on between us?"

"She didn't hate you."

"Yeah, right." Truth be told, Regan hadn't been a fan of Lindsey either. She had tried to get along with her for Ky's sake, but deep down, she had always known Lindsey wasn't right for her.

"She didn't," Ky repeated. "She just felt insecure around you."

Regan snorted. "When did I ever make anyone feel insecure?"

"You didn't. I did. According to Lindsey, I didn't pay enough attention to her and was never really in the moment with her."

Regan hurled an angry stare at the door, where Lindsey had disappeared. "Bullshit. That's one of my favorite things about you. You're always fully present."

Ky dug the toes of her boot into the bathroom tiles and shrugged.

"That wasn't why you two broke up, was it?"

Another shrug.

*Oh shit.* What her mother had told her last week came back into focus: *You're keeping each other from having it all. How is a partner going to compete with all the history you two share?* Was this what her mom had been trying to tell her? She grasped Ky's arm to get her to look up. "Was it?"

Ky glanced up, then back down at her boots. "No. Not really. But let's just say Lindsey's jealousy of you didn't help."

"If I was causing problems in your relationship, why didn't you tell me? I could have—"

"No!" Ky looked up sharply. "That's exactly why I didn't tell you. I didn't want you to feel bad or..."

"Or?"

"Or stop being you. Being...us."

Regan slid her fingers down Ky's arm and captured her hand. "We'll always be us, Ky."

Their fingers intertwined in a tangle, and they both looked down at them.

God. It was incredible how good Ky's strong hand felt wrapped around her own. Regan shook off the thought to focus on what she was going to say. "I want you to be happy." She held up her free hand because she knew Ky was about to interrupt. "If I...our friendship is keeping you from finding happiness with someone..."

"I know you're only looking out for me, but I *am* happy. I don't want to limit the time we can spend together or change the way we interact just so my girlfriend won't feel threatened." Ky looked into her eyes. "There's nowhere else I'd rather be right now."

Regan blinked against the burning in her eyes. "Ditto."

A bubble seemed to have formed around them. Regan no longer heard the drip-drip-drip of the tap or smelled the fake lemon scent of the toilet cleaner. All she heard was Ky's breath and her own heartbeat thrumming in her ears, and all she smelled was Ky's subtle perfume.

They stood like that for approximately fourteen eternities or maybe only a few seconds.

Finally, Ky cleared her throat. "Well, maybe except in there"—she pointed at the theater—"watching Grace Durand in those sexy scrubs."

That burst the bubble surrounding them. Regan disentangled her fingers from Ky's and forced a laugh. "You think women in scrubs are sexy?"

"You think they aren't? What kind of bisexual are you?" Ky held open the door for her with her arm.

As Regan slipped beneath it, another whiff of that pines-and-Ky scent tickled her nose. "The kind who thinks people are sexiest in their favorite pair of jeans." She glanced back over her shoulder—and right at Ky's jeans. *Shit.* She really should think before opening her mouth.

Luckily, Ky didn't seem to think anything of it. "You've got me there. A worn pair of jeans on a woman…totally hot."

Regan stared down at her own jeans, which had been washed so often that they were a shade lighter than when she'd first bought them. *She doesn't mean you, doofus. Just women in general.* She ducked into the dark theater, where Ky couldn't see her flush.

When they climbed the steps, the seat in front of theirs was empty.

Regan couldn't wrestle up any real compassion. Ky was the most loyal, faithful person she knew. Anyone who accused her of cheating didn't deserve to watch Grace Durand in her sexy scrubs.

Although Regan had to admit that moment in the restroom probably hadn't looked very platonic. It hadn't *felt* very platonic either. She had touched Ky a hundred or probably a thousand times before, giving her a foot or a shoulder massage, touching her arm to make a point, or holding her hand in support. But none of it had felt any different from touching Heather or Eliza or any other friend.

She paused and stared at the screen without actually watching. No. That wasn't quite true. Her friendship with Ky had always been different—deeper and fiercer in a way she had never been able to put into words. The few times they had argued had hurt much more than an argument with other friends.

Maybe it had been naive to be so sure these dates wouldn't trigger a reaction. With how intense their friendship was, perhaps some sort of reaction was to be expected.

That didn't mean it was a romantic or—Regan gulped—a sexual one. It was exactly what she always tried to teach her students: not everything that appeared like a chemical reaction was one, no matter how spectacular it looked.

Ky burst out laughing at something that had happened in the movie.

Regan had completely missed it, but she couldn't help chuckling along with her in response to Ky's mirth.

*See?* She reacted to Ky. Always had. It wasn't new; it was just this pretending-to-date situation that made it feel that way. Next weekend, they would wrap up this experiment and go back to more predictable reactions.

"Oh my God!" Regan's booming laughter filled her small car, making something inside Ky's chest vibrate. "That scene in the grocery store was the best ever! So hilarious!"

Ky laughed along with her. "I don't know about best scene ever, but yeah, it was great. I'll never look at sponge cake the same way again."

Both burst out laughing again.

"So what was your favorite scene?" Regan asked as she steered the car toward Ky's apartment building. "Let me guess. The shower scene. Grace Durand with her head flung back, trailing one hand down her belly and—"

"No," Ky said quickly before Regan's narration could make her body temperature skyrocket.

That scene had been tastefully done, more hinting at what was happening than showing too many explicit details. But Grace Durand with dark, constantly tousled hair was still messing with her head. Even though her eye color was all wrong—blue instead of Regan's melted-chocolate brown—she reminded her of Regan a bit too much for Ky's peace of mind.

"Which one's your favorite scene, then?" Regan asked.

"The faking-an-orgasm conversation. No, wait. The Griffith Observatory scene. Or maybe when Grace's character loses a patient and they kiss. Or…"

Regan chuckled. "So basically the entire movie."

"Pretty much. I know Grace is happily married to the woman who wrote the script for the movie, but she and Amaya had amazing chemistry."

"I think they're friends in real life, and it shows."

"So are you saying friends can have chemistry, Ms. Chemistry Teacher?" Ky snapped her mouth shut, but the words were already out. What was she doing? Was she flirting with Regan?

"Of course." The grin Regan flashed back was almost sensual.

A shiver chased through Ky. *Don't read anything into it.* Regan was just being Regan. She had always been a flirt. It was merely a bit of good-natured fun to her, but Ky could no longer brush it off with a carefree laugh.

Somewhere between Regan coming up with this harebrained dating idea and now, something had shifted for her. It was as if a protective mask of denial had been pulled from her eyes, and now those rare flashes that she used to get had become a constant awareness of how goddamn attractive her best friend was, especially when she laughed.

Which she was no longer doing. "Um, I mean, friendship chemistry. That's a thing, right?" Regan added. "Of course, it's totally different from the let's-heat-up-the-sheets kind of chemistry."

"Totally." Earlier, in the restroom, she had thought for a second Regan might be feeling more than friendship chemistry too, but now that she could think more clearly, she realized it had probably all been in her head. She had to accept that they would never heat up the sheets together. No way would she make the same mistake her father had and destroy her life because she was never happy with what she had.

So what if she was attracted to her best friend? Not a big deal. She would ignore it until it faded into the background, the way it had when she'd been a teenager.

She just hoped she would do a better job at hiding her attraction than Grace Durand's character had in the movie because life wasn't a romantic flick. With her track record, instead of getting a happily ever after, she'd screw it all up and lose Regan forever.

*Not. An. Option.* She dug her nails into her palms. Come hell or high water, she would make it through their last date, then go back to being in denial.

She already had a fail-safe plan for date number three: Next weekend, she would take Regan to see her favorite singer in concert. They would drool over Jenna Blake in her tight leather pants together, and any kind of chemistry happening between them would be strictly of the friendship kind.

# *Chapter 7*

Ky's plan wasn't as fail-safe as she'd thought.

The next Saturday at the concert, Jenna Blake wasn't wearing leather pants, at least not on the poster shown on the huge video screen behind the stage, and the only drooling going on happened whenever Ky looked at Regan for any length of time.

Cargo pants weren't supposed to be sexy, but Regan had paired them with what Ky secretly called her milkmaid top. Its short, puffy sleeves left her arms bare, and its square neckline revealed a tantalizing glimpse of her collarbone and a hint of cleavage. So much for no cleavage-flashing on their third date! Apparently, Regan hadn't gotten the memo. White laces crisscrossed up her belly, ending just below her breasts. Their ends dangled loose, and Ky caught herself wondering what would happen if she—

*Don't even think about it!*

"Aren't you cold?" Ky asked with another quick glance.

"No, not at all. I'm too excited." Regan bounced along the rows of seats, her denim jacket casually thrown over her shoulder. "Where exactly are our seats?"

Ky pointed up ahead. "Third row."

Regan stopped abruptly and gripped Ky's arm. "You got us third-row seats in the floor section, with a direct view of the stage? Oh my God, Ky! Please tell me you didn't have to sell a kidney. I would have been fine with nosebleed seats, really."

"Don't worry," Ky said. "No essential organs were harmed in the procurement of the tickets. Lilia got them for me. Her cousin's queerplatonic partner is friends with Jenna Blake's wife."

"Wow. Small world."

Traffic around the Moda Center had been horrible, so they had arrived later than expected. By the time they took their seats, the huge arena had already filled, and it wasn't long before the concert started.

The air around them seemed to vibrate with excitement as the lights faded to black. A single beam flared on and danced across the stage until it found a solitary figure, shrouded in artificial fog.

The audience surged to their feet and cheered.

Bass notes and the wild beat of a drum reverberated through Ky's chest. She owed Lilia big time for these tickets.

The look of awe on Regan's face was even better than the up-close view of the famous singer. Ky smiled as she watched her out of the corner of her eye. Regan's almost childlike enthusiasm was one of the things she loved most about her.

"'Odd One Out,'" Regan shouted to her.

The crowd roared in approval, then fell silent as Jenna Blake's husky voice filled the arena.

Amazing how such a lithe woman could glide through four octaves without any noticeable effort. The singer roamed the stage, high-fiving fans left and right while she belted out the lyrics. The leather pants and skin-tight tops she'd worn in the past were absent, as were the scantily clad dancers. Instead, she seemed completely at ease in ripped jeans, boots, and a red tank top.

Well, they had both agreed that nothing looked sexier on a woman than her favorite pair of jeans, so maybe Ky's plan for them to salivate over Jenna Blake was working after all.

"Good evening, Portland," Jenna shouted when the song ended.

Regan cheered so loudly that Ky winced and plugged the ear closest to her.

For the next song, Jenna sat on a stool at the edge of the stage, dangling one long leg and strumming her guitar as if she were merely playing for a few friends on a lazy summer night. She sang the heartfelt ballad with her eyes closed.

With a glance at the rows behind them, where people were starting to take their seats, Ky and Regan sat down too so they wouldn't block anyone's view.

Regan whipped out her cell phone and waved the flashlight above her head. The move made her milkmaid top slide up, revealing a strip of bare skin above the waistband of her pants.

Ky's mouth went dry. Too bad she'd refused to spend five dollars on a bottle of water at the entrance.

"Come on!" Regan nudged her. "Get your phone out!"

Ky tore her gaze away and pulled the device from her back pocket, adding it to the ocean of lights filling the arena.

All around them, the crowd swayed to the beat of the song, thousands of glowing phones held high above their heads.

*Great.* Just what she needed—a ridiculously romantic atmosphere.

Regan's shoulder pressed against hers, and her bare arm rested against Ky's as they swayed in time to the rhythm.

Every now and then, Ky got a respite since Jenna seamlessly switched between love ballads and faster pop songs.

Regan and the rest of the crowd were spellbound through it all, watching Jenna Blake's every move. Ky, however, couldn't take her eyes off Regan. In the glow of dozens of cell phone screens, she was prettier than ever, her expression soft and dreamy. She didn't always hit the right notes as she sang along, but her enthusiasm was endearing.

Finally, the concert seemed to draw to a close. Jenna handed her guitar to a staff member and walked to the edge of the stage with a cordless microphone. "There's one song that I've never performed on stage. Not because it's not good. I'm admittedly biased, but I think it might be my best. It's just too personal. But tonight is special because exactly one year ago today, I got married to the most wonderful woman on the planet, and I feel like shouting from the rooftops how lucky I am to get to share the rest of my life with her."

An earsplitting cheer rose from the crowd, and a group of young fans higher up in the arena waved rainbow flags.

Regan pressed her hand to her chest. "Awww, happy anniversary!"

Her booming voice pierced through the chaos and reached Jenna Blake, who flashed her a smile that seemed amazingly shy for such a successful superstar.

"Oh my God!" Regan bounced on her seat. "Did you see that? She smiled at me!"

Ky bit back a grin. Fangirling Regan was cute, reminding her of their teenage years.

With a giddy laugh, Regan threw her arms around Ky in an exuberant hug.

Ky returned the embrace, soaking up Regan's joy. That and the softness of her body and the amazing way she smelled—no heavy perfume, just Regan. Her eyes fluttered closed.

"Isn't it incredible?" Regan asked, raising her voice over the cheers from the crowd.

Her breath on Ky's ear made her shiver. She forced her eyes back open. "Yeah. Incredible."

A hush fell over the audience as Jenna sang the opening line.

Regan let go and slid around on her seat to face the singer. One hand fluttered up and touched her chest as if she, too, could still feel their embrace imprinted on her skin. Her eyes, however, were intently focused on the stage as she listened.

Jenna sang with the mic in one hand and a single red rose in the other, hitting every note just right. She clearly put her heart and soul into the song. The blend of strength and vulnerability in her voice was mesmerizing.

While Jenna had seemed to make eye contact with every fan in the floor section during the earlier songs, her focus now remained on one person in the first row. She sang only to her.

The emotional intensity sent goose bumps rippling up and down Ky's body. A deep ache welled up inside of her and lodged in her throat.

Regan reached over and took her hand as if sensing her need for connection. Like last week, in the movie theater restroom, their fingers meshed to a perfect fit.

The ache in Ky's chest increased. She peered at Regan's face, but her friend was still focused on the singer. Did she even realize she was holding Ky's hand?

The big video screen showed a close-up of Jenna as she jumped down from the stage and sang the last line while extending the rose toward an auburn-haired woman in the first row.

Once the last note of the song faded away, silence reigned for several heartbeats.

Then the lights came back on. Jenna and her wife shared a tight embrace. The crowd around them cheered, whistled, stomped, and clapped, but Ky barely heard any of it. Her focus was still on Regan's hand in hers.

Regan didn't let go for several more seconds. Finally, she loosened her grip one finger at a time, as if reluctant to let go. "Should we get out of here so we've got a head start and beat the worst of the traffic?"

Ky glanced at the now empty stage. "Won't she give an encore?"

"After that last song?" Regan shook her head. "I don't think anything could top that."

"True. This time, our friends can't accuse us of not trying hard enough to create a romantic mood."

"Definitely not. We get an A-plus for creating the perfect setting for our little experiment."

As Ky followed Regan toward the exit, she wondered what the lab report would say if this really were a chemistry lesson. Would Regan write, *no indications of a chemical reaction,* or had this series of dates affected her in unexpected ways too?

Regan pulled into the parking lot of Ky's apartment building and turned off the car. For several seconds, they sat in silence, interrupted only by muted sounds of traffic and the barking of a dog.

It was getting late, and she had to catch up on her grading tomorrow and make a mnemonics video for her AP students. She really should just drop Ky off, but she didn't want the evening to end.

"So," they said at the same time.

Their voices were hoarse, probably from singing along with Jenna and shouting comments to each other earlier. Ky might pretend to barely like Jenna Blake's music and be unimpressed by the pop star, but Regan saw beneath that cool facade. She had caught Ky singing along at least twice.

"Come on," Regan said. "I'll walk you to your door."

"It's right there." Ky pointed. "You don't have to—"

"You don't want to downgrade my A-plus as a date to a B-minus, do you?"

Ky held up both hands and chuckled. "Wouldn't think of it."

They got out of the car and walked to the front door, close but not touching. When they reached it, they paused and turned toward each other. The light was on in the apartment, bathing them in its glow.

Ky slid one hand into her pants pocket as if to pull her keys out but then didn't. Instead, she swiped her bangs out of her eyes with her other hand—a gesture that always made Regan smile because of its awkward cuteness.

"So," Regan said, "this was it. Our third and final date."

Ky shoved her other hand into her second pocket. "Yeah. Don't think I'm going to kiss you good night just because it's the last one."

"Chicken." Regan made a bawk-bawk sound. "But maybe it's for the best. You couldn't handle me." *Or maybe you'd be the one who couldn't handle it,* a voice in the back of her mind said. Regan ignored it.

Instead of bantering back, Ky smiled softly. "No. I don't think I could."

Regan looked into Ky's eyes, and her playful mood shifted. "Thank you for tonight, Ky. For the tickets and for indulging my fangirl moments." She couldn't even remember when someone had last gone out of their way to plan such a great evening for her. Probably Ky for her last birthday.

"My pleasure," Ky said quietly, and Regan could feel that she meant it.

She put one hand on Ky's shoulder to avoid losing her balance and leaned up for a quick thank-you-and-good-night kiss.

Ky stood very, very still. Her cheek was smooth and warm beneath Regan's lips. God, she smelled incredibly good, even after hours in the crowded arena. Regan deeply inhaled her scent while she lingered close.

A splotch of color rose where Regan's lips had brushed Ky's cheek, and Regan lifted her free hand to tenderly trace it with her fingertips.

Ky pressed into the contact, bringing their faces even closer. She peered down at Regan from mere inches away, her eyes wide and silvery in the dim light.

Regan couldn't look away. Neither could she rein in her much-too-fast breathing or her thrumming heartbeat.

Ky's gaze flicked down to Regan's mouth.

A wave of heat rolled through Regan, and she licked her dry lips.

They were even closer now—so close that their breaths mingled. Someone groaned. Regan had no idea who'd moved or how it happened, but their lips met in a gentle caress as if it was the most natural thing in the world.

Regan's eyes fluttered shut, and their surroundings fell away, leaving only them. She melted against Ky until their thighs brushed.

Ky's hand came up, and she touched Regan's face in a mirror gesture. The slide of her lips against Regan's was tender yet intense, making her head spin in the most delicious way.

A low sound escaped Regan, half gasp, half moan. So soft. So good. So—

Ky jerked back as if she'd been zapped, breaking the kiss so abruptly that Regan's wobbly legs nearly buckled.

So...wrong. Even though it had felt completely right, this was Ky, for Christ's sake! Her best friend. Regan blinked as if waking from a trance. She stared at Ky, into those familiar eyes that all of a sudden did completely unfamiliar things to her. Her hand had coiled into Ky's shirt without conscious thought, and now she quickly let go, breaking the last connection between them.

Ky stared back, one fist pressed to her lips as if hiding the evidence of their kiss.

God. They had kissed!

"I, uh... I'd better go." Ky pointed vaguely in the direction of her front door. "Lil is probably..."

"Yeah."

Ky stumbled to the door. Her keys jangled as she searched for the right one. Then, with one last "night" tossed over her shoulder, she was gone.

Regan placed both hands against the wall to hold herself up. *Oh. My. God! What just happened?*

She didn't know. The only thing she knew for sure was that their experiment, meant to prove that there was no chemistry between them, had been a complete and utter failure.

# Chapter 8

*Holy hell. Did we really just...?* Ky sank against the closed front door and dropped her keys without caring where they landed. She rubbed one hand over the cheek Regan had kissed, then pressed her fingers to her still-tingling lips.

Lilia rushed over from the living room. "Kylie! What happened?"

Ky lowered her hand and gave her a dazed look. "Wish I knew," she mumbled.

"Are you...drunk?"

Ky laughed—a surprisingly rough and husky sound. "No. I'm stone-cold sober." Or maybe she was drunk on the feeling of Regan in her arms, her mouth moving against hers.

Once or twice, years ago, she had wondered what it would be like to kiss Regan—really kiss her, not just share an awkward peck the way they had when they'd been six. Clearly, her imagination sucked. None of her immature teenage fantasies came close to what it had actually felt like when Regan had kissed her.

And that's what she had done. Regan had kissed her. Or had Ky made the first move?

She wasn't sure. It was all a blur of hot breath, pounding hearts, and then Regan's soft lips on hers. But she didn't think she would have initiated the kiss, no matter how much she secretly longed for it. At sixteen, she'd shoved her crush on her best friend into an airtight container and had written the words *Do not open* across it in big, fat letters, with a permanent marker.

She would have never done anything to risk opening that particular Pandora's box, but now Regan had blown it wide open, and Ky had no idea how to deal with it.

*Dammit, Regan!* Ky let out a growl and slammed her fist against the door. Why did she have to do that? Before, whenever her thoughts had strayed in that direction, it had been easy to rein them in and be happy with what they had because she'd been convinced that Regan would never have the slightest interest in her beyond friendship.

But did she really? Was she interested in Ky in a romantic way, or had she merely reacted to the tantalizing atmosphere at the concert? Maybe it had been a spur-of-the-moment thing for her—one of Regan's infamous spontaneous impulses that turned out to be a bad idea and got them both into trouble.

"Kylie?" Lilia stared at her with wide eyes. "You're starting to scare me. What happened?"

Ky shook her head. How could she explain what she didn't understand herself?

"Did you and Regan have a fight?"

"No."

"Are you sure?" Lilia asked. "You seem kinda angry."

Ky fisted her hair with both hands. "I'm not angry. I'm—" She bit her lip hard.

Lilia eyed her. "You're what?"

*Scared to death.* Of course Ky would never admit that. She pushed past Lilia and marched to the kitchen. "I'm fine. Just hungry." She really was—but not for food. Her lips still tingled, and every inch of her body was sensitized, yearning for more. Now that she knew what kissing Regan felt like, how was she supposed to go back to strictly platonic hugs? Could she place the lid back on the box?

*You have to.* She grabbed a chocolate bar and a beer and slammed the fridge shut so hard that the condiments in the door rattled.

Even if there was a certain amount of chemistry between them, Ky knew from the warning signs all over Regan's classroom that some chemical reactions could get dangerous. If she wasn't careful, her entire life could explode into fragments.

Ky had long ago come to the conclusion that she, like her parents, sucked at relationships, and Regan didn't have the best track record either. Even if Regan was interested in trying, they would probably mess it up, and that would be so much worse than any of her previous breakups.

Regan was her rock, her safe place, the person who knew all her secrets. Well, all except for one. Every single one of Ky's happy childhood memories included her. Most of the happy moments as an adult too. She couldn't risk losing her. She *wouldn't.*

With a sharp plop, she twisted the cap off her beer bottle.

As it flew across the kitchen and ricocheted off the wall, Lilia quickly ducked. "Yep, you're clearly just peachy."

Beer bubbled up, splashing over Ky's fingers.

*Damn.* She stared at the dripping mess. Yeah, putting the lid back on was definitely the safest bet.

The next morning, Regan's face felt as if it were stuck in a cement mask, so grinning into the camera took a real effort. Instead of making chemistry seem easy, she probably made it appear as much fun as cleaning cat vomit from a shag rug.

"BARF," she said into the camera, which fit her thought about cat vomit. "Break, absorb, release, form. When a bond is broken, energy is reformed. No. Absorbed. Shit." She stabbed at the stop button on her cell phone, deleted the video, and screamed into one of the throw pillows.

This was her seventh attempt to record the mnemonics video that was supposed to help her students remember bond formation. She tossed the pillow aside and gulped down the remainder of her coffee. Even though it was only nine o'clock on a Sunday morning, it was her third cup, but all the caffeine in the world wouldn't help her focus after tossing and turning for most of the night.

The only bond she could think of had nothing to do with the AP exam.

Her night with Ky at the concert kept playing through her mind in full HD glory: Ky's face in the glow of a dozen cell phone flashlights, both of them swaying to the beat of Jenna's song, all the emotions the romantic lyrics had stirred in her. Each continuous loop ended with the kiss.

She pressed the pillow to her burning cheeks again.

God, that kiss. She could still feel Ky's lips on hers, yet at the same time, the thought of her and Ky kissing was so surreal that she could almost convince herself she had only dreamed it.

But even in her dreams, she had never kissed Ky…had never even thought about kissing her. Sure, lately, she had noticed how good Ky looked in her dating outfits, and there had been that confusing moment in the movie theater restroom, but that was a far cry from kissing her. Why on earth had she done that?

The question had kept her up, but she still hadn't found an answer—at least not one that sounded convincing.

Had she just been on a romantic high after the concert? Maybe it had put her brain on autopilot, so she had walked her date to the door and kissed her good night.

Even though that theory sounded logical, it didn't quite ring true. At least not the part that made Ky seem completely replaceable.

Would she have kissed any of her friends if they had been with her last night? No, she couldn't imagine that.

But then again, neither could she have imagined kissing Ky.

And yet she had. She had known whom she was kissing too. There was no confusing Ky with some random date. She had kissed her not despite her being Ky, but *because* of it. Last night, she had felt so close to her and had needed to be even closer. Maybe the kiss had been an unconscious attempt to make that happen. Apparently, her mind had mistaken one form of closeness for another. Just because she loved Ky didn't mean she loved her romantically, right?

Her silent apartment held no answers.

God, she was so confused.

The worst part was that she couldn't even call her best friend to talk it out and help her see it more clearly, as she normally would have done. Ky had always been her go-to person whenever she needed to talk, but now she was the one person she couldn't call.

She wondered how Ky was dealing with this mess of a situation? Was she pacing her apartment, wishing she could call too? Had she slept or—?

Her phone rang.

"Aargh!" Regan nearly flung it across the room. She pressed her free hand to her wildly pounding heart. Oh jeez, was that Ky?

She peeked at the name flashing across the screen.

*Eliza.*

A complex mix of disappointment and relief rushed through her. She swiped one damp finger across the screen and lifted the phone to her ear. "Hi."

"Sorry for calling so early," Eliza said.

Truth be told, Regan was glad for the distraction. Neither her video recording nor her ruminating about the kiss was producing any good results. "That's all right. I've been up since six."

For a moment, only silence answered. "On a Sunday? I thought you hated mornings?" Eliza paused again. "Unless...something happened to change that. Which is what I'm calling to find out."

Regan's exhausted brain was lagging behind, so it took her several seconds to figure out what Eliza was implying. *Great.* She flopped down face-first onto the couch. Now she couldn't even get angry at her friends' constant teasing and hinting about her and Ky anymore because something *had* happened between them.

"Regan? You still there?"

"Yeah, sorry. The connection must have cut out for a sec. And to answer your question, I still hate mornings."

"Ah, too bad." Eliza's sigh drifted through the phone. "I was hoping you and Kylie..."

"Eliza."

"I know, I know. Wishful thinking. I still think you've got great chemistry, but you two gave it a try, like you promised, so I'm gonna shut up about it from now on." Eliza made a zipping sound.

Regan bit her bottom lip. Shutting up their friends had been their goal when they had agreed to the chemistry experiment, but now she couldn't be happy about it. She felt awful about lying to Eliza, even though it was only a lie of omission. But she wasn't ready to talk. Not before she'd talked to Ky.

"...Saturday?"

Eliza's expectant tone jerked Regan out of her thoughts. Damn. Eliza was clearly waiting for a reply, but Regan had no idea what she'd just asked. "Um, sorry, I missed that."

"I asked if you and Kylie are still up for helping me move in with Denny on Saturday."

"Oh, yeah, of course. We'll be…um…" Regan bit her lip again. If she wasn't careful, she'd leave a permanent mark.

Their friends tended to treat them like a couple, expecting each of them to have the right to answer for them both. And up until now, Regan had never had a problem with that, and neither had Ky. Why bother pretending they didn't spend most of their spare time together?

But was that still true now?

The mere thought that their dynamic might change sent a sharp stab to Regan's heart. Had she forever harmed their friendship because of an impulse she didn't even understand?

"Regan? If you've got other plans, that's okay. My bosses have insisted on helping, and, of course, Heather, Salem, and Matt will lend a hand too, so we should be all set."

"No, no," Regan quickly said. "We'll be there."

"Great. We're meeting at my place—my *old* place—at eight." Eliza let out a giddy chuckle. "I still can't believe I'll be living with Denny this time next week. No more waking up alone. No more saying good night at the door."

The memory of saying good night to Ky started playing through Regan's mind again. As much as she tried to focus on Eliza and her obvious happiness, the autorepeat wouldn't stop.

"—could you let Kylie know?"

Shit. She had missed part of the conversation again. "Um, let her know what?"

"That we're meeting at eight. I'll call her myself, but if you talk to her first, could you let her know?"

"Sure. Will do." She would have to face Ky eventually, and at least that would give them something to talk about…something other than the kiss.

"Are you okay?" Eliza asked. "You're acting a little strange."

Regan held back a sigh. "I've got a busy week ahead. My kids take the AP chem exam on Friday."

"Are you sure you're up for lugging around moving boxes and dismantling furniture on Saturday, then? I'd really understand if you want to hibernate all weekend."

"I'll be there," Regan said firmly. More softly, she added, "We'll be there."

They talked for another minute, then Eliza went back to packing moving boxes, and Regan was once again alone with the images playing through her mind.

She stared at her phone. Should she call Ky?

*No.* What she had to say couldn't be said on the phone. Not that she knew what she wanted to say.

Starting with an apology was probably a good idea.

*But it wasn't all me,* a voice in the back of her head pointed out. *She kissed me back.*

Regan shook her head to silence that voice. Ky kissing her back didn't necessarily mean anything. Maybe she had just gone along with it the way she went along with all of Regan's spontaneous ideas, even if she thought they were silly.

Other than how wonderful Ky smelled and how soft her lips were, what Regan remembered most about last night was how stunned, almost panicked Ky had looked afterward.

She had seen that kind of look on Ky's face only once before: when she'd told Regan that her mother was filing for divorce and they were moving away. Back then, Regan had been the one to comfort her, hug her, and tell her it would be all right.

Never in a million years had she thought that she would one day put that look on Ky's face. Regan's stomach clenched into a tangle of knots. She had messed up, and this time, she wasn't sure whether a hug would make it all right—or make it worse.

# Chapter 9

On Thursday morning, the cafeteria kitchen was a whirlwind of organized chaos as their team worked to prepare lunch and get the day's deliveries squared away.

At least Ky's busy workday left her no time to think about Regan.

Okay, that was a lie. She thought about her as she prepared sandwiches, the only thing Regan could "cook." She thought about her as she lugged a box of frozen cookie dough—chocolate chip, Regan's favorite—out of the walk-in freezer. She thought about her as the PE teacher popped in to grab a snack. Would Regan find the time to do the same? Would she come through Ky's lunch line? Or would she avoid Ky, as she had all week?

If that was what she was doing. Ky couldn't be sure. With the AP chemistry exam coming up tomorrow, Regan had her hands full with last-minute lessons and pep talks to reassure her nervous students.

Still, even in the middle of exams, they had never gone four days without speaking.

Ky was just as much to blame; she knew that. The phone worked both ways. She could have called or at least sent a text. But what was she supposed to say? *Hey, how are you? Have you recovered from the kiss?* Or maybe: *Why the hell did you kiss me?*

She wasn't prepared to hear the answer to either of these questions. What if Regan said it had merely been an impulse and didn't mean a thing? What if she said it meant *everything*? Even worse, what if Regan asked her these questions?

A trickle of sweat rolled down between her shoulder blades, making her school polo stick to her back.

She had no idea what to say or how to face her. Regan had always been able to read her like a book, and now Ky was afraid of what she would see. After the kiss on Saturday night, she needed time to get her platonic-friend game face on.

"Damn." Fran slapped her clipboard onto the worktable next to Ky, wrenching her out of her thoughts and making her flinch. "Our bread order didn't come in."

Ky stared at the chicken breasts she had just seasoned. "So no chicken sandwiches?"

"Not unless you can magically turn two crates of zucchini into ciabatta rolls." Fran sighed. "We'll have to think of something to avoid a mutiny."

Ky flipped through her mental recipe collection and compared the ingredient lists with what she knew was in the walk-in cooler. "How about we make chicken parmesan instead? If there's time, we can even do zucchini noodles."

Fran tapped her pen against Ky's shoulder. "You're good. Must be why they're paying you the big bucks."

"Fourteen dollars an hour is big bucks?" Ky muttered.

"Lilia," Fran called over the hum of the industrial can opener. "Get a cart ready. You're on second-chance breakfast duty in the science wing."

"Can't do it, boss," Lilia shouted back from the double sink. "I'm elbow-deep in apples that need to be washed. Can Kylie do it instead?"

*Me? Go to the science wing?* Ky gulped and hurled a glare at her roommate. Lilia was usually happy to take the cart over to the main entrance or the science hall, where she got to interact with students instead of slaving away in the kitchen. She was obviously convinced that Ky and Regan had had a fight, so she was trying to get them to talk.

Fran looked back and forth between them. Finally, she nodded. "Okay. Kylie, you go. If you want the assistant cafeteria manager position, it might not be a bad idea to show your face over there more often." She nodded toward the main building and the west wing beyond. "By the way, you should let me know about that soon. I need to make a recommendation for the position before the end of the school year."

Ky gulped again. She couldn't deal with this on top of everything else. When had her nice, predictable life become so complicated and overwhelming? "I will."

Fran eyed her. She was probably wondering what the holdup was. Any of the other cafeteria workers would have jumped at the chance to earn more money.

"I need to talk it over with, um, a couple of people first." Only one person, really. With everything that had been going on, she hadn't had a chance to bring up the topic with Regan again, just to make sure she was making the right decision for the right reasons. But for that to happen, she needed to stop being such a coward and finally face her.

Ky grabbed the stainless-steel breakfast cart. They always prepared it the day before, so now all she needed to do was to slide cold packs beneath the dairy in the bottom shelf and check the fruit in the baskets on the slanted top shelf. Then she wheeled the cart through the double swinging doors and over to the west wing.

With every step, her throat tightened more until she felt as if she were breathing through a straw.

Regan's classroom was at the end of the hall, overlooking the football field, not exactly close to where Ky set up the cart. She would only be here for fifteen minutes, so she might not even see her.

Her heart pounded anyway as she folded down the side shelf and set up the POS system so the kids could enter their IDs.

A bell blared through the loudspeakers, signaling the end of the first period.

Classroom doors swung open, and students flooded the hallway. Several stopped by the cart to grab a Pop-Tart, a blueberry muffin, or some juice.

Shoes squeaked on the floor, locker doors slammed, and kids called out to each other. But even over the noise, Ky immediately picked out one voice. She glanced up from the cartons of chocolate milk.

Regan was walking toward her. She wore the T-shirt Ky had given her for her last birthday. The *If you're not part of the solution, you're part of the precipitate* slogan written across its front peeked out from beneath her navy-blue blazer. Her hands were moving without pause, forming round shapes that might be atoms or molecules or something. The two students flanking her hung on her every word.

Ky couldn't look away either. She drank her in like a glass of cold water after a march through the desert. God, she had missed her. The four days without her had been the longest of her life.

As Regan came closer, Ky zeroed in on her face. She was pale, which made the light sprinkle of freckles across the slope of her nose stand out. Her brown eyes, surrounded by faint shadows, looked even larger than usual, and her hair seemed to have lost a fight with her comb. For the first time since the day Ky had met her, Regan's petite frame appeared fragile and vulnerable.

Ky's stomach churned. Damn. Regan looked like crap. Obviously, she had slept as little as Ky had the last few nights.

This immature not-talking bullshit had to end—right now. She wouldn't stand by and watch Regan hurting. Ky opened her mouth just as Regan looked up from her conversation.

Their gazes met.

Ky's lips froze in position, forming a word that had completely slipped her mind. Muffled music drifted through someone's earbuds, but Ky barely heard it over the buzzing in her ears. Time seemed to slow.

Regan said something to her students and gave a see-you-later wave.

They shuffled down the hall, throwing curious glances over their shoulders.

Very aware of all the people watching them, Ky tried to appear cool, calm, and collected as Regan bridged the remaining space between them and stopped in front of the cart. Nothing to see here. Just a lunch lady offering breakfast to one of the teachers.

"Hi," Regan said quietly.

"Hi." Ky tried to shove her hands into her pants pockets, then realized she was wearing an apron and white-knuckled the cart's push handle instead.

Silence lingered between them, as dense as fog in October. Ky wasn't exactly chatty around other people, but she had never been tongue-tied with Regan before. Aargh, she hated this sudden awkwardness between them.

*Come on. Say something.* Anything to break that damn silence. She swept her hand over the goodies in the cart by way of invitation. "Second-chance breakfast?"

*Kind of fitting,* her anxious mind supplied. A second chance was exactly what they needed.

"Um, yeah, thanks." Regan turned her attention to the bottom shelf as if she was glad for the excuse to look away from Ky. She regarded the food as if nothing appealed to her, then finally picked a pre-packaged piece of banana bread and a carton of chocolate milk.

Comfort food. Ky had eaten too much of it in the past few days too. Regan needed something more nutritious. She grabbed the most beautiful apple from the top shelf and held it out.

Regan stared at it as if Ky had morphed into Eve and were offering her the forbidden fruit.

"School regulations," Ky said quickly. "One of the items needs to be a piece of fruit."

Normally, Regan would have made a joke about the banana bread classifying as fruit. Not today. "Oh, right. Of course." As she took the apple, their fingers brushed.

A tendril of heat twisted through Ky.

Regan licked her lips. "Thanks."

Ky glanced away. Looking at Regan's mouth—that graceful Cupid's bow of her upper lip—was what had gotten them into this trouble.

"So," they both said at the same time.

Quickly, Ky waved her hand for Regan to speak first. Regan had always been the brave one, and she hoped that wouldn't change now.

Regan rubbed the apple along the outer curve of her thigh in a slow, probably unconscious movement, and Ky realized looking at her legs was as dangerous as looking at her lips.

"Um, did Eliza call you?" Regan asked.

Ky ducked her head. She had, and so had Heather, but Ky hadn't answered, afraid they would ask about their date. "I haven't talked to her in a while. Why?"

"She's moving in with Denny on Saturday and asked if we can come over to her old place at eight. Are you still up for it?" Regan's eyes were deep and searching, as if she was asking about more than helping their friends move.

"Always," Ky said firmly.

They gazed into each other's eyes for what seemed like a long time.

"Good. Very good." Regan shifted her breakfast goodies to her other hand. "Do you maybe want to—?"

"'Scuse me," a teenager towering over Regan called from behind her. "Can I have a Pop-Tart?"

*No! Not now,* Ky wanted to shout. Her polite smile probably looked more like a predator baring its teeth. "Here." She shoved two Pop-Tarts at the boy, then, as an afterthought, added a banana. "On me."

"Uh, thanks." He stared back and forth between the Pop-Tarts and Ky before shrugging and sauntering off.

Ky leaned across the cart to be closer, very aware that they could be interrupted again any moment. "You were saying?"

"Did you want to meet up before Saturday? Maybe take a walk up Mount Tabor and...talk?"

Every bit of air escaped Ky's lungs. Mount Tabor, the park on top of an extinct volcano, was the place they went to whenever they needed to talk about serious stuff. It had been there, high above the city, where Regan, overwhelmed by the stress of her first year of teaching, had confessed she wasn't sure she was cut out to be a teacher. And it had been there where Ky had voiced her doubts about whether her mother's death had really been an accidental overdose or suicide.

Well, a very much nonplatonic kiss probably qualified as serious.

Ky forced herself to inhale and stand up straight. They had made it through those conversations. This time wouldn't be any different. "Yes," she croaked out. "I'd like that."

A hint of a smile quivered about Regan's lips. "Okay. Good. I've got a faculty meeting right after school, but how about afterward? Meet me at half past seven at the reservoir?"

Ky nodded. She would have said yes, even if Regan had suggested midnight. Suddenly, she couldn't stand going another day without talking to her. She wished they could go somewhere and talk right now, but abandoning the cart was not an option. Plus she had to get back to the cafeteria.

"Good." Regan let out a shuddery breath. She looked left and right as if to make sure no one was watching, then reached across the cart. Inches from touching Ky's arm, she froze and pulled her hand back.

Ky's fingers twitched with the need to cover hers and establish some kind of contact. Instead, she wrapped them around the cold metal of the push handle.

"We're going to fix this, okay?" Regan spoke so quietly that Ky had to strain to hear her over the din of conversation in the hallway.

Ky's vocal cords felt stuck together, so she again just nodded.

Regan nodded back.

They stood without saying anything else, simply looking at each other.

Then two students walked up and peered over Regan's shoulder at the breakfast goodies.

Regan backed out of the way and gave a wave that appeared unusually timid. "See you tonight."

All Ky managed was another nod. As she tracked Regan's path down the hall, Regan's words echoed through her mind. *We're going to fix this.* Instead of reassuring her, they weighed her down like an iron band around her chest. *Fix this.* So her suspicion had been correct—Regan indeed thought kissing her had been a silly impulse, a mistake, something to fix.

Ky should have been happy with that. Fixing their friendship should have been all she wanted. But thanks to that magical moment at her front door, it no longer was. Her most important rule had always been to be happy with what she had and avoid wanting more in every part of her life. Now she had broken that rule big time.

*Shit.* She was in so much trouble.

In her six years as a teacher, Regan had learned to turn off personal worries when she walked into a classroom. But as soon as the last lesson of the day was done, the faculty meeting was over, and she got home, all of her thoughts were with Ky again.

She would see her in about half an hour for their walk up Mount Tabor, and she still had no idea what to tell her.

In the last few days, while her AP students took their last practice exam, she'd had plenty of time—too much time—to think about what had happened. The sensations of Ky's lips on hers still lingered, but now she could push back those images and look beyond.

Had that kiss really come as out of the blue as she'd first thought, triggered by the ridiculously romantic evening and Jenna Blake serenading her wife with a love song?

If she was honest with herself, she hadn't been thinking of Jenna Blake or her wife when they had said good night outside of Ky's front door. The only person she'd been thinking of was Ky—in a way she never had before.

Or had she? Had she experienced similar feelings in the past?

Memories from their first two dates flooded her. She had laughed them off when they had happened, blaming them on their friends' meddling, but now she remembered being breathless at seeing Ky in that formfitting sweater, with Charlize Theron-style hair, and how she had suddenly noticed her perfume in a new way.

A shiver went through her as she flashed back to the moments in the movie theater restroom. At the time, she had put it down to the intensity of their friendship and avoided thinking about it too much, but now that she was forced to examine her reaction more closely, she had to admit that curing Ky's hiccups had been the last thing on her mind when she had slid her fingers down Ky's upper chest. She had focused solely on how soft Ky's skin was and how good it felt to touch her.

Regan stretched out on her couch, then put one leg up the wall, which always helped her think. *Okay.* She inhaled and exhaled deeply.

It was probably safe to say she was attracted to Ky. The thought sent shockwaves through her entire body.

*Calm down.* It didn't need to be a big deal, right? After all, attraction was just chemistry—the brain releasing a heady cocktail of dopamine, norepinephrine, and serotonin. It didn't have to mean anything.

But then again, maybe it did.

Had it merely been a physical reaction, something that, like the physical changes she taught her students about, altered only the appearance of the substances involved and could easily be reversed? Or was it more than purely physical attraction? Was it possible she was developing romantic feelings that, like a true chemical reaction, would change the very identity of their relationship into something completely new?

And the scariest question of them all: What if it was one type of reaction for Regan but something entirely different for Ky?

Well, she would never find out if she didn't get going. Parking was usually bad at Mount Tabor Park, so she needed to leave now to make it on time.

She swung her leg down and hopped up from the couch.

When Regan had been little, her parents had taken her and her siblings to Mount Tabor Park a few times. Back then, she had imagined the turn-of-the-century gatehouses with their turreted tops and arched windows as castles where princesses lived.

Once she was older, she had found out they actually controlled the flow of water in the reservoirs, but that feeling of the park being a magical place, set apart from the bustling city, had never quite left her.

As she crossed the street and climbed up the long set of stairs to the reservoir at the base of Mount Tabor, she hoped that slivers of magic still lingered—she could sure use it for the conversation ahead.

An unlikely princess waited for her in front of the first gatehouse. Since Ky's apartment was less than half a mile from the park, she usually made it there before Regan. At least this one thing hadn't changed.

Ky had one hand shoved deeply into her pants pocket while she repeatedly swiped her bangs from her face with the other hand. One of her feet tapped out an unheard rhythm, but when Regan approached, she stopped. A look of apprehension crossed her face, then was gone so fast that anyone else might have missed it.

Not Regan.

That look made her want to walk up to her and hug her tightly. But hugging might lead to kissing her cheek, which might lead to capturing Ky's soft lips with her own again.

No. This conversation was too important to mess it up with one of her impulsive moves, so Regan forced herself to stop a few feet away. She dredged up a smile. "Hey."

"Hi." Ky bobbed up and down on the balls of her feet as if trying to get rid of some nervous energy. "How was the faculty meeting?"

Regan made a show of dramatically rolling her eyes. "Could have been an email."

Silence descended again.

God, Regan missed their usual easy banter. "Shall we?" She pointed toward the promenade encircling the rectangle-shaped reservoir, separated from it by an ornamental wrought iron fence. At least walking would give them something to do apart from awkwardly avoiding eye contact.

Ky nodded, and they turned right to get to the other side of the reservoir.

Since it was a weekday, not as many joggers and cyclists passed them, making the silence between them even more obvious.

Neither of them said much, other than pointing out a squirrel darting across the paved path and then scrambling up a tree.

They climbed the hundred-plus stairs that would take them to the next reservoir, halfway up the hill. The steps were narrow and steep, forcing them to walk single file. Talking was impossible anyway because Regan was breathless. Her heart pumped fast, but admittedly, it wasn't just because the climb gave her quite the workout. She knew what would happen once they made it up: they would sit in their favorite spot and talk.

When they reached the end of the stairs, they paused to catch their breath.

Regan took a moment to study her favorite castle. The gatehouse up here was round, not square like the two on the lower level.

They easily fell into step, matching each other's pace without effort as they circled the oval-shaped reservoir to get to their spot. The scent of pine trees tickled Regan's nose. Maybe the scent was part of the Mount Tabor magic for her. It reminded her of Ky's perfume and the tree house from their childhood.

Everything in her life reminded her of Ky. Hell, Ky *was* her life—or at least a big part of it. She couldn't lose her.

Their bench at the edge of a grassy area was empty, without any people nearby.

Wordlessly, they steered toward it and sat next to each other. A foot of space separated their thighs. Each inch hurt, making Regan aware of how much was on the line.

Despite her Catholic grandparents, she wasn't a religious person, but now she prayed she wouldn't say the wrong thing and screw everything up. If only she knew what the right thing was.

Ky was quiet too—not her usual laid-back calm but a tense silence, as if she had no clue what to say either.

They both watched the clouds reflected in the green-blue water of the reservoir below them as they slowly drifted across the sky. Beyond the gatehouse on the other side, they had a scenic view of downtown and the West Hills in the distance. Slowly, the sun dipped toward the dusky hills.

*Great.* A romantic sunset. Just what she needed for this conversation.

"I hate this," she burst out. Wait, that wasn't what she'd wanted to say. "Not that." She gestured toward the reservoir, the view, and the sunset. "This." She pointed between them.

Ky merely nodded without saying anything.

Her silence was unnerving, so Regan tried to fill it with whatever came to mind. "I had the shittiest week."

"You think mine was great?" Ky grumbled.

Regan slid around on the bench to study her in the slowly fading light. Where had that come from? Ky wasn't usually one for snarky comments. But something seemed to seethe beneath the surface, like the dormant volcano that was Mount Tabor. Her strong jaw clenched, and the hand closest to Regan tightly gripped her own leg.

Regan desperately wanted to reach out and stroke her fingers until they relaxed. It almost physically hurt to know that she couldn't. "No." For the first time in her life, she chose her words carefully when talking to Ky. "Of course I don't think that. I'm trying to work up the courage to apologize, okay?"

Ky once again stared straight ahead across the reservoir.

Had that not been what she'd wanted to hear? But Regan felt she had to say it. "I'm sorry, Ky."

Now Ky turned her head and looked at her. Her eyes had taken on the greenish color of the water in the reservoir, and they were just as inscrutable—for once, Regan couldn't see what lurked beneath. "Sorry… for what?"

Wasn't it obvious? "For kissing you."

The words seemed to echo across the water, even though she'd spoken them quietly.

Ky's eyes appeared to turn an even mossier shade of grayish green.

Regan felt as if she were tiptoeing through the dark, slamming into obstacles with every step. Clearly, that hadn't been the right thing to say either. What on earth did Ky want if not an apology? Maybe she didn't even know. Regan sure as hell had no idea what she, herself, wanted. "I know that wasn't part of the plan when we agreed to our little chemistry experiment, and I've been trying to understand it ever since it happened." She paused. Should she tell Ky about her surprising realization? See if Ky possibly felt that spark of attraction too? Heart pounding, she decided to be brave and put it out there. "Do you think maybe—?"

Ky slashed her hand through the air as if she didn't want to hear an explanation. "This isn't a fun little experiment to me. You're the most important person in my life. I can't lose that. I can't lose you." Her voice, sharp at first, became quieter and more anguished with every word until she whispered the last one with trembling lips.

*Oh God.* Ky wasn't angry. Not really. She was terrified.

Nothing in the world could stop Regan from touching Ky now. She put her hand on top of Ky's shaking fingers, but that wasn't enough, so she slid closer and wrapped both arms around her in a hug that was fierce yet tender.

At first, Ky stiffened. Just when Regan thought she would pull away, Ky slumped against her and returned the embrace. She clung to her with a desperate intensity Regan hadn't felt from Ky since her dad had been caught embezzling, tearing Ky's life apart.

Ky's knee dug into her leg, but Regan didn't care. She curled both hands into the corduroy of Ky's jacket and deeply inhaled her scent.

Regan's sweater had slid up a bit, and one of Ky's hands rested on the bare skin along the small of her back. Goose bumps rose beneath her touch, but Regan ignored them. One thing was clear to her now: Whatever it was she had felt on Saturday night…whatever she might still be feeling, she had to push that spark of possibility to the back of her mind until it extinguished. If the last few days had proven one thing, it was that this had the potential to do what even Ky moving away after her parents' divorce hadn't managed: to pull them apart.

She tightened her grip on Ky. For once, she'd adopt Ky's risk-averse approach to life. She couldn't risk hurting her or losing what they had for something that might not work out. "You won't lose me," she whispered into Ky's ear. "Never."

Ky's hold on her increased, and she pressed her face to Regan's shoulder. "I've had a lot of breakups over the years, but I was always fine after a little while. Because I had you. But if I lose you…"

"You won't," Regan said again. She would repeat it until Ky believed it. "Forget"—she bit the inside of her cheek and forced herself to say it—"that kiss." *And that moment in the restroom. And holding hands at the concert.* She ignored that annoying voice and forged on. "I mean, the idea of us dating for real… It would be even sillier than when we taped Ms. Noyes's remote to the SMART Board, right?"

"You did that; I just acted as the lookout."

"Yeah, yeah. My point is, like you said, we both suck at relationships."

"Mm-hmm." Ky hummed against her skin, causing more goose bumps to erupt. "We're pretty good at the friendship thing, though. I don't want to mess with that."

"Right. Why mess with perfection, right?" *Stop saying* right, *dipshit!* Regan cleared her throat. "We'll leave all of this behind and go back to how it was."

"You think we can?" Ky asked, her voice muffled by Regan's sweater.

"Of course," Regan said, as much to convince herself as Ky. "It's up to us to define our relationship and what we want it to be, right?"

Ky shrugged without loosening their embrace, barely avoiding an uppercut to Regan's chin. "I guess. I just want my best friend back. I want *us* back."

"We will get us back." It felt like speaking an oath, and Regan knew she would take it as seriously. "I promise I'll never allow anything to come between us again."

Ky blew out a long exhale.

Her warm breath washed over Regan's neck and drifted beneath the V-neck of her sweater. A shiver raced down Regan's chest, but she vigorously tamped down on her body's traitorous reaction.

They hung on to each other for a while longer. Slowly, Ky relaxed her grip on Regan's back, let go with one arm, and leaned against the back of the bench, with her other arm still around Regan.

Regan peeked over at her.

Was it only the remaining pink glow of the sunset, or did Ky really look more at peace? Was it that easy for her? Had she already forgotten about their kiss and moved on?

On the one hand, that was a relief. Ky had had enough hardship in her life; she shouldn't have to be afraid of losing anyone else. On the other hand, Regan felt a bit of the sadness she wanted to spare Ky. Even though she had been the one to say they'd leave the kiss behind them and go back to how things had been before, not knowing what could have been made her strangely melancholic.

They sat with their arms loosely around each other and watched as the sky grew darker until even the glimmer of orange hovering over the hills faded away. Regan could no longer make out any details, only Portland's skyline in the distance and the black silhouettes of towering Douglas firs surrounding them. The lamps around the reservoir came on, their glow reflecting off the water. Beneath them, the lights of the city twinkled to life.

*Magical.* That made her think of castles and princesses again. Well, these two princesses wouldn't get their classic fairy-tale ending, but they would continue to slay life's dragons together. That was a happy ending in its own right, wasn't it?

"What are you thinking about?" Ky asked quietly.

"Dragons."

Ky burst out laughing, maybe a little too loudly, as if all the emotions of the last few days needed an escape valve. "What?"

With a mild smile, Regan shook her head. "Oh, you know. Just my brain being weird after a long day…long week teaching."

Regan felt Ky's gaze on her in the dim light, but Ky didn't say anything.

"What about you?" Regan asked, partly to stop Ky from digging deeper, asking about her thoughts, and partly because she really wanted to know. "What are you thinking about?"

She felt more than heard Ky sigh, her chest lifting and falling next to her. "*Heart Trouble.*"

As if recreating Ky's words, Regan's heart ba-bummed. "Um, what?"

"Sorry. Guess my brain is as weird as yours. I meant the movie we watched. The one with Grace Durand."

*Oh. That Heart Trouble.* "What about it?" Truth be told, Regan would have to watch the movie again at some point because most of the scenes after the restroom incident were a blur.

Ky swept her arm toward the glowing lights beneath them. "This reminds me of that scene when they are up at Griffith Observatory, looking down at the lights of LA."

That comparison felt dangerous. Her life was not a romantic movie with a guaranteed happy ending, and if she wanted to forget she was undeniably attracted to her best friend, she needed to remind herself of that. "Yeah, well, but anyone who's ever seen my bank account knows I'm not Grace Durand, and unlike her co-star, you at least had the sense not to come up here without a jacket."

"But you didn't."

Regan had been occupied thinking about what she would say to Ky, so she had forgotten to grab a jacket. "Teacher's brain."

"Aren't you getting cold?" Ky asked.

"A little." Before Ky could offer her jacket, which was totally like her, Regan added, "But we should go anyway. It's getting late, and I have a super early day tomorrow."

Ky got up immediately. "All right. Let's go."

As they walked around the reservoir and passed the gatehouse, Regan glanced over her shoulder at her favorite castle. Of course, there were no princesses inside, only old pumps and other equipment. Maybe Mount Tabor didn't have any magic left or had never had any to begin with.

She should have known there was no such thing as magic; it was all just chemistry.

Regan had insisted on driving her home, refusing to let her walk back to her apartment in the dark, and Ky was too drained to put up a fight.

The latest Jenna Blake album played through the Toyota's speakers, and, of course, it had to be one of the love songs the pop star had sung at the concert.

Ky tried not to grimace.

This late in the day, the neighborhood was even quieter than usual, so it thankfully took only two minutes until Regan pulled into the parking lot of Ky's apartment building. She shut off the engine but made no move to get out and walk Ky to the door.

Considering how the evening had ended the last time she'd done that, maybe that was a good thing.

They sat without speaking for a few moments while the song continued to play.

"I hope tomorrow goes okay," Ky finally said.

Regan sent her a questioning look.

"The AP exam."

"Oh, that." Regan chuckled as if she had completely forgotten about it. "The chem test is one of the most challenging, but my kids have put in the prep work. They'll be fine."

"Good." Ky hesitated, but she couldn't leave without making sure.

"Are we?" they both asked at the same time.

They paused and looked at each other. A slow grin formed on Regan's face, and Ky mirrored it.

Thank God. They were still on the same wavelength.

Ky felt as if she had been wrenched back from a deep chasm at the last second and was now back on steadier ground. It was as if she could finally breathe after holding her breath for the last five days.

But a tiny little voice in the back of her mind remained, wondering what she would have found at the bottom of the abyss if only she'd had the courage to jump.

*A broken neck, that's what.*

"We'll be fine," she said firmly.

"Yeah." Regan nodded, but Ky knew her well, so she couldn't help noticing the hint of tension in her voice. "Just keep talking to me. About everything. Okay?"

"Okay." Ky felt like the shittiest liar ever because she already knew it was a promise she wouldn't be able to keep. If she wanted to put the lid back on Pandora's box and tape it shut, she couldn't tell Regan how complex her feelings for her really were. She wasn't even sure she understood it herself. "You do the same, all right?"

Regan nodded again, her lips slightly compressed.

Ky knew that particular shape of her mouth. That was how Regan looked when she forced herself to shut up so she wouldn't get into even more trouble. Was Regan holding back something too?

*Whatever it is, you don't want to know,* she firmly told herself. *Put the lid on and keep it shut.*

Ky climbed out of the car. "Do you want me to leave you a snack on your desk tomorrow since it'll be a long day?"

"Would you?" A quiver went through Regan's voice.

Ky bent a little to see her better. The way Regan looked up at her with her big, vulnerable eyes made Ky want to crawl back into the passenger seat to draw her into her arms. "Of course."

"I don't want you to have to get up even earlier to deliver it," Regan said.

Ky waved her hand. "Nah. It's on my way to work anyway."

"I'd love to have a snack, then. But don't stay up too late, baking." Regan pointed her index finger at her. "I know you, Kylie Wells."

"Yes, you do," Ky said softly. "Don't worry about it. I won't go overboard. Please drive carefully and send me a text when you get home."

"Will do. Good night."

"Good night." Ky shut the passenger-side door between them. She waited for Regan to pull out of the parking lot but then realized Regan was waiting for her to reach the front door.

She waved and walked toward her apartment. As she slid her key into the lock, Regan started the car.

Ky unlocked the door but didn't enter yet. Instead, she turned.

Their gazes met through the car's side window. Then Regan backed out of the parking space, and soon, her taillights disappeared around the corner.

"We'll be fine," Ky repeated to herself as she swung the front door open. After all, she had done it before—put her crush on Regan aside and focused on their amazing friendship.

It would take more effort to do it again, but she would manage somehow.

But this damn door needed a new coat of paint in a different color so it would stop reminding her of their kiss.

She closed it sharply behind herself, as if that would also close that chapter, and marched to the kitchen to see if she had any almonds and chocolate chips to bake chocolate biscotti. The yummy biscuits Regan's grandmother had made for them when they'd been kids seemed like exactly the right snack for Regan's long workday tomorrow.

# Chapter 10

On Saturday afternoon, Denny's two-story townhouse in Lents looked like the headquarters of the local women-loving women community. Ky didn't even know all of the helpers, but most of them pinged her gaydar.

A tall woman in a Portland Police Bureau T-shirt was up on a ladder securing a new shelf to the wall. Her strawberry-blonde partner handed her a bracket. Eliza's bosses—a lesbian couple—were putting up new curtains, while Denny and Eliza were carefully navigating a nightstand upstairs.

Ky deposited the box she was carrying on the kitchen counter, then stepped aside so Regan, who was following closely behind, could place hers next to it.

Regan groaned as she swung her box back to gather momentum.

Before Ky could take one side of the box to lift it up together, one of the only two male helpers walked over and tried to take the box from Regan. "Let me."

"Thanks. I've got this." Regan heaved her box up without his help.

*Go Regan!* Ky couldn't help grinning proudly.

The guy blushed and held up both hands. "Sorry, that was…um…"

"Right out of the *Sexist Moves 101* handbook," Ky muttered.

Regan elbowed her. "Be nice."

"I'm really sorry," the man said. "I didn't mean to imply… It's just that I'm taller."

Regan laughed. "*Everyone*'s taller than me. I appreciate the offer, but if I let my height—or lack of it—stop me from doing things, I'd never get anything done."

Most of the time, Ky didn't think of Regan as short, because her personality and her presence were larger than life.

Instead of being put off by Regan's frank words, the guy smiled. "Fair enough. But if you would like some help with anything, let me know."

"Don't worry; I will. I've always been told that my mouth is bigger than the rest of me, so if I need help, you can be sure I'll speak up."

He hooked his thumbs into his front pockets and regarded her. "What if *I* need help?"

Ky narrowed her eyes at him. Was he flirting with Regan?

So what if he was? That was great, wasn't it? One of them getting involved with someone else might actually be a good idea.

If he was indeed flirting, Regan apparently hadn't noticed—or wasn't interested. She measured him with a friendly, but not flirty look. "You don't look like you'd be afraid to speak up either."

"I'm not. So, to be honest, I could use some help with the dresser." He pointed toward Denny's former bedroom, which they wanted to convert into a sewing room for her. "I'm Oliver, by the way. Matt's brother. Please call me Ollie." He shook Regan's hand, holding on too long for Ky's liking.

Christ, what was he doing? Trying to decide her ring size by touch? She struggled not to glare at him.

Finally, Oliver let go of Regan's hand and offered his to Ky too.

She reluctantly took it but couldn't bring herself to return his smile.

He regarded her with a curious look. Then his eyes widened. "Wait… Oh, shit. Are you two…?" He let go of Ky's hand to slap his own forehead. "Man, I'm so barking up the wrong tree, aren't I? Again, I'm really sorry. I swear I'm not normally so obnoxious."

Heather walked by with a lamp, the lampshade playfully perched on her head as if it were a hat. It wobbled precariously as she shook her head at Oliver. "Everybody thinks they're a couple, but these two conducted a little study, and apparently, the results are just in. No chemistry. You could strip them buck naked and tie them together for the rest of the weekend, and nothing would happen."

"Um, thanks for that mental image." Oliver fanned himself with one hand.

Ky barely resisted the urge to do the same. She hurled a glare at Heather. *Yeah, thank you so much. Some of us have a visual imagination, you know?*

When neither of them commented, Heather pushed the lampshade off her forehead so she could see them better. "What? You're the ones who always insist you've got zero chemistry. Right?"

"Right," Ky and Regan said in unison.

"Wow." Heather shook her head. "That sounded convincing." She tipped the lampshade and walked past them to the new workroom.

"So." Oliver looked back and forth between them before focusing on Regan. "Bedroom? Um, I mean, how about that dresser?"

"Lead the way." As Regan followed him, she glanced back at Ky and playfully rolled her eyes.

Ky stared after them.

Denny joined her, and they stood silently for several moments. Except for her, Denny was the quietest person in their friend group, and Ky had always enjoyed her kind, unassuming personality.

Finally, Ky forced her attention away from the old bedroom and turned toward her. "Do you need my help with something?"

"Join me in the backyard for a second, will you?"

"Sure." Ky followed her through the sliding glass door into the tiny, fenced-in backyard. She had expected to find some kind of project Denny needed help with, but except for some potted plants hanging down from the wooden fence, there was nothing to see. She sent Denny a questioning look.

"I, um, thought you might need a little timeout."

"Why would I—?"

Denny nodded toward the house.

The old curtains had been removed so they could see directly into the bedroom, where Regan was talking to Oliver, waving a screwdriver and clearly giving him instructions.

"Denny, it's not—"

"You and I, we haven't been friends for that long, but have I ever mentioned that Eliza and I were just friends for some time when we met?"

Ky held back a grin. "You did." With Regan, Heather, and Eliza being the chatty ones in the group, Denny didn't say much, but when she did, she mostly talked about her girlfriend. It was cute, even though Ky didn't quite understand it. Her relationships had never been her sole focus. But then again, maybe that was why she was single, while Denny was setting up house with the love of her life.

"I thought she was straight—and Eliza thought so too."

Ky waited. Where was Denny going with this?

"She was the queen of disastrous first dates," Denny continued. "We laughed at each one afterward, and I started to believe that it would always be like that. Just the two of us enjoying each other's company, with no one to come between us. Until she met a guy who looked like Chris Hemsworth."

Ky drilled her nails into her palms and stared through the window at Oliver. Was that what Denny thought would happen? That Mr. Let-me-carry-that-box-for-you would come between them?

Eliza stepped outside with a potted cactus. "He looked like Henry Cavill, not Chris Hemsworth." She hung the prickly plant next to the others on the fence and brushed a soft kiss on Denny's lips. Her hands came to rest on Denny's love handles, and she stroked them tenderly. "And he had nothing on you, my love."

Then she was gone again and closed the glass door between them.

Denny blinked as if she had trouble refocusing her eyes. She cleared her throat. "What was I saying?"

Ky laughed. "Eliza was completely straight and going out with Chris/Henry."

"That's what I thought. I was convinced a wonderful friendship was all we would ever have."

Ah. So this was where this was going. "Denny, that's different." Eliza and Denny had been friends for only a few months, while she couldn't even remember a life without Regan. If she tried for more, she wouldn't be merely risking one friendship among many; she'd be gambling everything she had, as her father had.

Denny didn't listen. "So I tried to date someone else too. Did Heather ever tell you she and I went out once?"

Ky felt like a cartoon character whose eyes were popping out of its head. "You and Heather? I had no idea!"

"It won't go down in history as the best date ever. I mean, Heather was her usual funny, beautiful self," Denny added. "But—"

"There was no chemistry," Ky finished the sentence for her.

"She wasn't Eliza. And the guys Eliza went out with, they weren't..." Denny ducked her head. Her cheeks went red, even as a happy smile formed. "Me."

Ky wrapped her arms around herself, battling a vague feeling of nausea that threatened to rise. "Why are you telling me all this?"

"Have you ever thought that maybe your relationships never work out because your girlfriends aren't Regan? Or that hers always fail because her partners aren't you?"

A fist wrapped around Ky's stomach and twisted. She hugged herself more tightly. "No. Denny, you...you've got it all wrong. I'm just shit at relationships. Always was, always will be. Like parents, like daughter, I guess. That wouldn't suddenly change if Regan and I—"

The glass door slid open again, and Heather stuck her head out. "Ooh, what's this? Secret Butch Club meeting? Is there beer?"

Normally, Ky would have protested because she didn't apply any labels to herself. She was just Ky. But right now, she was Ky in an existential crisis, so she couldn't care less about what Heather called her.

Heather's grin faded away. "You okay, Kylie?"

Ky let go of her middle and tried for a casual stance. "Yeah, I'm—" Her phone rang. *Phew. Saved by the proverbial bell.* She pulled it out of her back pocket and slid her finger across the screen without bothering to check who it was. Even having to deal with telemarketers would be worth it if only she could escape this conversation. "Yeah?"

For several moments, only silence answered.

Had the connection cut out? Just as Ky was about to move the phone away from her ear to check, someone—a man—cleared his throat.

"Kylie, it's me." The voice hit her like a punch between the ribs, leaving her unable to breathe. "Your father."

# Chapter 11

Ky was a gold-medal-worthy champ at pretending to be fine when she wasn't. Or maybe just silver-medal-worthy because Regan could usually tell.

Right now, Ky was not okay.

Regan kept glancing over at her as she drove them the three miles from Denny's place to Ky's apartment. "What's going on?"

Ky's head jerked up. "What? Nothing. I'm fine."

*Sure.* Regan didn't believe it for a second. What the hell had happened?

At first, Regan had put it down to the two of them having to find their footing with each other again. But Ky had joked around with her and Heather on the first few trips between the moving van and the house. Only later had she started to act withdrawn.

Had she been bothered by Ollie's less-than-subtle flirting?

Why would she be? She had made it clear that she wanted their friendship to remain the way it was. No, that couldn't be it. While Ky clearly wasn't amused by Ollie, it had to be something else.

She had been more or less fine until she had disappeared to the backyard with Denny. Something must have happened out there because when she had stepped back inside, her emotions had seemed shut off, as if she'd pressed the emergency button due to emotional overload. She had barely even touched the pizza Denny and Eliza had ordered.

Regan had seen her like this only once, at her mother's funeral, when Ky's father had tried to talk to her afterward, chatting about the weather. He'd seemed to think they could just pick up where they'd left off before he'd gone to prison, without acknowledging Ky's grief or admitting that his crime might have played a role in his ex-wife's death.

Back then, Regan had taken her to Lake Oswego, where they had hid in their tree house for the rest of the afternoon.

But it was after eight and getting dark now—too late for a trip to the tree house.

When they approached the intersection where she would have to either continue straight ahead to Ky's apartment or take a right to head to her own place, Regan looked over at Ky again. "Come home with me."

That seemed to wrench Ky from the dark place she'd withdrawn to. She stared at Regan with almost comically wide eyes. "Um, what?"

Laughing, Regan slapped the side of Ky's leg. "Not like that. Jeez, Wells! Although…" She took her gaze off the road for a second to bat her lashes at Ky. "I'm inviting you over for the most fun, relaxing thing two adults can do together."

Now Ky seemed to catch on. A hint of a smile replaced the unmoving mask her face had become. "If you really can't think of anything for two adults to do together that would be more fun than Netflix and chill—and I mean literally Netflix and chill—I think you need a lesson or two."

"Are you offering?" Regan shot back before she could think about it.

Ky opened her mouth. For a second, heat flared in her eyes.

*What are we doing? Are we…flirting? Okay, silly question.* They clearly were. *Dammit, focus on whatever's going on with Ky.*

Ky looked away. "No, of course not. Good old Ollie seemed interested, though."

Regan squinted over at her. Maybe this was about Ollie after all. They definitely had to talk. She took a right onto SE 60th Avenue.

"Um, you missed my apartment."

"No, I didn't. You are coming home with me. I will make you a sandwich, we can watch some Netflix or Hulu if you want, and then you'll tell me what's going on."

Ky folded her arms across the seat belt. "You aren't even giving me a choice?"

"Remember all the times when we hid in the tree house so you didn't have to go home because your parents were either screaming at the top of their lungs or giving each other the silent treatment?"

Ky's face turned several shades lighter, as if all blood had drained from it. "Why are you bringing them up now of all times?"

"Because when we were in the tree house, we promised that we would never do what they were doing. We promised that we would always talk everything out. I've never broken a promise I made you, and I'm not about to start now."

Ky let her head fall back to rest against the seat. She glanced out the window as they drove past Mount Tabor Park, then turned her head to look at Regan. "All right." Despite her earlier protest, she actually sounded relieved. "But only because you promised to make sandwiches."

Ten minutes later, Regan rummaged through her fridge, hoping she had enough stuff to make the promised sandwiches.

"Jeez, what kind of Italian are you?" Ky said from directly behind her. "Your fridge is practically empty!"

"The kind whose culinary skill is eating." Ky's presence—so close at her back that Regan thought she could feel her body heat—made her squirm. She resisted the temptation to turn around, very aware that this was the first time they were alone at her place since the kiss. "Why are you hovering? Take a seat." Since when did Ky wait for an invitation as if she were a guest?

"Um, I'm all sweaty."

"Then take a shower. You know where your stuff is." Once the warmth at her back moved away, Regan could finally breathe.

The water started in the bathroom as Regan spread her meager bounty on the counter. She tried to focus on her attempts at preparing sandwiches, so she wouldn't think about Ky undressing and stepping beneath the steamy spray.

*Focus. On the sandwiches. What do we have?* Exactly one tomato. A few slices of cheese. No bacon or ham. At least she had enough onions to feed a family of five.

She opened cupboards and drawers. Pasta. Cornflakes. Pasta. Applesauce. More pasta. "See?" she muttered even though Ky couldn't hear. "I'm perfectly Italian."

Finally, she found two small cans of tuna. *Ooh. Tuna melt sandwiches!*

She worked quickly, draining the tuna, chopping dill pickles, an onion, and some parsley, and mixing it all with the last of her mayonnaise.

When the bathroom door swung open, she was buttering two slices of bread.

The sound of Ky padding barefoot through the hall toward her made Regan's pulse quicken.

She threw a glance over her shoulder to show herself that it was just Ky. They had spent evenings like this a thousand times before, with Ky showering at her place and then preparing dinner together. But convincing herself this was nothing out of the ordinary, only her lifelong best friend, would have been a hell of a lot easier if Ky hadn't looked so sexy with her sweatpants riding low on her hips, the *Culinary superhero* T-shirt sticking to her still-damp skin, and her wet hair combed back, revealing the gap in her eyebrow.

Regan bit her lip. *Damn.* It was as if someone had flipped a switch—or taken off a blindfold—and now she couldn't look at her as *just Ky* anymore. "I need a cold shower. Um, I mean, I got a bit sweaty lugging around those moving boxes, so I need a shower too. Could you take over?" She gestured at the skillet that was heating on the stove.

"Sure."

As Ky squeezed past her in the small kitchen, a whiff of her apricot-scented shower gel tickled Regan's nostrils. *Mmm.* How strangely intimate it felt to have Ky use her shower gel—even though she had done it dozens of times before. It definitely smelled better on Ky than on her.

Regan hurried through her shower, not allowing her thoughts—or her hands—to linger on anything. After a minute, she turned off the water, reached for a towel, stepped out—and froze.

*Oh shit.* Apparently, she had been a little too successful at shutting off her brain. She had forgotten to bring a fresh set of clothes to the bathroom. Muttering every Neapolitan curse she knew, she looked around for something to wear.

But unless she wanted to put her sweaty clothes back on or stick sanitary pads over strategic places on her body, the only thing she had to cover herself with was her towel.

*Deep breath. It'll do.* Ky wouldn't see her anyway. It was only two steps from the bathroom to her bedroom, and Ky was busy in the kitchen, without a direct line of sight to the hall.

She dried off with unsteady hands, wrapped the towel around herself, and tucked the ends into a knot between her breasts. The seam brushed her thighs. *See? Basically like a miniskirt.*

Feeling like a burglar in her own apartment, she opened the door a few inches and peeked out.

Dishes clinked in the kitchen. The coast was clear.

Regan slipped out of the bathroom and tiptoed to the bedroom door. Just as she reached it, steps crossed the living area.

"Great timing. Dinner is—" Ky appeared at the end of the hall, carrying two plates. Her gaze traced down Regan's bare shoulders, lingered on the place where the knot barely held her towel up, then slid down the length of her legs before snapping back up to Regan's face. "Uh..."

They stared at each other like a rabbit and a wolf who'd unexpectedly come across each other in the forest, though Regan couldn't tell who was the predator and who the prey.

The look in Ky's eyes was wild and scared at the same time.

Regan glanced away, afraid to telegraph her thoughts.

As if finally freed from a hypnotic trance, Ky whirled around to face the coffee table, where she put down the plates with an audible *clunk*. "Sorry. I was just bringing the sandwiches to the table."

"I'll be right there." Regan rushed into her bedroom, kicked the door closed behind herself, and sank against the mirrored closet door. The cold surface on her burning skin made her shiver—or maybe it was the memory of Ky's gaze roaming down her half-naked body. "Get yourself together, Regan Romano. You're not fifteen."

Not that she would have reacted like this to her best friend seeing her half-naked at fifteen. She still couldn't fully understand how it had all changed so quickly, but, at least to herself, there was no denying that it had. And clearly, it wasn't all one-sided either. That look in Ky's eyes had been unmistakable.

*It doesn't matter,* she firmly told herself. She had promised Ky not to risk their friendship, no matter what. Besides, there was something else going on with Ky, and she needed to focus on that.

She pulled her oldest pair of sweatpants and one of her chemistry T-shirts from the closet. At the last second, she glanced at the dialogue bubble above the cartoonish Erlenmeyer flask, saying, *We've got great chemistry.*

*Oops. Maybe not that.* She shoved it back into the closet and chose another. This one said: *I periodically tell chemistry jokes, but there's no reaction.* Much better.

Once she was dressed, she walked out into the living room.

Ky sat in one corner of the couch, staring at the sandwiches. Either she had suddenly discovered she was hungry after all, or she couldn't look Regan in the eyes. "Sorry," she said again.

"No big deal," Regan answered as casually as possible. "How were you supposed to know I was modeling the latest towel fashion?"

A dimple formed in Ky's cheek as if she was about to say something funny…or maybe flirty. But then she shook her head and gestured at the plates. "Your culinary creations are getting cold."

The loud growl of Regan's stomach broke the tension. She hadn't had more than a few bites of pizza earlier because she'd been too worried about Ky.

She plopped down on the couch next to Ky and picked up her sandwich. It was still warm as she took the first bite. The gooey cheese practically melted in her mouth, and something spicy contrasted perfectly with the tartness of the pickles. "This is good," she said as soon as she'd swallowed the bite. "Maybe *I'm* the culinary superhero."

"I added a few of the chili flakes your dad uses on his pizzas to spice things up a little. Hope you don't mind."

"Mind?" Regan took another bite and hummed her appreciation. "Not at all. We make a great team."

"Yeah," Ky said quietly. "We do."

Something resonated in her tone, and Regan peered over at her.

Instead of making eye contact, Ky looked at her sandwich and ate in silence.

Okay. Ky clearly wasn't ready to talk. Regan turned on the TV and flicked through shows and movies on her streaming service for something to watch while they ate, knowing Ky needed some time to get used to the idea of telling her what was going on with her.

*Rizzoli and Isles* was their usual fallback option, so she started it where they had last stopped watching. Too late, she realized it was the episode in which the detective and the medical examiner went undercover in a lesbian bar and had a friendly sleepover.

Maybe watching a TV show about two supposedly platonic friends with more chemistry than her entire prep room hadn't been a genius idea.

Ky seemed to eat in slow motion. Regan had long since finished her sandwich by the time Ky swallowed her last bite.

Normally, Ky would have stretched out to watch the rest of the episode and thrown her legs across Regan's lap, hoping for a foot massage. But now everything was different.

It sucked.

Regan missed those affectionate little touches.

Ky stayed on her side of the couch and looked toward the TV, but Regan could tell she wasn't really watching.

When she caught Ky sneaking a peek at her out of the corner of her eye, she grabbed the remote and shut off the TV.

"Hey, I was watching that," Ky said.

"No, you weren't."

"Yes, I was." Ky lifted her chin. "Try me."

"Okay. What was our favorite scientist wearing for their sleepover?"

Ky mumbled something that sounded like, "She's not my favorite scientist." Then, more loudly, she added, "That thing with the ruffles."

"Nope. That was in the episode one sleepover. Besides, it was a trick question. We haven't even gotten to that scene yet—which you would know if you had actually watched." Regan threw the remote onto the coffee table. "Will you please tell me what's going on with you? I'm starting to worry."

Ky put one foot on the couch and hugged one knee to her chest.

"This isn't about Ollie, is it?"

"Ollie?"

"Oliver…whatever his last name is."

One corner of Ky's mouth twitched into a humorless smile. "I wish it were."

"Okay, so it isn't him. But there is something going on with you, so don't pretend otherwise. I mean, something other than…" Regan swung her feet up on the coffee table and stared at her toes, then peeked over at Ky and pointed back and forth between them.

Ky offered her a tired smile. "What, that's not enough?"

They were joking about it. Kind of. That was good, right?

Regan slid a little closer. "Come on, Ky. Get it off your chest. Is it the promotion? You haven't mentioned it in a while, and I didn't want to put any pressure on you by bringing it up."

Ky sighed. She let go of her knee and put her feet on the table next to Regan's, but not touching. "Fran keeps nudging me to make a decision soon, and I still haven't."

"Why not? Are you still afraid of not being good enough?" Regan waved at their clean plates. "Hello? You could cook circles around Fran and anyone else on staff."

"Thanks."

"But?"

"Even if I could do the job, I'm not sure I want to."

Regan studied her. "Because you honestly don't want it or because you think you shouldn't want it?"

Ky stared at her, then touched her fingertips to her temples as if that helped her think. "Um, the former. I think. I'm just not sure if it's the right job for me."

"Then don't take it."

Ky turned her head and looked at her. "It's that easy?"

"I figure if you really wanted it, you would know."

Ky's attention seemed to turn inward, as if she was listening to the echo of Regan's advice deep inside of her. Finally, she gave her a look full of admiration. "When did the little girl who used to ride down her steep driveway on a wheeled desk chair become so wise?"

Regan grinned. "Probably when she spent the rest of that summer in a cast."

"Nah. That can't be it. I remember all the ways you tried to get rid of that cast. None of them were what I'd call wise."

Regan covered her face with her hands. "It's a wonder I survived my childhood."

"It's a wonder *your parents* survived it, not to mention me!"

"That too." Regan dropped her hands to her lap and regarded Ky. Despite their joking, she still seemed as relaxed as a kid waiting to see the dentist. "The promotion isn't really what's on your mind, is it? There's something else."

Ky wrinkled her nose at her. "It's kind of annoying how well you know me."

"You know you can tell me anything, right? No judgment. But if it's something you're not ready to talk about, I won't judge you for that either."

"No, I want to tell you. It's just not an easy subject."

Regan racked her brain. Besides whatever was going on with them, there was only one thing…one person who had the power to upset Ky this much. "You heard from your dad."

Ky stared. "How did you…?"

"Because I know you annoyingly well. So you really heard from him?" After his two-year stint in prison, Ky's contact with her father had consisted more or less of short calls on Christmas and birthdays. Regan had witnessed a few of them, and she'd cringed every time at how stiff and formal they were with each other. She'd had more animated conversations with the barista when she got coffee on the way to work. After her mother's death, Ky had even stopped talking to him for a while. During the past three years, their tense calls had turned into postcards from all over South America.

"Yeah." Ky rubbed her eyes with her knuckles. "He called earlier."

"When you were in the backyard, with Denny." She didn't phrase it as a question, but Ky nodded anyway. "What did he want?"

Ky hunched her shoulders as if protecting her vulnerable core. She looked so pale that, for a second, Regan worried she would be sick.

Without hesitation, Regan slid across the couch, bridging the space between them, and took her hand. Ky's fingers, usually strong and reliable, were trembling. Regan interlaced their fingers into a tight bond. "Breathe. It would look really bad on my culinary résumé if you pass out on my couch after eating my sandwich."

Ky let out a startled laugh. "Can't have that." She drew in a deep breath, then slowly let it escape. "He's back from Brazil or Chile or wherever he was last. And he wants to see me."

*Hell, no.* Regan bit back the words before they could slip out. Trevor had left deep wounds on Ky's heart, and now that most of them had finally scarred over, he wanted to come back into her life and do it all over again? Over her dead body. But, of course, she knew it wasn't her decision to make. "What did you tell him?"

"I hung up on him." Ky stared down at their joined hands. "I couldn't deal with him on top of…everything else."

A part of Regan cheered, but deep down, she knew that wasn't the resolution Ky needed. "What will you do if he calls again?"

"I don't know. Hang up again? I really have no idea. What do you think I should do?" Ky looked at her in a way she hadn't for at least ten years, as if she were searching for a lifeline in an ocean that threatened to drown her.

Regan wrestled down the impulse to tell her to get a new phone number. Her overprotectiveness wasn't what Ky needed right now. Closure was. "Can I be honest?"

"Since when do you have to ask me that?"

Their gazes met, then veered away like two repelling magnets.

While Regan had never lied to her, she also hadn't opened up completely lately.

"Yes, of course you can," Ky finally said. "I don't want you to start censoring yourself around me."

*Are you sure?* Regan bit her lip. Now wasn't the right moment for a question like that. One crisis at a time. "Okay. Do you want the impulsive Regan or the wise Regan response?"

Ky chuckled. "There's a wise Regan?"

Regan tapped Ky's knee with her own. "You were the one who called me wise earlier."

"Guess I did. Okay, then. Give me both."

"Impulsive Regan thinks you should flush your phone down the toilet and get a new number."

"Hmm, I like impulsive Regan."

"Me too, but the last time I listened to her was—" Regan cut herself off. No need to bring up the kiss. "Um, when I invited you over for sandwiches without considering the lack of food in my fridge."

"Oh, I don't know. I think it turned out all right," Ky said with a vague gesture that seemed to indicate their joined hands more than the empty plates.

"Yeah?"

"Mm-hmm."

God, there was more subtext going on here than in an average *Rizzoli and Isles* episode. Was she interpreting the look in Ky's eyes correctly or indulging in wishful thinking? It was all so damn confusing.

"So?" Ky prompted.

"Hmm?"

"What does wise Regan think?"

*That I should slide to the right and put at least a foot of space between us.* But, of course, Regan had rarely listened to that wise voice, so she stayed where she was, with her thigh pressed along Ky's, holding her hand. "There's a lot of unfinished business between you and your dad. Between you and both of your parents," she added very quietly. "But you'll never get any answers or closure from your mom."

Ky's fingers flexed around hers, yet she nodded for Regan to go on.

"So maybe…maybe you should get whatever closure you can from your dad. Not for him. You don't owe him a thing. But maybe you need to do it for yourself."

"I don't know, Regan. What if all he wants from me is money?"

Regan let out a growl. "Then I'll flush *him* down the toilet."

That made Ky smile, if only for a moment. "Or what if he tells me he got married while he was in South America and has a new family now?" Shadows lurked in Ky's eyes, darkening them to a mossy gray.

"Even if he did, that wouldn't mean he replaced you." Ky was such a kind, unique woman. No one could ever replace her.

Ky finally looked from their hands into Regan's eyes. "You really think I should meet him?"

"Only if you feel it could help you in the long run."

"Maybe it would. It's just… The thought of seeing him brings up a lot of stuff."

Regan softly squeezed her hand. "I know. Would you want me to come with you if you decide to see him?"

Ky looked at her as if she'd offered to go through hell and trim the devil's claws. "You'd do that?"

"I'd do anything for you, Ky." Regan reached over with her free hand to brush back Ky's bangs so she could see how much she meant it. "Don't you know that by now?" *Shit.* Where was wise Regan when she needed her to stop impulsive Regan from blurting out whatever was going through her mind? Still, she refused to take it back.

Ky's eyes misted over, but she didn't look away. Her gaze dove deeply into Regan's, searching, connecting.

Heat swept from their intertwined hands through the rest of Regan's body. "I mean," she mumbled, her voice low and hoarse, "it's in the best-friend contract, next to not being allowed to watch *Rizzoli and Isles* without you ever."

"Best-friend contract. Right." Ky brushed back her bangs as if retracing Regan's touch. "Thank you. Just you offering…that helps a lot, even if I end up not meeting him or not taking you up on it."

"Any time."

They sat in silence for a while, until Regan became overly aware that they were still holding hands, even though Ky's need to be comforted seemed to have passed. "Want to stay for a while and finish the episode?"

"Yes, of course. I still need to win our bet."

"Bet? What bet?"

"Your sleepover wear question from earlier. I still think Maura was wearing that thing with the ruffles down the front."

"Let's find out." Under the pretense of reaching for the remote, Regan disentangled her fingers from Ky's—then immediately missed the contact.

Ky curled her hand around her own knee as if it felt empty too.

Dammit. Their friends might have been right. There was an undeniable chemistry between them, and maybe it truly could be something other than friendship chemistry. But she had promised not to pursue that train of thought because it had the potential to leave Ky—and her—just as destroyed as her father's prison sentence and her mother's death had.

Suppressing a sigh, Regan restarted the episode.

Ky was having the best dream she'd had in years. A warm body was cuddled up to hers. Even in her sleep, she knew it wasn't just any warm body. She was holding Regan. Or maybe Regan was holding her. It didn't matter.

Regan was trailing her fingers over Ky's cheek, her temple, the arc of one eyebrow, and Ky nuzzled closer, never wanting the dream to end.

"Ky." Regan's voice, soothing and tender, vibrated through her. It was so close that it almost seemed to come from within her.

"Mmmh." Ky pressed her face against soft cotton and buried deeper against her comfy spot.

"Come on, Ky. Come to bed with me."

Ky slowly drifted awake. She opened her eyes, but all she saw was the navy-blue fabric that she'd pressed her face to, probably a pillow or something. For a moment, she had no idea where she was. She just knew wherever it was, she didn't want to move. The scent…the warmth…the gentle caresses… This was heaven.

Her eyes closed once more—then popped open again.

Wait! Heaven was moving. Breathing.

*Oh shit!* It hadn't been a dream, and the blue fabric wasn't a pillowcase; it was Regan's T-shirt. She must have fallen asleep and had curled up on Regan's lap, with her face pressed to her belly and one hand on Regan's thigh, pillowing her cheek.

Ky tried to scramble back, but Regan held on with one hand against her back.

"Careful. If you fall off, you'll hit your head on the coffee table."

Finally, Ky managed to disentangle herself and sit up. "Sorry. I didn't realize how tired I was." She massaged the crick in her neck and touched her chin to check for drool. Thankfully, there was none.

"It's okay."

Was it? Were they okay? Ky peeked over at her.

The look in Regan's eyes was soft and so at peace that Ky wanted to sink back onto her lap.

"Come on." Regan slid off the couch. "Let's go to bed."

Ky stared. Was she saying she wanted them to share the bed? They had done it more than once in the past because Regan's fake leather couch had started to sag in a couple of places over the years, so it wasn't the comfiest place to sleep the entire night. But that had been before Regan's dating experiment had reawakened her damn crush.

A part of her longed to crawl into bed with Regan, yet another, bigger part was scared of what would happen if she did. "That's okay," she croaked out. "I won't be able to sleep anyway. I'm totally wired, so if you give me your car keys, I could—"

"Ky, you were sound asleep a minute ago. Stop being stubborn and come to bed with me." A flush rose up Regan's neck, making her look even lovelier. "Um, I mean, you should stay over. Neither of us is driving all over town at this hour."

Ky glanced at her wristwatch. *Oh my God.* It was two in the morning! When had that happened? She must have been asleep on Regan's lap for quite some time.

Regan walked toward the bedroom as if it was already decided Ky would stay.

*Guess I'm sleeping over.* The thought of sleeping so close made her pulse pound, but at the same time, the way Regan had taken charge—bringing Ky to her place and then deciding she was staying—was unexpectedly comforting. It proved that Regan was still there. She hadn't lost her.

Weariness tugged at Ky, and she wanted nothing more than to wrap herself around Regan, as she had earlier, and find some peace in the safest place she knew.

Finally, she gave in to that pull and followed her to the bedroom.

Regan had kicked off her sweatpants and unfastened her bra. She pulled it out through the sleeve of her T-shirt.

Ky's mouth went dry, and she looked away, even though there was nothing to see, other than Regan's legs. Quickly, she escaped to the bathroom and closed the door behind her.

*Sleep,* she firmly told her reflection in the mirror above the sink. *You are going to sleep.* Her toothbrush was in the cup holder next to Regan's. The sight of it was soothing, reminding her of how often she had stayed over. Tonight would be no different.

After the drama with her dad, she wasn't up for anything other than sleeping anyway, even if Regan were.

*Which she isn't. Stop thinking and go to bed.*

She brushed her teeth, splashed cold water onto her face, then left the bathroom.

In the hall, Regan passed her with a smile that looked nervous.

Was this as awkward for her as it was for Ky? For the first time ever, there was something Ky couldn't ask her.

She slid into bed on her side. Funny that she had one. Had any of Regan's partners ever had a side?

God, she really needed some sleep.

The sheets smelled of Regan, and Ky snuggled into them with a sigh. She'd just started to relax when the door opened and Regan padded toward the bed.

As Regan pulled back the covers, Ky slid to the edge of the bed to make room for her.

Regan got in and turned off the light. They both lay on their backs, carefully not touching.

Ky stared into the near darkness. The dim shapes of Regan's furniture were as familiar as her own. She turned onto her side, her back to Regan, but the position felt all wrong, so she rolled onto her belly. No, that wasn't comfy either. With a grunt, she turned back toward the window.

"You're making me seasick," Regan mumbled.

"Sorry. I'll stay still." Ky flopped onto her back and pressed her arms to her sides to keep herself motionless.

Regan sighed. "This isn't working. Neither of us will get a wink of sleep."

"If you want me to leave, I—"

"Spoon me."

Ky sucked in a breath. Surely she hadn't heard that right? "Um, what?"

The bed shook beneath Regan's laughter. "Jeez, you're acting like I said, 'Spank me and take me doggy-style.'"

Her words sent a jolt through Ky. She stared at Regan, trying to make out her features. As far as she could tell, Regan was looking back defiantly.

Then they both burst out laughing.

"Come on," Regan said once their laughter had trickled off. "Spoon me. That's how we'll end up anyway as soon as we fall asleep." She turned away from Ky, offering her back.

God, the curve of her neck was so lovely, even in the near dark. Ky shook her head to get rid of that thought, then slowly inched across the mattress until she felt the heat of Regan's body. She had planned to settle down with the tiniest bit of space still between them, but magnetism or something took over, pulling her in, and she found herself cuddled up to Regan's back. The fit of their bodies, as different as they were, was as perfect as that of their entwined fingers earlier.

She wrapped one arm around her, then hesitated. What was she supposed to do with her hand? Where did she usually put it?

As if to answer the unasked question, Regan took her hand and pressed it to her belly, with her own on top.

Ky froze. *Oh God!* If she moved her fingers even a little, she would cup Regan's breasts!

"You comfy?" Regan asked, her voice husky.

Comfy wasn't the first word that came to mind. Or even the twenty-first. She was too intensely aware of Regan's body tucked into the curve of her own and the press of her breasts against Regan's back. "Um, yeah." She hoped Regan couldn't feel her heart racing. "This is…nice."

"Mm-hmm. It is." Regan trailed her thumb over Ky's wrist in a caress that was probably meant to be calming but instead sent a prickle of awareness up her arm.

Ky pressed her overheated cheek to Regan's shoulder. This was the sweetest torture she had ever endured.

It took quite some time, but eventually, Regan's familiar scent and the quiet sound of them breathing in the same pattern lulled her to sleep.

# Chapter 12

For the first time since they had kissed more than a week ago, Ky woke up feeling well-rested. She couldn't have slept more than a few hours, but her head was clear and her body relaxed.

She knew she wasn't at home before she even opened her eyes. But then again, maybe she was. She was with Regan.

They had changed positions during the night so that they now lay facing each other, with Regan using Ky's arm as a pillow. The faint light of dawn filtered through the closed blinds, painting stripes of gold and shade across Regan's face.

Ky drank in her features—the curve of her mouth, with her lips slightly parted, the slope of her nose, the sweep of her long lashes, and the untamed tousle of her hair. God, she was beautiful.

Regan sighed in her sleep and nuzzled closer.

Ky wrapped one arm around her and held her close, inhaling Regan's sleepy scent. Her heart ached. Not with the sharp pain that came with the thought of messing it all up and losing her. This felt more as if her heart was too full, spilling over all the emotions she had stored there and suppressed over the years.

It was as if that barely patched-up lid to Pandora's box had been blown off while she'd slept, and now the contents were staring her in the face.

She was not over her crush on her best friend.

And it wasn't merely a little crush either—and maybe it had never been.

This was way scarier. This was love.

Not the kind of love she'd shared with her girlfriends in the past. Those feelings felt superficial in comparison. Regan hadn't just touched her heart; she had engraved her name across Ky's very soul.

As if the shockwaves reverberating through Ky had woken her up, Regan's eyes fluttered open.

She didn't flinch or seem surprised when she saw Ky there, in her bed, holding her, as if that was where she belonged.

For the first time, Ky allowed herself to think that maybe she did. Maybe this was how she was supposed to wake up every day. Her panic receded as she looked into Regan's sleepy eyes. Maybe she could have this and not mess it all up.

Regan didn't say anything—morning was the only time when she wasn't talkative—but she gave Ky a groggy smile. "'kay?"

"I'm fine." *I'm in love with you.* For a second, she wasn't sure which one she'd said out loud, but when Regan smiled again and settled back down on her shoulder, she assumed it was the former.

"'s early," Regan mumbled. "Go back to sleep." Her words brushed warm air against Ky's neck, causing a trail of goose bumps.

Ky knew sleep was out of the question. Her mind was racing along with her heart. She stared past Regan's tousled hair to the nightstand. A swath of light fell across the framed picture Regan kept there.

It was a photo of them, cheek to cheek, their arms around each other. Their friends pressed close around them so they would all fit into the photo. Heather had one arm around Milena and was gazing at her instead of at the camera.

Had they been just friends at the time the photo had been taken, or had it been during their short-lived relationship? Ky couldn't remember, and neither could she ask, because Milena and Heather were no longer talking, and no one dared bring it up.

A lump lodged in Ky's throat and refused to budge, no matter how often she tried to swallow it down.

What if that happened to her and Regan too? What if she allowed herself to want this…to have this…and then lost it, like Heather had lost Milena and Ky's mother had lost her marriage, her home, and, eventually, her life?

Cold sweat broke out along her spine. Could she really risk that, now that she knew how deeply ingrained in her Regan was?

Regan cuddled closer. It turned that sweet ache in Ky's heart into a stabbing pain.

She needed to leave. Now.

As fast as she dared, she slid out from beneath Regan, who mumbled a protest.

Ky fought back the tears that burned in her eyes. She whispered something about needing the bathroom and fled, not knowing where she was running—or even if she could.

Regan drifted into wakefulness in a cocoon of warmth and happiness. The pillow her head rested on smelled like Ky, but she didn't feel the familiar arms around her anymore.

Hadn't Ky mumbled something about needing the bathroom? She would probably be right back. A soft sigh escaped her as she imagined Ky slipping under the covers, cuddling up against her back, and brushing a kiss against her neck.

Wait. No. Despite the intimate way they had slept, it wasn't like that between them.

But she wanted it to be.

That realization squeezed all air from her lungs as it filled every last inch of her, leaving no space for doubts. She wanted to be the one to hold Ky when she was upset and feed her sandwiches after a long day. Granted, she could do that as a friend—heck, she *had* done that all their lives—but she also wanted to kiss her goodbye at the door without either of them panicking. Or even better: she didn't want to say goodbye at the door. She wanted to follow Ky in and leave a trail of clothes to the bedroom.

Her cheeks heated, followed by the rest of her body, as she imagined Ky exploring her bare skin with her hands and lips.

Most importantly, she wanted to do that every night of their lives and kiss her awake every morning. It wasn't only a one-time physical thing that would fade away once her curiosity was sated. No. She would never get enough.

This could be *it* for her—a true chemical reaction that would change her forever. But what about Ky?

Regan glanced at the closed door leading to the hall. Was Ky hiding in the bathroom, struggling with the fears Regan had seen in her eyes up at the reservoir? Did she feel the same? No doubt she felt *something.* This connection between them went too deep to be one-sided.

They really needed to talk. But Regan had promised to let it go and not do anything that might risk their friendship.

*Shit. What now?* Should she stick to it or, for the first time ever, break a promise she'd made Ky?

Her phone rang on the nightstand next to her, sending her already racing heart into overdrive. She quickly reached for it.

*Mom. Of course.* Her mother had a talent for calling in the middle of an emotional crisis.

Regan glanced at the door again. Weird that the ringing phone hadn't brought Ky running since she probably assumed Regan was still asleep.

It rang again, and Regan finally accepted the call. "Hi, Mom."

"Hi, daughter of mine." Her mom sounded awfully cheerful for the early hour. How late was it anyway? "How does parmigiana di melanzane sound?"

Regan's mouth watered reflexively. "Um, good, but—"

"I thought you'd say that. Your dad and I decided to lure you home for some family time. With the opening of the Vancouver restaurant coming up, this might be our last chance for a while. Twelve o'clock. Be on time. And bring Kylie."

"But—"

"Don't tell me she's got plans."

"I have no idea. Wait, let me ask." Too late she realized she had given Ky's presence in her home away. But her mother probably wouldn't think anything of it since she was used to their sleepovers.

Regan threw back the covers, climbed out of bed, and padded across the hall. "Ky," she called through the closed bathroom door. "My mom's on the phone. Do you want to go to Lake O for family dinner?"

No answer.

After a quick knock, she peeked into the bathroom.

It was empty.

With a growing feeling of dread, she checked the rest of her apartment.

Ky wasn't in the living room or the kitchen either. A note lay on the counter, with a banana on top—either to make sure the sheet wouldn't fall to the floor and get lost or because Ky wanted her to eat the piece of fruit.

But food was the last thing on Regan's mind. She shoved the banana aside and picked up the note.

*Regan,* it said in Ky's scrawly handwriting. *I woke up early and couldn't go back to sleep. I'm walking home to get some air. Will call you later. Hugs, Ky.*

Regan stared at the note, then crumpled it up in her clenched fist. Ky had left, just when Regan needed to talk most? Goddammit.

"Regan?" her mother's voice drifted through the phone that hung forgotten in Regan's grip.

Quickly, she brought it back to her ear. "Sorry, Mom. Looks like it'll be just me after all."

"What? But why? Kylie loves eggplant parmigiana!"

"I know." Regan had to swallow down the lump in her throat before she could continue. "But she left."

"Then call her and tell her you'll pick her up on the way over."

One-handedly, Regan unfolded the crumpled paper and smoothed it out with her palm. *Will call you later,* Ky had written. That was a "don't call us; we'll call you" if she'd ever heard one. "I can't."

"What do you mean? Why can't you call her? What happened?"

The urge to spill her guts to her mom gripped Regan. She needed someone to talk to, and her go-to person had snuck out on her. But she couldn't do this on the phone. "I'll tell you later, when I come over."

"All right. Do you want me to call Kylie and use my mom voice that will make her drag her ass over to our place?"

"No!" Regan realized she was shouting and lowered her voice. "No, Mom. Please promise me you won't call her." The last thing she needed was for her overprotective parents to get involved in her love life—not that it could really be called that.

"Okay, okay, I won't. I'll tell your dad to make something chocolatey for dessert. You sound like you need it."

Regan sighed. If only this was the kind of problem that could be solved by chocolate. "Thanks, Mom. See you later."

She stabbed the *end* button and re-read Ky's note. Against all hope, she even turned the piece of paper around to check the back for anything Ky might have added, but there was nothing.

Ky had left, and Regan was alone with all those feelings.

Cursing, she crumpled up the note again and hurled it across the kitchen.

Normally, it was a fifty-minute walk to get home from Regan's apartment in Montavilla. Ky made it in thirty-five. She walked fast, trying to get rid of the anxious energy, only to realize that it didn't help at all.

When she unlocked her front door—which she still couldn't look at without reliving the kiss—her T-shirt stuck to her chest and her hair was damp with sweat.

"What happened to you?" Lilia called from the couch as Ky strode in.

How was she supposed to explain? *I jumped out of Regan's bed and ran like a scared rabbit?* Instead, she just mumbled, "Power walk," and marched to the fridge.

"In your jeans?"

Ky guzzled down a bottle of water so she didn't have to answer.

Her phone rang in her back pocket.

The bottle slid from Ky's sweaty grasp, splashing water all over the kitchen, before she caught it. *Oh, shit.* Was that Regan? What was she supposed to say to her? She was making a mess of things, and she wasn't talking about the puddles on the kitchen floor.

But it wasn't Regan's name flashing over the screen. For a second, Ky was equal parts relieved and disappointed.

The phone continued to ring.

"Aren't you going to answer?" Lilia asked.

Ky didn't normally answer calls from unknown numbers, but what the heck. Her day couldn't get any worse, right? She reached for a dish towel and started to mop up the water while she accepted the call. "Hello?"

"Hi, Kylie. It's me—your dad. Please don't hang up again. I'd really like to talk."

So much for her theory. She sent a helpless glance down at the wet floor.

"Go," Lilia mouthed. "I've got this."

Ky hesitated, then nodded gratefully. She went to her room and closed the door. "This is not a good time."

"Will there ever be a good time?" He wasn't shouting, as he had in the past. His voice was quiet and sounded sad.

"Fourteen years ago would have been good. Before—" She bit back the words at the last second.

"Before what?"

She slipped out of her sneakers and kicked them against the wall. "Before you fucked up our lives and made Mom kill herself!"

His sharp intake of breath reverberated through the phone. "I didn't… She didn't… It was an accident, wasn't it? She forgot she wasn't supposed to mix Xanax with alcohol."

Ky massaged her temples with her free hand. She hadn't meant to say what she had, but it had been on her mind all these years, and she wasn't taking it back. "I guess we'll never know."

He didn't say anything for a while. Only the sounds of him blowing his nose drifted through the phone.

Oh man. Was he crying? She wouldn't feel sorry for him. She wouldn't. He wasn't the victim here; he was the one to blame for it all.

"I know I fucked up, okay?" This time, he did sound angry, but maybe not at her. "That's why I'm calling. To apologize and to…to explain."

Ky said nothing. She didn't want his excuses.

"I did a lot of soul-searching while I was gone, trying to understand how it all went to hell. Your mother and I, we didn't have the best of marriages."

That was the understatement of the century. What Ky knew about loving relationships and honest communication, she had learned from the Romanos, not from her parents.

"That wasn't the only part of my life I wasn't happy with. I hated my job and that most of our friends seemed to make more money than I did."

A huff escaped Ky. "You were a lawyer. Do you really expect any sympathy from a cafeteria worker?"

"I don't want your sympathy, Ky. I—"

"Don't call me that," she said sharply. Only Regan got to call her Ky.

He swallowed audibly. "All right. I won't. Just listen, okay?"

"So talk."

"I hated most parts of my life. I realize now that I should have worked to change it. I should have quit my job, gone to marriage counseling, whatever it took."

"Then why didn't you?"

He hesitated, then said, "Because I was scared shitless."

She hadn't expected him to admit that. He had always been the bragging kind, never showing any weakness. "Scared of what?"

"Of admitting I wasn't God's gift to trust law. Of your mom leaving me if we aired my dirty laundry in therapy. My life was like a house of cards, and I was afraid that if I started pulling at one corner, it was going to collapse. So I was stuck. I started doing stupid things—embezzling money—to prop up that damn house of cards." He cleared his throat. "Can you understand that, even a little?"

Dammit. Ky didn't want to admit it, but yes, she understood it only too well. She had been gently cradling her own house of cards for the past fourteen years. Less than an hour ago, she had snuck out of Regan's bed because she'd been terrified of pulling at one corner and having the whole thing come crashing down.

"Kylie?" he asked when she didn't answer.

"I'm not ready to forgive you." The words burst out of her. "You ruined Mom's life—and you nearly ruined mine too, just because you couldn't face your problems like an adult. We lost everything when you got caught. And I don't mean only the house. The clients whose money you took weren't strangers. A lot of them were our friends, neighbors, my classmates' parents."

"Don't you think I know that?" A defensive tone crept into his voice.

"It didn't stop you from doing it. They all shunned us when you got caught. Mom stopped talking to me as she got swallowed up in her depression. If it hadn't been for Regan and her family..." She shuddered and cut off that line of thought. "I can't forget that."

"I'm not asking you to. I just want a chance."

"To do what? Rebuild the house of cards?"

"No. The cards are down," he said quietly. "I just want to get to know you."

Could she let him do that? Get to know her—the real her that, for the most part, she showed only Regan? Could she take that risk?

She suppressed a sigh. Apparently, she got that unwillingness to take emotional risks from him. That thought stung. She didn't want to resemble him in any way. "I can't make any promises," she finally said.

"I'm not asking for that either. Just… I don't know… Let's keep talking. And maybe we could meet up in person. Whenever you're ready."

"Not now." Maybe never. Certainly not without Regan, who had offered to come with her. But by now, she had probably realized Ky was gone and was upset with her.

Ky's house of cards was wobbling precariously, despite all of her efforts to prevent that—or maybe *because* of those efforts. God, she really was like her father in that regard.

"Whenever you're ready," he repeated. "Just call me or text me or whatever it is you millennials do." Humor colored his tone, as if he was poking fun at his own struggle to keep up with her generation. Maybe he had changed. When she had been a child, he never once admitted to any shortcomings.

"Okay. I mean, maybe I will. Like I said, no promises. Oh, um, D—" She stopped herself. She couldn't bring herself to call him Dad, but calling him Trevor didn't feel right either.

"Yeah?"

"If we do meet, there's one thing you should know about me." She forced herself not to pause. She didn't care if he was fine with it or not, right? "I'm gay."

"I figured." He sounded very calm.

Maybe it should have been a relief—he was still her father, after all—but Ky realized she had half hoped he'd explode or not want anything to do with her, so she wouldn't have to make that decision. "How did you…?"

"It wasn't hard to guess, even when you were what…fourteen? I mean, you and the Romanos' youngest…"

Ky sank onto the edge of her bed. Even her father, who couldn't have been a less attentive parent if he tried, had sensed there was something between them?

"I have to go," she said instead of answering.

"All right. Talk later…maybe."

"Yeah. Bye." Ky ended the call and dropped the phone onto the bed next to her. Acid seemed to burn a hole into her stomach and all the way up to her throat. God, she was so exhausted—not physically, but mostly emotionally. She wished she could crawl back into Regan's bed and start the day over.

But life didn't come with a rewind button. She had to choose how she wanted to go forward—if she dared to. Regan was her only constant, her one true stability. How could she risk that?

*How can you not?* a little voice whispered. Refusing to deal with her feelings might wreck their friendship as surely as confessing them, just as her father's inability to face his problems had ruined all of their lives.

Groaning, Ky curled herself into a ball on her bed and pulled the covers over her head.

A knock came at the door. "Kylie?" Lilia called from the hallway. "You okay?"

Ky stuck her head out from under the covers. "Yeah. I'm fine."

Her phone buzzed with a text message.

*No, no, no.* Why couldn't they all leave her alone?

But what if it was Regan?

The thought made her throw off the covers, sit up, and reach for the phone.

The text wasn't from Regan—it was from Regan's dad.

Ky swallowed heavily. Had Regan told her parents what had happened? What if they hated her now?

*Come on. Be an adult.* Besides, even as close-knit as the Romanos were, she was fairly sure Regan would never tell them.

She opened the text.

*What's this about you not coming for family dinner?* Joe had asked.

Apparently, they had invited her and Regan over. Ky blew out a breath. Now she felt silly for thinking, even for a second, that Regan might tell them.

*Sorry,* she texted back. She didn't want to lie to him, especially since she had no idea what reason Regan had given for her not coming, so she just added, *Maybe next time.*

*I'll hold you to that,* Joe answered. *Quick question: Are brownies still Regan's favorite chocolate dessert?*

Ky barely had to think before replying. *Actually, I made her a chocolate panna cotta with espresso syrup last month, and she declared that her new favorite. Want me to send you the recipe?*

*That would be great.*

A quick search and she copied in the link.

*Thanks!* Joe replied. *I'd better hurry now before the hungry masses arrive.*

It sounded as if Regan would be spending the day in Lake Oswego. Maybe she had already left. So even if Ky wanted, she couldn't head back to Regan's place, and getting to Lake Oswego without a car was impossible.

Sighing, she flopped back onto the bed and stared at the ceiling. Now what?

There was nothing she could do at the moment. Not that she had to do something right away. She could wait until Regan got back and talk to her tonight…or next week. Maybe wait until the weekend so they had plenty of time to talk.

But deep down, she knew she was only propping up her house of cards. If she waited, she would chicken out and go back into denial for another ten years. But now that she had admitted her feelings to herself, she would have to work that much harder to keep them in check. Did she really want that—always having to hide that part of herself from Regan?

It wasn't fair, not to herself, not to their friendship, and certainly not to Regan. Ky dug her nails into her palms as she imagined how Regan must have felt when she had woken up this morning and found her gone. Regan deserved better than that. She deserved to be loved, not just the way her previous partners had loved her, but the bone-deep, carved-into-my-soul way that Ky knew she would be capable of…if only she opened herself up to the possibility. And, of course, if Regan wanted that kind of love from her.

Ky thought maybe she did, but she couldn't be sure.

*Ask her.*

She needed to trust that they would be able to work it out, no matter what, and that letting herself want more wouldn't necessarily lead to disaster. *Do it now, before you chicken out.*

With trembling fingers, she reached for her phone again. Not giving herself time to change her mind, she tapped out a quick text message. *Are you busy? I have a favor to ask.*

Then she waited with her heart hammering wildly.

# Chapter 13

Regan's father tsked and gave her half-empty plate a chiding look. "Eat! You barely touched your food!"

"Dad, this is my second plate."

Her brother, Robbie, reached over to take her plate, but Regan slapped his hand away. "Mine!"

He rubbed his fingers. "I thought you were done."

"Yeah, but that doesn't mean you can have it. I'm taking leftovers home with me."

"For Kylie?" her sister, Mac, asked. "Where is she anyway? Busy with her new girlfriend?"

The thought of Ky with someone else made the eggplant parmigiana sit like a brick in Regan's stomach. It hadn't been like that in the past, had it? She hadn't been a big fan of most of Ky's girlfriends, but that had nothing to do with jealousy, right? Granted, it had been a while...okay, more like years...since either of them had been in a relationship. "She doesn't have a new girlfriend. Why would you think that?"

Mac shrugged and tried to steal some of the cheese crust from Regan's plate, earning her a slap on the hand too. "Because that's the only time the two of you aren't joined at the hip. I never got why you don't just date each other."

Regan's cheeks burned as if they were about to catch fire. "Because... because... You wouldn't understand." She was no longer sure she understood it herself.

Their mother pushed back her chair and got up. "Regan, would you mind helping me with dessert?"

Regan had never been so glad to help out in the kitchen. She jumped up. At the last second, she snatched her plate up from the table and took it to the kitchen with her before her siblings could steal all the cheese. She set it on the wooden center island, then opened her parents' giant fridge to see what her father had made for dessert.

"Top shelf," her mother said.

Not that Regan could have missed the dozen individual glass bowls. Her father had garnished each one with fresh strawberries. Regan took the first two from the fridge and stared at the chocolate dessert. Her throat tightened. "Is that…?"

"Chocolate panna cotta. Kylie said it's your new favorite."

Regan whirled around. "You promised you wouldn't talk to her!"

"I didn't. Your father sent her a text."

"Like that's any better! What did he tell her?"

"Nothing. He only asked for the recipe. It's not like he could have told her anything, even if he wanted, since we don't have a clue about what's going on." Her mother rounded the center island, took the two bowls from her, and closed the fridge with a nudge of her hip. "Sit and tell me."

"But the others are waiting for the panna cotta."

"They can come in and get it." Her mom guided her to the small, round table in the hexagonal breakfast nook. When Regan reluctantly dropped into one of the chairs, she put a bowl and a spoon in front of her.

Regan clutched the spoon but made no attempt to eat. "I don't even know where to start."

"At the beginning, please." Her mother sat across from her, not touching her panna cotta either. Her full focus was on Regan.

"I kissed her," Regan blurted out.

Her mother smiled. "Ah."

"What's that supposed to mean?"

"Nothing, nothing." Her mom waved her spoon. "Go on, please. What did Kylie do? She kissed you back, right?"

"Yes. At least for a moment or two." Then Regan's overloaded brain caught up with what her mom had just said. "Wait! How did you know I was talking about Ky? There are other women in Portland, you know?"

Her mother gave her the same smile as before. "Let's call it a mother's intuition. So, what did you do next?"

"Nothing."

Her mom stared at her. "Nothing?"

"It's not like I planned to kiss her. It was more like...an accident."

"An accident?" Her mom eyed her with a skeptical look. "Like you tripped and fell onto her mouth?"

"Haha. Really funny, Mom." Regan shoved a spoonful of panna cotta into her mouth to help fight down her frustration, but it didn't work. "Our friends talked us into going on a date, and at first, I thought these feelings were only a temporary reaction to it. I didn't want to risk our friendship on a fluke that won't last."

Her mother snorted. "Yeah, only a little twenty-five-year fluke."

"What do you mean by that?"

That annoying smile reappeared on her mom's face. "It's been clear to everyone in this family—well, everyone but you—that it's always been Kylie for you. You even scandalized your grandparents by declaring that you'd marry Kylie when you grew up."

Regan couldn't remember that. "Uh, I did?"

"Oh, yes. You kept insisting Kylie would be your husband one day, and nothing anyone said could convince you otherwise."

Regan rubbed her burning cheeks. "I was a child. Everyone thinks they are going to grow up and marry their best friend, right?"

"Not me. I thought I would grow up to marry Robert Redford." Her mom let out an exaggerated dreamy sigh.

Regan laughed. "Is that where Robbie got his name?"

"No. He's named after my grandfather. By the time I had Robbie, I had long since gotten over my childhood crush. But I think you never did. You just didn't realize it."

"No, Mom." Regan shook her head so firmly she nearly became dizzy. "You've got it all wrong. Ky was always just...Ky to me. I never thought about her like that before."

"I'm not saying you dreamed of turning the tree house into a love shack and luring her up there to seduce her."

Regan's spoon clattered onto the table. "Jesus, Mom!" She fanned herself.

"I'm just saying Kylie has always been your person. The one you confided in. The one you told your dreams to. The one you—"

"That's called having a best friend…isn't it?" Regan searched her mother's face for the answers to the questions that had kept her up for the past week.

"Yeah, but Kylie has always been more than that to you. She's your yardstick—the one you compared all of your girlfriends and boyfriends to. And they always fell short." When Regan opened her mouth to interrupt, her mother raised one hand to stop her. "At first, when you never brought anyone home, I thought you were holding out for the perfect man. Then I realized maybe it would be the perfect woman. And finally, it dawned on me that maybe the person who's perfect for you has been right there, by your side, all this time."

Regan gripped the edge of the table as she wobbled on her seat. This very realization had started to dawn on her too, but hearing it phrased like that still took her breath away. "If you knew, why didn't you tell me?"

"Excuse me? Last time I tried, I got an earful about letting you and Kylie decide what your relationship is and what it isn't."

Regan ducked her head. Yeah, she had said that, hadn't she? That conversation had happened only three weeks ago, yet it felt as if her entire life had shifted since then.

"Besides," her mother added, "I had nearly given up hope of the two of you ever recognizing what's right under your noses."

"I might never have if not for that little chemistry experiment our friends talked us into."

"Hey, what's taking so long? You two aren't in here, eating all the—" Her sister froze in the doorway and looked from Regan to their mother and back. "Uh, never mind." She beat a hasty retreat but not before snatching two bowls of dessert from the fridge.

Regan loosened her white-knuckle grip on the table and rubbed the red lines where the edge had dug into her palms. "What do I do now?"

"You eat your panna cotta." Her mom nudged the glass bowl toward her.

"No, I mean, what do I do about Ky? About us?"

"You knock on her door and ask her if she wants to have panna cotta with you for the next sixty-plus years."

It sounded so simple. "That's a lot of panna cotta."

"Not if it's your favorite dish and you share it with your favorite person," her mother replied.

"But what if Ky doesn't want to have panna cotta with me?"

Her mother let out a huff. "Please! That girl loves Italian dishes more than you do!"

"She's not a girl, Mom, and we're not really talking about panna cotta. What if Ky doesn't think I'm the perfect person for her? She made me promise I wouldn't..."

Her mother tilted her head. "Wouldn't...what? Have panna cotta with her? Love her?"

"No. Yes. I don't know." What exactly had she promised Ky up at the reservoir? Her head was pounding. "That I wouldn't risk our friendship for anything." She lowered her voice to a whisper. "Not even for a chance at love."

Her mom leaned across the table and gently took hold of Regan's shoulders. "Are you sure that's what she wants? Or is it just fear talking? I mean, it's scary to have so much wrapped up in one person."

Regan nodded. It was terrifying.

"And unlike you, Kylie has always been the cautious type, not someone who leaps into things without thinking," her mom added. "Usually, she didn't leap at all, unless you did it first."

Regan jumped up. "Keep Mac and Robbie away from my panna cotta, okay?"

"Where are you going?" her mother asked.

"Outside. I need some time to clear my head." Stepping onto the elevated deck for a moment wouldn't be enough. Regan rushed downstairs, where tall firs grew right in her parents' backyard, surrounding her with their familiar scent.

"Maybe this was a bad idea," Ky mumbled as Denny safely navigated them up and down the hills of the Palisades neighborhood. Making impulsive decisions wasn't her thing; it was what Regan did, and most of the time, it had gotten them into trouble.

But then again, all the shenanigans had helped forge their friendship into the most important relationship in Ky's life.

"What was a bad idea?" Eliza asked from the passenger seat. "Having dinner with Regan and her folks?"

"Um, no." Before Ky could decide whether she wanted to explain the real reason why she had asked them to drive her to Lake Oswego, Denny's old Subaru Outback made it around the last bend.

They passed the house in which Ky had lived for the first sixteen years of her life. Usually, the sight of it made her insides clench into a knot, but today, she hardly paid it any attention.

Instead, she zeroed in on the Tudor-style home next door. Two cars were parked in front of the attached garage. Ky's heartbeat sped up as she recognized one of them as Regan's. She had to clear her throat before she could speak. "You can stop here. This is it."

Denny whistled through her teeth. "I had no idea Regan is so…um…"

"Loaded," Eliza finished with a good-natured laugh.

Ky's hackles rose. "She's not. It's her parents' money. Regan has never relied on the bank of Mommy and Daddy. Besides, the lot was much cheaper when they bought it in the early eighties."

Eliza peered through the gap between the seats and gave her a curious look. "No need to get defensive. You know I couldn't care less about how much money her family has or doesn't have."

"Sorry." Ky swiped her fingers through her bangs. "I just…"

Eliza and Denny exchanged a long look, then Eliza turned back toward Ky. "It's not really the thought of being late for meatballs or whatever they are having that is making you so anxious, is it?"

"No." Ky took a deep breath.

Before she could spill her guts, the Romanos' front door swung open. For a second, Ky clutched the seat belt, expecting to come face-to-face with Regan. But it was only her siblings who stepped outside, both loaded down with bags that, as Ky knew from experience, contained enough leftovers to last a week.

Since Denny's car was blocking the driveway, they paused and peered inside.

Ky undid her seat belt. "Thanks so much for driving me. I owe you. I'll take you out for a thank-you dinner sometime soon."

"I'll never say no to dinner, but you don't owe us a thing," Denny said. "Are you sure you don't want us to wait? We could take a walk through town or go down to the lake, then come back for you."

"It's fine. I'll ride back with Regan." God, she really hoped she would and that the trip back wouldn't be spent in awkward silence. With another "thanks," she slipped from the car and then waved as they drove off.

"Kylie!" Mac rushed over and gave her a hug so tight any boa constrictor would have been proud.

Robbie followed suit, and Ky found herself engulfed in one of the Romano family hugs. She had missed this. It was the closest she had ever come to having siblings.

"I thought you weren't coming," Robbie said when he let go.

Ky rubbed her neck. "Um, yeah, it was kind of a last-minute change of plans."

"Are we going back in with her?" Robbie gave his sister a hopeful look.

"No, I told you I have a date. I need to drop you off and get ready. Besides…" Mac glanced from Ky to the house. "I have a feeling Kylie isn't here to see us."

"Huh? Why else would she—?"

"I'll explain in the car." Mac gave her another hug and whispered, "Good luck."

"What for?" Robbie chuckled. "You aren't here to propose to our baby sister…" His laughter trailed off. "Are you?"

Ky's cheeks and ears burned. "Uh, no."

"Too bad." He hugged her before opening the door on the passenger side.

Ky waved, then stood in the driveway until Mac's car had disappeared around the bend. Slowly, she turned toward the front door behind the arched entryway. Her finger shook as she raised it to the doorbell. Great. Now she felt as if she were really here to propose!

The door was opened within seconds, as if someone on the other side had been waiting for her.

"Kylie! Come on in!" Tammy hugged her, then dragged her to the kitchen.

Joe looked up from a dozen different containers. He instantly put down the serving spoon and engulfed her in a hearty embrace. "I was just packing up the leftovers. Sit and I'll heat up a plate for you."

"No, thanks." If she tried to eat even one bite, she would probably be sick. "I, um… Is Regan here?" The moment she said it, she wanted to slap herself. *Her car's in the driveway. Where else would she be?*

But it was weird that Regan was nowhere to be seen and no sounds came from other parts of the house.

"She's outside, clearing her head," Tammy said.

Ky instantly knew what that meant. "May I…?"

"Of course." Tammy patted her shoulder. "Go."

Ky knew the house as well as her own apartment. Her heart pounded twice for each step she took as she made her way down the stairs. She pushed open the sliding glass door and crossed the patio.

Except for a couple of birds singing overhead, everything was quiet. Ky stepped out from beneath the deck of the main floor, which formed a roof over the patio, and walked over to the tall Douglas fir at the edge of the property.

Their tree house looked a bit weathered but, overall, in good shape. Its little porch, eight feet up from the ground, was empty, and the rope ladder that led through a hole in the platform dangled down. As kids, they had always pulled up the ladder so Regan's siblings wouldn't be able to follow them.

Was Regan really up there?

Something kept Ky from calling out. With sweaty palms, she reached for the rungs of the rope ladder, hoping that Tammy still checked the tree house and the ladder for necessary repairs every summer. One deep breath, then she started to climb.

Regan lay on the wooden platform, her legs propped up against the wall to help her think, and stared up through the plexiglass skylight her mom had built into the roof.

She had lost count of how many times she and Ky had lain like this while she had made up wild tales about ships and pirates and, later, had dreamed about them going to college together.

As much as the stories and conversations had changed over the years, they all had one thing in common: it was always the two of them together, braving every adventure.

Now she was up here alone—which felt wrong beyond words—and neither of them had been brave.

For once, it hadn't been Regan talking Ky into taking a risk. This time, it had been the other way around—Ky had talked her into playing it safe.

But the more Regan thought about it, the more she realized she didn't want safe. She wanted Ky.

And it was up to her to make that happen. Her mom was right: Ky was too scared, and she wasn't one to take risks. Even if she felt the same, she would never tell her. Ky would do anything not to lose her, including denying herself a chance at love.

Regan couldn't allow that. Ky's happiness had always been the most important thing in the world to her, and that meant she had to break her promise. Somehow, Regan had to find a way to talk her into going on the biggest adventure of their lives—provided Ky wanted it too. Wanted *her*.

Only one way to find out.

She swung her legs down from the wall, jumped up, and rushed to the hole in the platform.

Ky peered upward. One more rung, then she could pull herself up. She still had no idea what she'd say or do once she found Regan, but she tried not to think about that.

A sneaker-covered foot appeared through the square opening in the platform, aiming for one of the rungs.

Ky tried to duck out of the way, but unless she let go of the ladder, there was nowhere to go. *Shit,* was all she had time to think before the heel hit her just above her left eye.

Pain flared through her forehead. Her feet slipped, and only her desperate grip on the rung kept her from plummeting down farther. She grunted as her entire weight hung on her sweaty palms.

For a moment, she dangled helplessly while she fumbled to find a rung with her feet.

The sneaker above her disappeared. A second later, Regan's pale face loomed above her. "Oh my God, Ky!"

Ky finally managed to slide one foot onto a rung, followed by the other.

Regan reached down, clutched a handful of Ky's shirt in a death grip, and helped pull her up.

As soon as she made it through the hole, they both collapsed onto the platform, with Ky resting half on top of Regan.

Her heart pounded wildly, and she wasn't sure if it was from the near fall or from Regan's sudden closeness. She tried to roll off, knowing she was heavier, but Regan held tight.

"God, Ky! I nearly kicked you off the ladder! Are you hurt?" She ran her hands along Ky's back and shoulders.

The sensations trailing through Ky's body were definitely not pain. She struggled to suppress a moan. "Uh, no, I don't think so." Then, as Regan stopped moving her hands over her body, Ky became aware of the mild pounding in her head. "Ouch. I take that back. I think you managed to kick my eyebrow. The one with the scar."

"Let me see." Regan pulled her into the back of the tree house, away from the opening, carefully guided her into a sitting position, and knelt next to her. Despite a light tremor, her fingers were incredibly gentle as she ran them over Ky's forehead and traced her eyebrow. "Here?"

"Uh." Ky had no idea. All she could feel was Regan's tender touch.

"Thank God it's not bleeding. It's just a bit red. Let me get some ice from the kitchen." Regan moved toward the ladder.

"No!" Ky took hold of her ankle, preventing her from leaving. "I don't need ice."

"Are you sure?"

Ky nodded. "It barely hurts." She ran one finger along her eyebrow to prove it, then couldn't stop herself from flinching.

"God, I'm sorry, Ky. I had no idea you were down there."

Ky waved her hand to stop her. "You don't have to apologize. I do. I shouldn't have left this morning."

Regan sat with her arms wrapped around her knees. "Is that why you're here? To apologize?"

"Yes. No. I…I think we need to talk."

"Yeah, I think so too. That's why I was climbing down. Ky, I..." Regan buried her face against her arm, then peered at her over the top of her knees. She spoke so quietly that Ky had to strain to make out the words over the birdsong in the trees around them. "I'm not sure I can...or want to...keep the promise I made you."

Ky's heart slammed against her ribs. Oh my God. That sounded like a breakup speech...when they weren't even together!

"I realized that my mom is right. Everyone's right." Regan cleared her throat. "I want your toothbrush in my cup holder."

Either Ky's brain had been scrambled too hard from the kick to her head, or this was the weirdest friendship breakup speech ever. She stared at Regan openmouthed. "What?"

"Oh damn." Regan let out a sound that was half giggle, half groan. "Is it just me, or did that come out like a euphemism? That sounded so much better in my head. I swear I didn't mean it like that." Then she paused and, in a breathless mumble, added something that sounded like, "Or maybe I did."

Every word only increased Ky's confusion. She held up both hands. "Let me say something here before I chicken out. I ran this morning because I wanted to stay more than anything."

Regan lifted her head from where she had buried it against her arm. "I wanted you to stay too."

Ky's heart gave a happy thump. But she needed to make sure because too many things had remained unsaid between them in the past few weeks. She filled her lungs with the soothing scent of the trees, then asked, "You wanted me to stay like I stayed before? For a sleepover between friends?"

Regan took an audible breath as if she had to brace herself for what she was about to say. The seconds she took to answer seemed to tick by in slow motion. "No." Her voice came out raspy. "I'll never stop being your friend if that's all you want, but if...maybe...you could imagine staying for something more...something different." She searched Ky's face with an intensity that made Ky's heartbeat quicken.

"I can." Distantly, Ky realized she was whispering. "That's the reason I wanted to stay too."

"Then why did you run?"

"Because I was so afraid of messing it all up and losing you. Still am." She paused to peek at Regan.

"I know," Regan said, understanding in her dark brown eyes. "Me too." She slid over to Ky's side of the tree house and took her hand. Their fingers instantly settled into that familiar tangle. "But that's the thing. We've both been operating under the assumption that things won't work out. That we're risking destroying what we have if we try to turn it into something it wasn't before."

Imagining it hurt more than the kick to the head. She gripped Regan's hand tightly. "Yeah."

"But that's not how chemical reactions work," Regan said with her passionate science geek expression. "Sure, some of the old bonds might be broken, but new ones form, and no atoms are destroyed." As if to demonstrate, she disentangled their fingers, then laced them again in a new position that had Regan's instead of Ky's thumb resting on top. It felt different, but just as wonderful. "We wouldn't be destroying our friendship. We'd be building on it."

Despite her tension, Ky couldn't help cracking a smile at how adorable she was. "When you use chemistry to explain something, I know you mean it."

Regan held her gaze. "I've never meant anything more."

Ky pulled her closer by their joined hands until they were both kneeling in the middle of the tree house. She drank in Regan's familiar features, her eyes that looked so deeply into her own. Then her attention was drawn to the beautiful curve of Regan's mouth. "Are you sure?" she asked in a husky whisper. "Once we cross that line, we can't go back."

"I don't want to go back." Regan's voice was quiet but intense. She didn't break their eye contact, not even to blink. "Do you?"

Ky sucked in a breath, then blew it out, imagining she was toppling over that fragile house of cards so she could build something stronger. "No. I want to go forward." So she did—right into Regan's arms. Still on her knees, she slid one hand onto Regan's hip while keeping hold of Regan's fingers with the other.

Regan wrapped her free arm around Ky's shoulder and pressed closer until her body heat engulfed Ky.

Ky's breathing sped up, but none of the oxygen seemed to end up in her lungs. She felt a little dizzy. Tunnel vision set in, and the only thing she could see was Regan's face. Her eyes. Her lips. "Can I—?"

"Yes," Regan breathed.

Ky raised their joined hands and pressed a kiss to Regan's knuckles, almost like a test to see what it would be like. It wasn't weird; it was electric. It made her want more, and now, for the first time, she allowed herself to have it. She disentangled their fingers and brought her hand to Regan's cheek as she slowly leaned forward.

Regan let out a shuddery breath and met her halfway.

Warm air caressed Ky's mouth, only to be replaced by Regan's lips.

The birds stopped singing, or maybe Ky was no longer aware of them because all she could hear was her own heartbeat, and all she could feel was the slide of their lips against each other.

At first, it was slow and careful, a tentative exploration, with neither of them taking possession of the kiss but sharing it as they'd shared everything else—as equals. Maybe this was really building on their friendship rather than destroying it, Ky thought.

And then she stopped thinking as Regan slid her fingers up the back of her neck and into her hair and deepened the kiss. She tasted faintly of chocolate and something else, equally addictive.

Heat sizzled over Ky's skin. Her moan mingled with Regan's. She wobbled on her knees and clutched Regan's hips with both hands to keep herself upright. Their bodies pressed together along their lengths, turning up the temperature even more.

Finally, Regan broke the kiss with a gasp, and Ky became aware that the throbbing in her body wasn't just the pleasant kind. "Ouch. My knees are killing me."

Regan smiled, her lips still lingering against Ky's. "Yeah. Mine too. Maybe we should have picked a different place for our first kiss. Well, second kiss."

"No," Ky said. "This was perfect."

"Yeah?" Regan murmured against her mouth, and Ky could hear the same faint insecurity in her voice that remained deep inside of her.

"Yeah."

Their lips met again, and this time, there was nothing tentative about their kiss. It lasted until Ky was breathless and could no longer ignore the pain in her knees.

They sank onto the wooden floor and lay on their backs next to each other, holding hands in their tree house, like teenagers. With the butterflies fluttering in her belly, Ky certainly felt like one.

Regan turned her head and looked at her. Her cheeks were flushed, her lips red from their kisses, and a leaf had gotten caught in her hair.

Ky reached out to remove it, then remembered that she no longer needed an excuse to touch her. Besides, Regan looked good like that—carefree and happy.

"I realize this might take some getting used to," Regan said quietly. "But if you want to touch me, you can."

Ky's cheeks burned. "It's not that." She bit her kiss-swollen bottom lip. Great. Two seconds into this relationship and she was already making a mess of things. "I mean, of course I want to touch you." She reached out her free hand and tenderly traced Regan's cheekbone with her fingertips. God, her skin was incredibly soft.

Regan's eyes fluttered closed, then opened. She sent Ky a questioning look as if sensing that there was more.

*Oh.* Ky had lost her train of thought. "You've got a leaf stuck in your hair."

"Where?" Regan patted her locks on the wrong side of her head. "You'd better remove it, or my parents will think we had a little tumble in the tree house."

Ky groaned and hid her face in the bend of her elbow. "Oh God." She wasn't sure she could sit down at the dinner table with the Romanos after kissing their daughter. "Do you think we can get away with sneaking out to the car?"

Regan laughed.

The booming, happy sound made Ky tingle all over.

"You basically grew up with them, so I think you know the answer to that."

Ky sighed. "They would show up on my doorstep with the leftovers, wouldn't they?"

"The leftovers and a guilt trip the size of a blue whale."

Ky reached over and tenderly removed the leaf from Regan's hair, then let her hand linger, just because she now could. "Do you want to tell them? I mean, today?"

"Do you?"

They looked at each other, then shook their heads at the same time.

"Part of me wants to call everyone in my contacts list and tell them right this minute," Regan said with the most adorable grin. "But my family and all of our friends have been up in our business for years. Maybe it would be nice if this"—she touched her own chest, then laid her hand on Ky's, right above her heart, which promptly picked up its pace—"could grow without being the focus of everyone's attention for a while. What do you think?"

Ky put her hand on top of Regan's. "I think you are a wise woman."

"Oh, you think I'm wise again now?" Regan's eyes twinkled as she leaned over her. "I thought I was impulsive?"

"That too. But I kinda love that about you." Damn, that had practically been a declaration of love just minutes after their second kiss. But Ky didn't want to play games with Regan and pretend she didn't care when she really, really did.

"Yeah?"

"Yeah."

God, this was intense. Their eye contact made it hard to breathe.

Then one corner of Regan's mouth curled up into a playful smile as if she knew Ky needed to ease up on the emotional intensity. "So if you like my impulsiveness, you might like this…" With her hand still on Ky's upper chest, she leaned down and—

"Girls?" Joe's voice drifted up through the opening in the platform. "Are you up there? Your mom said to leave you alone, but Kylie hasn't had anything to eat yet."

Regan let her head fall against Ky's shoulder and moaned into the cotton of her shirt. "You were right. We should have tried to sneak out."

"Too late." Ky ran her fingers through Regan's hair and enjoyed the shiver she felt go through her. "Come on. Let's go get some dessert." She would have preferred more kisses, but for now, some chocolate panna cotta would have to do.

The sun was starting to set when Regan pulled into the parking lot in front of Ky's apartment building. She shut off the engine, and they both turned and looked at each other without saying anything.

Regan couldn't believe how much had changed since the last time she and Ky had been in her car together, less than twenty-four hours ago. She felt as if she could float all the way home, yet at the same time, a heavy weight settled on her chest because she was very much aware of how much this mattered. It wasn't like the start of any other relationship since emotions were already higher and they both had so much more to lose—or to gain.

Ky took her hand, then studied their intertwined fingers with the same look of wonder on her face that Regan felt. "This is..."

"Yeah," Regan said on a long exhale.

Ky cocked her head and smiled at her. "How do you know what I wanted to say when I haven't even decided on the right words yet?"

"Surreal, wonderful, scary. Pick any of them. I think they all apply, for me anyway."

"Yeah, for me too."

Being able to be completely honest with each other once again felt so freeing. Holding back anything from Ky, even for a little while, had been excruciating.

"So," Regan finally said, "what do we do now?" It had been easier up in the tree house because it was their safe spot, removed from their adult lives.

Ky gave her a crooked smile. "I have no idea."

Maybe that answer should have scared Regan even more, but instead, it gave her hope. She knew how hard it had been for Ky to make herself vulnerable in past relationships, and it was a relief to see that the trust they had built as friends still existed.

"Do you, um, want to come in?" Ky tilted her head toward her front door.

Mutual teasing had always been a part of their relationship, so Regan didn't even try to hold back the joking reply that was on the tip of her tongue. "Isn't that a little fast, considering we haven't even had a real date yet?"

Ky's cheeks took on the loveliest tinge of red. "Get your mind out of the gutter, Regan Romano. I meant for a hot chocolate or something. Besides, we've had three dates. You kissed me after the third, and I've already been introduced to the family too."

"Hmm, maybe I should come in, then." But Regan didn't undo her seat belt. As tempting as it was, this was a big change for both of them, and they needed some time to adjust.

"Seriously, though, could I interest you?" Ky's eyes widened, and she quickly added, "Uh, I meant, can I interest you in going on a date? Not in coming in for…um…"

Regan couldn't help smiling. Such cuteness. How had she managed not to fall in love with her years ago? Then it was her turn to freeze, wide-eyed. Had she really just thought that? But was it that much of a surprise? She had loved Ky deeply for years, and she wouldn't have risked their bond for a hookup or a little crush.

"Regan?" Ky swiped her thumb along Regan's index finger, sending a tingle up her arm.

"Um, sorry. Yes."

"Yes to what?"

*To everything.* Out loud, she said: "To a date." She trailed her own thumb along the web of Ky's fingers. "For now."

Ky shivered visibly and cleared her throat. "Great. And this time, we won't set out to prove that there's no chemistry between us."

Regan chuckled. "No, I think it's safe to say that experiment was a complete failure."

"Depends on your point of view." Ky's voice dropped an octave. "I'd say it was an outright success."

Their gazes locked, and the temperature in the car seemed to climb a few degrees.

Finally, Regan blinked, interrupting their intense eye contact. "Friday?"

"Sounds like a plan. Where would you like to go?" Ky asked. "If we want to keep this…us…to ourselves for a while, it should probably be somewhere where we won't run into anyone we know."

"I've got this. I know the perfect place—and don't worry, it's not my parents' restaurant."

Ky laughed. "Phew. What about Saturday? Are we still on for Netflix night?"

"Of course," Regan said. "I mean, we're still best friends, right? That doesn't have to change because we…um…we're dating now. Or do you want things to change?"

"No! I just wasn't sure what the rules are for dating your best friend."

"I don't think there's a rule book, Ky. We'll have to make it up as we go along."

Ky sent her an affectionate smile. "Well, you've always been great at improvising."

"And you're great at following my lead," Regan answered. "We'll be fine."

They looked at each other for a while.

"I should get home," Regan finally said. "As much as I'd love to spend more time with you, I've got a stack of papers as tall as me to grade."

Ky opened her mouth, a twinkle in her eyes.

With a faux stern look, Regan pressed a finger to Ky's lips. "No jokes about my height."

"Wouldn't think of it," Ky murmured. Her breath tickled the pad of Regan's finger. "You're perfect, height and all."

They had bantered about Regan's shorter frame for years, but now every inside joke seemed to have taken on a new, deeper meaning.

Slowly, Regan slid her finger from Ky's lips, but her gaze lingered for a moment longer before it darted to the brightly lit kitchen window. *Damn.* Ky's eagle-eyed roommate was likely home, and if she walked past the window, she would have a perfect view of the car.

How were they supposed to say goodbye now? A casual "see you tomorrow"? A hug? A kiss?

"Huh." Ky rubbed her eyebrow. "This is kinda complicated."

Or maybe they were making it more complicated than it needed to be. They were two consenting adults. If she wanted to kiss her girlfriend, she would. She had already reached for Ky but then froze with her hand halfway to Ky's shoulder. "Oh wow."

"You okay?"

"Yeah." Regan shook her head and laughed. "I just realized you're my girlfriend now."

Ky looked at her the way she had when Regan had given her some of the Pokémon cards from her own collection for her birthday when they'd been ten. "Which also makes you my girlfriend."

"That would be a correct conclusion."

"So if I wanted to kiss you good night…" Ky's voice lowered with every word as she undid her seat belt and leaned across the center console.

Regan tried to pretend her breath didn't catch. "Well, if you must…" She let out a long-suffering sigh and puckered her lips.

Ky burst out laughing. "You goof." Her laughter faded away as she ran her fingers up Regan's arm and across her shoulder, raising a trail of goose bumps. She stroked up the side of Regan's neck, then touched a single fingertip to the corner of Regan's mouth in a gesture that was tender yet incredibly erotic.

Heat coursed through Regan, and her playful mood instantly shifted. *Ky. Please.*

As if hearing the silent plea, Ky bridged the final inch between them and brushed her lips against Regan's in a featherlight caress.

Regan cupped the back of Ky's neck and pulled her closer. Her mouth parted beneath Ky's.

Ky traced the curve of Regan's upper lip with the tip of her tongue before slipping inside. She explored with gentle strokes that quickly grew more confident.

Regan returned each touch and raked her fingers through Ky's hair.

A low groan escaped Ky, sending a thrill through Regan.

The taste, feel, and sound of her made Regan's head spin in ways she had never expected.

Finally, after one last, lingering kiss, Ky pulled back. "Good night," she whispered, her voice husky.

By the time Regan regained the power of speech, Ky had opened the door and climbed out on legs that looked a little unsteady.

"Good night," Regan answered through a dry throat. She stared after Ky as she closed the passenger door and walked toward her apartment.

When she reached it, she turned and lifted one hand.

Regan mirrored the gesture.

Somehow, Ky managed to unlock the door without fully turning toward it or breaking their eye contact. They stared at each other from across the parking lot for a few seconds longer before Ky stepped inside.

Regan slumped against the back of the seat and touched the corner of her mouth, recreating Ky's earlier caress.

Wow. Who knew?

# Chapter 14

On Friday, every student at Hamilton High seemed to be in the mood for pizza, and Ky felt as if she had single-handedly fed all one thousand thirty-six of them, even though not all of them ate in the cafeteria.

Finally, the stream of kids slowed to a trickle.

Ky checked the line to see if the cheese pizza would last.

A sixth sense drew her attention toward the double doors, which swung open.

Regan entered the cafeteria. Her energy filled the lunchroom as she smoothly sidestepped a group of students. She wore one of Ky's favorite outfits, a navy-blue wrap skirt and a simple white T-shirt. God, she looked good.

Ky drank her in as she approached. While they had talked on the phone for a few minutes every day, they had barely seen each other all week. With less than two weeks until senior finals, Regan had been busy creating study guides and review booklets. The sight of her was a special treat that brightened Ky's day.

As they made eye contact from across the room, a smile lit up Regan's face.

"Hey," the kid in front of Ky said as she handed him a tray without looking. "I wanted cheese pizza."

Grudgingly, Ky looked away from Regan and checked the tray. *Oops.* She'd handed him a slice of pepperoni pizza, Regan's usual choice. She switched it for cheese pizza and forced herself to focus on work but was very much aware of Regan as she made her way through the line toward her.

Finally, Regan reached her. Her gaze swept over Ky, making her flush more than the heat lamps that kept the pizza warm.

Ky had never cared how she looked in her work outfit, but now she cursed the unattractive apron and gloves and the baseball cap she wore to contain her hair.

"Hi." Regan tucked a curly strand of hair behind her ear. Tiny shreds of paper from the perforated edge of a spiral notebook stuck to her forearm.

Ky struggled not to reach across the counter and brush them off. While their school was pretty liberal, the principal supportive, and their co-workers aware she and Regan were queer, they had never before been queer together, and Ky had no idea how they would navigate their relationship at work now that the rumors weren't only rumors anymore. With all the students surrounding them, even the most platonic of touches was probably out.

"Hi," she said as casually as possible. "I should have known pizza day would lure you over."

"Of course. I'm Italian after all." But the look in Regan's eyes said that it hadn't been the pizza that had lured her to the cafeteria.

Someone in line behind Regan cleared their throat.

Ky kicked herself into motion, picked the most delicious-looking slice of pepperoni pizza, and slid the tray in front of Regan. "Here you go."

The corners of Regan's lips twitched into a smile. "Aren't you forgetting something?"

Ky stared at her. Did Regan really expect her to…?

"Fruit," Regan said. "Every lunch must include a serving of fruit or veggies, right?"

"Oh. Right." Ky added an orange to the tray, careful not to let their fingers brush.

"Thank you. See you tonight," Regan said but didn't seem in a hurry to walk away.

Tonight… The thought of their date made Ky's heart hammer with equal parts excitement and nervousness. This time, it would be real, not just going through the motions to prove a point to their friends. Her emotions would be out there for Regan to see.

"Kylie," Fran called from the back. "Can you come over here for a second?"

As Lilia slid in next to her to take over, Ky sent Regan a regretful look and a quick wave before crossing the kitchen to see what her boss wanted.

Fran glanced up from her ever-present clipboard. “I just found out that the district food service coordinator will drop by later today. If you want that promotion, you might want to stick around.”

Ky froze. In the past, she’d been afraid to let herself want more, scared that it would mean she would never be happy with what she had, like her parents. But now she had taken a huge leap of faith with Regan—and was happier than ever, so maybe wanting more wasn’t always a bad thing.

The question was just: Did she want this?

Regan’s words echoed through Ky’s mind: *If you really wanted it, you would know.*

“Um, about that…” When Fran lowered her clipboard, Ky leaned against one of the stainless-steel worktables for support. “I’m honored by your trust in me, but I’ve decided not to take the promotion.”

Fran nodded as if she had already suspected that answer. “Can I ask why not?”

“I don’t think it’s the right job for me.”

“Other priorities?” Fran peered at her over the rim of her glasses, and for a moment, Ky thought maybe her boss suspected that her focus was very much on her private life right now. Then a smile deepened the lines around Fran’s eyes. “Or is it the paperwork?”

Ky laughed. “That too. I just feel like all those forms and checklists would stifle my creativity. I’d rather stay out here, in the kitchen. But I do know who’d be perfect for the job.”

“I’m listening.”

Ky pointed at Lilia, who was talking a grumpy teen into taking an orange.

Fran slid her glasses back up her nose. “I’ll keep that in mind.”

That evening, Regan stared at the first batch of potato croquettes that she’d just dumped onto paper towels to drain. Ugh. She had conducted chemistry experiments that looked more appetizing. In desperate need of some help, she reached for her phone.

*Um, Dad? The recipe you texted me earlier this week… Are the panzarotti supposed to look like this?* She took a snapshot and sent it to her father.

Her dad answered with several cry-laughing emojis. *Not exactly. They're supposed to be torpedo-shaped. Why isn't Kylie cooking?*

Regan froze with her thumbs hovering over the phone. She and Ky had agreed not to tell anyone about their new relationship yet, but she didn't want to lie to her father—and she knew Ky wouldn't want her to either. *Because I'm trying to surprise her with one of Anonn's dishes for our date.* She held her breath until her father's reply popped up.

*Date? Is this still part of the dating experiment your friends talked you into?*

*No,* Regan answered. Before she could add more, her phone rang.

Sighing, she swiped her finger across the screen.

"So your mother was right," her father said. "She insists the two of you had a glow about you when you climbed down from the tree house last Sunday."

Regan's cheeks burned. "Dad! There was no glow!"

Her father laughed. "I don't want to know the details. But I'm really happy you finally figured it out. Couldn't wish for a better daughter-in-law."

"Jesus, Dad! I said I'm cooking for our date, not our wedding!"

"All right, then. Do you have any of the potato/egg mixture left?"

"Yes," Regan answered. "I only made a test batch."

"Why don't you make *Anonn*'s potato cake instead? It's based on the same mixture, and you just put it in the oven in a casserole dish, so it doesn't have to keep its form."

Regan blew out a breath. "You're a lifesaver. Okay, walk me through it—baby steps, please."

An hour later, a slightly frazzled Regan bounced up and down in front of Ky's apartment. After her cooking adventure, she had spent too much time trying to figure out what to wear, so she was running a few minutes late.

She knew it was ridiculous. After all, Ky had seen her in baggy sweatpants, grass-stained jeans, and geeky T-shirts more often than she could count. It was a bit late to suddenly start caring how she looked in front of Ky—but she did.

Truth be told, she had cared for a while. She had already obsessed over what to wear for their first let's-prove-we-don't-have-any-chemistry date, when she had taken Ky to La Casa Nostra. She had told herself she was only making an effort because of their friends. God, how oblivious she'd been! That should have been a big, flashing neon sign.

Lilia opened the door and regarded Regan with a smirk. "We've really gotta stop meeting like this."

Regan laughed. Maybe one day they would—when she and Ky would be living together instead. *Whoa! Take it easy. No U-Hauls anytime soon!*

Lilia escorted her into the apartment. "So is this still part of your little chemistry experiment? Or is this for real?"

*Shit.* If she continued like this, the entire population of the Portland metro area would know before the week was over.

Before she could decide on a response, the bathroom door swung open, and Ky stepped out.

Regan forgot how to form words other than "wow."

Ky was wearing the dark gray chinos she'd chosen for their date at La Casa Nostra—why mess with perfection, right? This time, she had paired them with a white button-up shirt with faint vertical stripes. She had rolled up its sleeves past her elbows, and it struck Regan as the sexiest thing she'd ever seen in her life.

Lilia looked back and forth between their faces and laughed. "Well, that answers my question."

Ky ignored her. She ran her gaze over Regan's sleeveless wrap dress, lingering on the knee-length hem and the V-neck for a second. "You look stunning."

The look in her eyes made Regan flush with pleasure. "So do you."

"Can I wear these?" Ky waggled her foot, which was covered by a white sneaker.

"They're perfect. There's no dress code where we are going."

"Oh, good. Where are we going?"

"You'll see."

As Ky joined her for the walk to the car, the fresh-forest-air scent of her perfume engulfed Regan, and she deeply breathed it in.

They both got in and clicked the seat belts into place, their movements so in sync that they ended up with their faces only a few inches apart.

"Hi," Ky murmured. "Since Lil now knows, can I kiss you hello?"

Regan loved how Ky always asked before kissing her. Consent was sexy. "Yes."

Their lips met across the middle console as soon as she'd finished her reply.

Ky's mouth was incredibly soft. She kissed Regan with a tenderness that made her ache, but there was also an undercurrent of desire buzzing between them.

"Speaking of knowing about us," Regan said when the kiss finally ended. She sank fully into the driver's seat so she wouldn't be distracted by Ky's lips. "I, um, told my dad about us. He asked, and I didn't want to lie." She glanced over to see Ky's reaction.

A gentle grin tugged on Ky's lips. "I know."

"You know? How?"

"I got a text from your mom while I got ready for our date." Ky pulled her phone from the pocket of her chinos, unlocked it, and held it out to Regan.

Her mother had written only four words: *Welcome to the family,* followed by a confetti emoji, a party hat emoji, and two bride emojis.

Groaning, Regan thumped her forehead against the steering wheel.

Ky laughed and lightly put her hand on Regan's back. The warmth of her palm drifted through the thin cotton, heating up Regan's body. "It's okay." More quietly, she added, "It's kinda nice to be part of a family again."

Regan took her head off the steering wheel and reached across the console for Ky's hand. "You always were, and you always will be."

Ky swallowed audibly, then lifted Regan's hand to her lips and kissed it.

The emotions vibrating between them were intense, especially for their first real date, but Regan realized she didn't want it any other way. She left their fingers melded together while she drove them toward her apartment.

"Ya Hala."

"No."

"Redwood."

"Nope."

"Oh, I know!" Ky stuck her finger in the air. "The Observatory."

Regan snorted. "No. Give up. You'll never guess."

Ky had thought they were headed toward one of the restaurants on Stark Street, but Regan continued north, then took a right onto Burnside Street and finally a left onto 74th Avenue. They weren't going to that greasy spoon diner two blocks from Regan's place, were they? Ky grinned as she imagined them walking in, all dressed up.

But Regan drove past the diner. When she finally stopped the car, they were parked in front of her apartment complex.

"Your place?" Ky swallowed.

"Is that okay?" Regan looked uncharacteristically insecure. "I mean, we said we wanted to go somewhere where we won't run into anyone we know, so..."

"No, it's fine. It's great." Ky had always loved spending time at Regan's place. She felt more at home there than in her own apartment—because Regan was there. But staying in, with the bedroom readily available, instead of having dinner at a public place would be a lot more intimate and enticing. Was Regan hoping to take things to the next level? And if she was, was Ky ready for that?

Regan studied her intently. "Are you sure?"

Ky pushed her nerves aside. She was being silly. Just because there was a growing, decidedly nonplatonic tension between them didn't mean they would jump each other's bones the moment they were alone. Besides, they would be at Regan's place for Netflix night tomorrow anyway. "Yes. It's perfect. I don't even care what we order. As much as I love food, I'm here for you, not for whatever's on the menu."

"O ye of little faith. We're not ordering."

"You cooked?" Ky was so stunned that she stayed in the car while Regan was already climbing out.

She walked around the car, opened the passenger-side door for Ky, and offered her hand. "I cooked. I wanted tonight to be special."

Ky's heart melted into a puddle of goo. She put her concerns aside and slid her hand into Regan's. When she got out of the car, Regan barely stepped back. They stood so close that their bodies almost brushed, and Ky could feel the heat emanating from Regan. "It already is."

"Then what has you so tense?" Regan brushed Ky's bangs out of her eyes.

She should have known she wouldn't be able to keep it from Regan—not that she wanted to. Ky glanced around. The driveway really wasn't the place to discuss their love life. "Um, can we maybe talk about it over dinner?"

Regan raised herself up on her tiptoes and placed the softest of kisses on Ky's lips. "Of course. Let's go in and check on my creation. It's in the oven, and I don't want to tarnish my spotless reputation as a chef by burning it."

Laughing, Ky let herself be dragged to the door.

Usually, they ate on the couch, but today, Regan had set the table in the dining area. The heavenly scent of sizzling cheese wafted over from the kitchen.

Ky's mouth watered. "Want me to help with anything?"

"No," Regan answered. "You cook for hundreds of kids every day. I've got this. You just sit and look sexy."

"I'll try my best." Ky slid the chair into a position that allowed her to watch Regan.

Regan turned on romantic music—the album of Jenna Blake's love ballads—before she went to the kitchen. She drizzled lemon juice and olive oil over the lettuce she must have prepared earlier, carried the bowl to the table, then bent over to peek into the oven.

Ky told her about turning down the promotion to assistant cafeteria manager, but her focus wasn't on the conversation. Watching Regan move around the kitchen was the most enjoyable thing Ky had done all week. The way the dress swirled with every graceful movement, how she closed a drawer with her hip, her smile whenever their gazes met… Ky couldn't look away.

"So, no regrets that you turned the promotion down?" Regan asked while she worked.

"None," Ky answered without hesitation. "It felt right." Just as right as being here, on a date with Regan.

"Good. I hope you know I don't care whether you're a lunch lady or a cafeteria manager as long as you're happy."

A ball of emotion lodged in Ky's throat. Both of her parents had cared too much about status and money, but she knew Regan truly didn't. "I know. I am happy."

They looked at each other until the oven timer went off.

Regan opened the oven door, releasing a cloud of steam and a delicious scent. She lifted out a casserole dish and set it on the table between them.

Ky stared at the golden-baked crust. "That looks like the potato cake your grandma used to make."

"That's because it is." With a proud grin, Regan put a generous portion onto Ky's plate, then served herself before she took a seat. "I hope it tastes like hers too."

"I'm sure it will," Ky said. Neither of them had had potato cake since *Anonn* had died shortly after her husband, and it meant the world to her that Regan had chosen to make it for her.

Regan jumped up. "Oops. I forgot our drinks."

"Let me get them." Ky pressed Regan back onto her chair. "That's one of the many advantages of dating your best friend. I know where the glasses are."

Regan's booming laugh filled the apartment, putting a smile on Ky's face. "Oh, is that the only advantage?"

"No," Ky said. "I also know where all your ticklish spots are."

"And that's an advantage how?"

Ky bit her lip. Her automatic impulse was to hold back the flirty comment that immediately came to mind—probably a result of years... or decades of keeping things strictly platonic. It would take some time and conscious effort to let go of that habit. "Well," she drawled, "I figure those sensitive spots might also be erogenous zones. And I already know each and every one of them."

Regan's eyes went hazy. "Maybe not *each and every* one," she said, her voice hoarse. "There might be one or two spots you haven't...tickled so far."

Heat rose up Ky's chest and shot into her cheeks. "Drinks," she got out.

"Yeah, I could use something cold too. Extra ice in mine, please."

Grinning, Ky took two glasses from the cabinet and opened the fridge. It was great to know that Regan felt the sizzle between them too.

"Top shelf," Regan said, her voice almost back to normal now. "I made us a pitcher of the blackberry lemonade you love."

*Aww.* Regan had really gone all out for their date.

"So," Regan said while Ky was pouring them each a glass of lemonade and adding extra ice to both, "what was it that made you so tense earlier?"

Lemonade splashed onto the counter. Ky rushed to the sink to clean up the spill and hide her flushed cheeks.

"Ky?" Regan's chair scraped over the hardwood floor, then her light footsteps approached. She gently laid her hand on Ky's back.

Slowly, Ky put the rag down and turned around.

"Are you okay?" Regan soothingly trailed her fingers up and down Ky's forearm, sending a delicious shiver through Ky's body.

"I'm fine." Ky decided to take a page out of Regan's book and just say what had been on her mind since Regan had pulled into the driveway. "I love having our first real date at your place, where we can both be ourselves. But I know you don't usually invite anyone over for a date or go to their place unless…um, you're ready to have more than dinner."

Regan's lips formed a startled O.

"It's not that I don't want that—eventually," Ky added quickly. "Believe me, the thought of having dessert in the bedroom is tempting. Very tempting." Her voice came out in a thick, scratchy whisper. "But I'm not sure we should rush things. Of course, after twenty-five years, no one can really accuse us of that, but…" Ky realized she was rambling and snapped her mouth shut.

"You're afraid we would mess up what we have if we move too fast," Regan finished the sentence for her.

Ky stared at her sneakers. One now had a deep purple stain from the blackberry lemonade. "Yeah. I am."

Gently, Regan tipped up her chin and placed a featherlight kiss on her lips. "Okay. Let's take things slow, then. I wasn't planning on dessert in the bedroom when I invited you over anyway."

Another flush swept up Ky's neck. Great. Now she had made an ass out of herself. "Sorry. I didn't mean to make assumptions."

Regan chuckled. "Nah. You weren't that far off. You know me. I'm the go-with-your-impulses kind of woman. I didn't invite you over for sex, but I don't think I would have protested too much if you'd suggested a nonplatonic sleepover."

The flush now reached the tips of Ky's ears, but it was no longer only embarrassment that heated her skin.

Regan stroked Ky's cheek with the back of her fingers. "And just for the record: Whatever I did when I was dating other people has nothing to do with you and me. All my dating rules went out the window the moment I, um, started dating my best friend."

For a second, Ky thought she had wanted to say something else—that she'd fallen in love with her. *Don't read anything into it. You are the one who wants to take it slow, remember?* "Ditto. This is completely uncharted territory for me too."

"But we'll navigate it together—at a pace we're both comfortable with, okay?"

Ky blinked against the sudden burning in her eyes. "Have I told you lately how wonderful you are?"

A rare blush dusted Regan's cheeks. "Tell me that after you've tasted my dinner." She took one of the glasses and nodded at Ky to grab the other.

Hand in hand, they went back to the dining area and took a seat at the table.

Ky cut off a small piece of potato cake with her fork and slid it into her mouth. The potatoes, mozzarella, parmesan, and ham blended together in perfect harmony, exactly the way Ky remembered.

"How is it?" Regan asked instead of tasting it for herself. "Do you still think I'm wonderful, or has this establishment just lost a few stars?"

Ky let out a hum. "You get top ratings both for being wonderful and for dinner." She took another forkful. "This is better than anything they serve at The Observatory."

"Good. Because I wasn't about to take you there and have Flirty Waitress interfere with our date." Regan shoved her fork into the potato cake, then chewed vigorously.

Ky couldn't help the broad grin stretching across her face. "God, I'm so slow sometimes! You were jealous, weren't you?"

"Maybe a tiny bit." Regan held the thumb and index finger of her free hand a fraction of an inch apart. When Ky gave her a doubtful look, she widened the distance between her fingers. "Okay, maybe more than a bit. But I convinced myself I was just pissed because it was disrespectful. After all, Blondie couldn't know our date was only a little chemistry experiment."

"I didn't even notice her flirting," Ky said. "I was totally focused on you."

Laughing, Regan shook her head at both of them. "How did we not know?"

"I have no idea." Ky reached for her glass and studied Regan over the rim.

"What?"

"Have you ever…?" Ky glanced into the depths of the blackberry lemonade while she thought about how to phrase her question. This was definitely not the usual first-date small talk. "Before you came up with the idea to go on a date to prove there was zero chemistry between us, had you ever felt anything other than friendship for me?"

Regan took another bite and chewed it thoroughly, as if needing time to think about it. "If you'd asked me that a month or two ago, I would have said no."

Ky hung on her every word. When Regan didn't immediately continue, she asked, "But now…?"

"Now I think deluding myself is apparently one of my many talents." Regan dug a few pieces of ham out of her potato pie. She stared at them for a moment, then ate them and peered at Ky. "Do you remember how I didn't date all through high school?"

"Of course." Back then, Ky had been incredibly jealous of all the boys who'd asked Regan out, but Regan had never given any of them the time of day.

"I assumed I was a late bloomer, but now I'm no longer sure. I mean, with everything else, I was always the first one to try out new stuff and follow my impulses."

Ky nodded. Regan had always dove headfirst into new adventures, eager to experience everything life had to offer. "Why do you think it was different with dating?"

"I'm not sure. Other people just didn't register for me romantically or sexually."

"Other people," Ky repeated. Her breathing hitched. "Meaning…I did?"

Regan fiddled with her fork while she seemed to think about it. "On an unconscious level…I think so. I mean, we kind of acted as if we were a couple, don't you think?" With a grin, she added, "Well, minus the make-out sessions under the bleachers."

Ky had never really thought of it that way. For her, they had always been Regan and Ky, an unbeatable unit, but she had never thought her crush might not be so unrequited after all. "Hmm, maybe you are right."

"Maybe? For Christ's sake, I took you to prom!"

"Causing quite the stir." Ky had admired her so much for standing up to parents and admin and for not caring what everyone else thought of her dancing with an out lesbian.

Regan shrugged. "I didn't care. I couldn't imagine going with anyone else."

"How do you know that wasn't just you wanting to share it with your best friend, even though I didn't go to the same school anymore?"

"I thought that's all it was, but I kept our prom picture on my bedside table until sophomore year of college."

Ky waved her hand in a "so what?" gesture.

"You looked incredibly hot in that suit."

Ky couldn't help grinning. "You thought so?"

"Melissa thought I thought so. God, she was so jealous of you. I finally had to put the photo away because she wouldn't let it go. It was ridiculous. After all, I was just admiring your cute bow tie—or so I thought."

"But you never had any inkling that maybe your feelings weren't completely platonic?"

Regan firmly shook her head. "I was totally oblivious. It's like I slapped the label 'base' on you and put you into the bases cabinet along with all the other bases, and when I was looking for an acid to create an interesting reaction, I rooted through the acid cabinet but never thought to look in the bases cabinet. It was only during our little chemistry experiment that I started to realize I had mislabeled you."

In high school, Ky had hated chemistry with a passion, but Regan's chemistry analogies were the cutest thing since evolution had come up with baby otters.

Chuckling, Regan slapped one hand in front of her eyes and peeked at Ky through her fingers. "Sorry, that probably made no sense whatsoever."

"No, it made perfect sense."

Regan dropped her hand back onto the table. "It did?"

Ky nodded. "I had you locked away tightly in a cabinet too."

"Wow. The next time someone plans to develop a hermetic seal for a spaceship or something, they should hire us. Considering that neither of us had the slightest idea, we seem to be quite good at it."

Ky smoothed her finger over her eyebrow. "Maybe they should hire only you. My seal would have made the entire ship explode at launch."

"You mean…you knew?"

Ky's cheeks burned. "Back in high school, I had a pretty big crush on you. God, I lived for those moments when you hugged me or held my hand, and I could never quite make up my mind whether our sleepovers were heaven or hell."

It was the first time since her teen years that she let herself remember those feelings, and they rushed over her with an intensity that made it hard to breathe.

"I…I don't know what to say." Regan shook her head as if wanting to get rid of molasses that suddenly filled her brain. "I really had no idea. Why didn't you ever say anything?"

"And risk losing you? No. I was convinced you were straight. By the time you brought home Melissa and I realized you weren't, everything had changed, so I stuffed my feelings into a box and convinced myself I'd outgrown my crush."

Regan reached across the table and took Ky's hand. "Not everything changed. Your dad going to prison, you moving away…none of that could change our bond."

Ky clasped their fingers in a tight grip. "It changed me. I didn't think I was great relationship material, and you deserve only the best."

Regan squeezed so hard it almost hurt. "You *are* the best, Kylie."

It had been years since Regan had used her full first name. It felt as if Regan was clutching her heart, not just her hand. "I'm not sure I'll ever see myself the way you do, but I'm starting to think that maybe I can be the best person *for you*."

"You are," Regan said without the faintest trace of hesitation. "No more doubts, okay? And no more airtight containers…unless there are cookies inside."

Ky burst out laughing, and the last bit of tension fled from her shoulders. God, Regan was so good at that! She was definitely the best person for Ky. "I'll drink to that."

They clinked glasses and looked into each other's eyes while sipping their lemonade.

Finally, Regan put her glass down and picked up her fork. "Now let's finish our food so I can indulge in another advantage of dating my best friend."

"Getting rid of the dressy clothes after dinner?" Ky asked with a grin.

"I thought you wanted to go slow? But, hey, if you want to get naked, I'm not stopping you." A mischievous curl of Regan's lips indicated that she was teasing, but the hint of desire in her eyes still made Ky tingle all over.

"Jeez! I was talking about getting rid of the dressy clothes to put on sweats!"

"I like that option too, but I actually meant licking the plate."

At the thought of Regan's tongue slowly trailing up and down the porcelain, a wave of heat engulfed Ky's entire body. She tugged on the collar of her shirt to fan herself. While they were still as comfortable around each other as before, some things had changed. Plate licking would never be the same again.

"If we keep this up," Regan breathlessly whispered against Ky's lips, "I'll develop a fetish for your front door."

Ky let out a hoarse chuckle and pulled back a few inches. "I was thinking of giving it a new coat of paint, but I think I'll keep it." She leaned one shoulder against the red-painted wood as if her knees had gone as weak as Regan's.

"Your landlord wouldn't allow it anyway—and neither would your girlfriend." Calling herself that still gave Regan a rush.

Ky's broad grin revealed that she felt the same. "I accept bribes."

"You want bribes? I already made you dinner."

"Yeah, but there wasn't any dessert."

Regan lightly tapped Ky's nose, then couldn't resist trailing her fingers over her cheek, the corner of her mouth, and the dip below her bottom lip. "You didn't want dessert, remember?"

"When did I say—oh. I said I didn't want dessert *yet*. Big difference."

"True." Regan smoothed her hand over Ky's collar to straighten it. Strange how she'd never consciously thought about Ky like that—and now couldn't stop thinking about it or touching her.

Ky sighed. "I should go in. It's getting late, and Lilia is probably pressing her nose against the window, watching us."

Regan playfully rolled her eyes. "She really needs a boyfriend…or girlfriend."

"We're not going to turn into two of those annoying people who are always trying to set up all their friends, now that we're together, are we?" Ky asked.

"Not planning on it. But you have to admit our annoying friends were right about us."

"I'd like to think we would have figured it out on our own eventually, but if I'm honest…yeah, I probably wouldn't have. I've gotten better at putting the lid on that hermetically sealed box over the years."

Regan hummed in agreement. "You have. Never in a million years would I have guessed that you ever saw me as anything but your best friend or maybe an adopted sister that you have to get out of trouble every now and then."

Ky firmly shook her head. "You were always family to me, but never like a sister."

"That describes it perfectly for me too." Regan shifted her car keys to the other hand. "Okay, I'll leave now."

"You've said that three or four times already." Amusement colored Ky's tone.

"You also said you really should get inside a few times before," Regan shot back.

Ky laughed. "Okay, okay. One last kiss, then we part ways."

"That was what stopped us from actually going the last six times."

"So you don't want me to kiss you?" Ky asked with a teasing grin.

"No." Regan leaned up and slid her free hand around Ky's neck. "Because I want to be the one kissing you." And then she did.

Maybe there really was something about that front door…or more likely it was its owner. This time, their kiss heated up within a second.

Ky's mouth molded to hers with the same perfection the rest of their bodies did. The velvety slide of her tongue made Regan clutch her shoulder.

Ky splayed both hands across the small of Regan's back, as if caught between the attempt to rein herself in and the urge to pull her closer.

Finally, the lights of a car that pulled into the parking lot broke them apart.

Regan blinked her eyes into focus and licked her tingling lips. They really had blown the lids off those airtight containers for good. On legs that felt wobbly, she took a step back. "Good night," she got out.

"Oh yeah." Ky cleared her throat. "Um, I mean, night, Regan. Sweet dreams."

When Regan slid into the driver's seat, a metallic jangle from the direction of the front door revealed that Ky had dropped her keys.

Regan smiled all the way home.

Half an hour later, as Regan crawled into bed, not sure if she would be able to sleep, her phone buzzed with a text.

She reached for it and wasn't surprised to find a message from Ky.

*How was your date?*

Um, Ky had been there for it all, from the first, slightly shy hello to the mind-blowing kiss good night. Why did she—?

Then realization hit her. It was the kind of text they had always sent each other whenever one of them had been on a date with someone else. Since they still hadn't told anyone but her parents and Ky's roommate about them, Ky was slipping into her best-friend role so Regan would have someone to talk to about their date!

Regan clutched the phone to her chest. Ky was so cute, it was killing her. Quickly, she lifted the phone to eye level and typed back.

*Promising. Very, very promising.*

*Good,* Ky replied. *So I don't have to kick your date's butt all over Portland?*

A giggle escaped Regan. *Now that could be interesting. But no, no butt-kicking required. What about you? How was your date?*

Ky took a while to reply, as if she had to search for the right words. *It was a clear 100 on the pH scale.*

Just when Regan had thought Ky couldn't get any cuter. Grinning, she typed back, *The pH scale only goes to 14.*

*It was a 14, then.*

Regan laughed out loud. *That's about the pH of drain cleaner. Are you comparing our date to drain cleaner?*

*Our date? I'm talking to Friend Regan right now.*

*Right. So, your date with Drain-Cleaner Woman was everything you could ask for?*

*It was the best date of my life,* Ky replied. *She even cooked!*

*Wow,* Regan typed back, thumbs flying across the small screen while she grinned widely. *She really must be head over heels in love with you.*

Then she froze. Shit, shit, shit. She hadn't meant to tell her. Not yet. Not via text. And especially not after Ky had requested they take things slow so they wouldn't get overwhelmed and mess things up.

Ky didn't answer for what seemed like an eon.

Shit! Should she try to laugh it off?

No. Ky had climbed up the ladder to the tree house even though she'd been scared. Now it was her turn to be brave. *Can I call you?* she typed with trembling fingers. *I mean, can Girlfriend Regan call you?*

*Of course she can,* Ky replied. *You can.*

Heart pounding wildly, Regan tapped on Ky's name at the top of her favorites list.

The phone rang for only a second.

"Hi," Ky said quietly. "Don't worry. I know you were just kidding around."

Regan swallowed against her tight throat. Ky was giving her an out, but she realized she didn't want it. "Actually…I wasn't. I mean, I was teasing, but I meant what I said. I didn't plan for it to come out that way, and I know you said you want to go slow, and it's totally all right if you aren't ready to hear it or say it, especially not on the phone and—"

"Regan, breathe."

She sucked in some much-needed air. "Sorry," she said, not even sure what she was apologizing for—tossing around the word *love* so soon or nearly passing out from rambling.

"No. Don't be sorry. I'm not."

Regan paused. "You're not?"

"No. Last Sunday, when I slept over and woke up holding you…" Ky drew an audible breath. "That's when I realized that I'm in love with you.

I've always loved you, but I never let myself comprehend how deep my feelings go."

The bedroom blurred before Regan's eyes as tears welled up. She had sensed it in every touch, every kiss, every baked good Ky had left on her desk this week. But hearing it made her heart thrum with joy. "I'm in love with you too."

Ky let out a long groan. "God, why didn't I stay over? You have no idea how much I want to hold you right now."

"I think I have a pretty good idea." Regan's voice shook with laughter and an overload of emotion. "Do you want me to come get you?"

"No," Ky said. Then, after a moment, she repeated, "No," as if talking herself out of it. "We said we'd take things slow."

"So far, we don't seem to be doing so well on that front, do we? We confessed our love after the very first date."

"Yeah, even if you count the dates our friends talked us into, that would be rushing things with anyone else," Ky said. "But it's different with us."

It was. Everything was different with Ky. "I know. I feel like our first date has spanned the past twenty-five years."

Ky laughed. "So when you puked on me because you had been—and I quote—conducting important scientific research on the flavors of different-colored M&Ms, that was really you asking me out?"

"Well, it worked, didn't it? I left quite the impression."

"That you did."

They chuckled together, then silence filled the connection for a few seconds.

"Ky?" Her voice came out breathless and with a bit of a quiver.

"Yes?"

"Would you sleep with me?"

Muffled noises drifted through the phone, as if it had slid from Ky's grasp and she was now fumbling for it.

Regan flopped onto her belly and buried her burning face against her pillow. "Uh, I didn't mean it the way it sounded. I meant will you stay on the phone with me while I fall asleep? I'm tired, but I don't want to end the call and miss a second with you."

"Aww. Of course I will. Want me to sing you a lullaby?" Humor entered Ky's tone.

Regan loved that their teasing banter hadn't disappeared from their interaction now that more tender emotions were involved. "No, thanks. I've heard you sing." They both laughed, then Regan turned off the light. "Just keep talking to me."

"Anything in particular you want me to say?"

In the darkness of her bedroom, Ky's voice sounded even more intimate, making Regan shiver. She wrapped her free arm around the pillow and pretended she was holding Ky. "Tell me you love me."

"I love you."

It wasn't the words alone; it was the way Ky said them—all soft and melting, as if the emotions were flowing out of her.

"I love you too," Regan whispered and realized she'd used the same tone.

It took her quite some time—and several more "I love yous"—to fall asleep, but she had never looked forward to waking up in the morning so much before. She couldn't wait to see Ky again and to tell her in person.

# Chapter 15

Early the next evening, Ky whistled a song as she tied her sneakers and got ready for Regan to pick her up.

"Jenna Blake?" Lilia asked as she passed her in the short hallway between their rooms. "I guess seeing her in concert turned you into a fan."

Ky shrugged and suppressed a grin. "She's growing on me."

"And since when are you the whistling type? Let me guess. You're heading over to Regan's for—"

"For our Netflix night," Ky finished the sentence before her roommate could imply something else.

"Ooh, Netflix and chill!"

Ky growled.

"No? Then maybe IMAX and cli—"

Ky pulled off the sneaker she'd just put on and threw it at her.

It bounced off the wall next to Lilia, who ducked and laughed.

"And to think I recommended you for the assistant cafeteria manager position," Ky muttered. Then she froze. Damn. She hadn't meant to let that slip, in case Fran would ignore her suggestion.

Lilia stopped laughing. "You recommended me? I thought it was Fran's idea."

"Oh, so she asked you?"

"Yeah, yesterday, when we were cleaning up."

"So, what did you say?" Ky asked. "Are you going to take the job if they offer it to you?"

"Only if you're sure you don't want it."

Ky firmly shook her head. "It's all yours."

Lilia did a victory dance. "I'm gonna be your boss! But don't worry; I'll be the best boss ever. I'll even put you on breakfast cart duty in the science wing every day so you can see your girlfriend." She teasingly drew out the last word as if expecting her to object to it—but Ky didn't.

A key rattled in the front door.

Wearing only one shoe, Ky padded to the wide archway connecting the hallway in front of their rooms with the living room and stuck her head out so she could see the entrance.

"Ky? Lil?" Regan called as she entered.

After last night, seeing her felt different. So far, being around Regan had always felt as if life was an inside joke that only she and Regan shared. Now life seemed like something precious, to be nurtured in their clasped hands.

Even though it hadn't even been twenty-four hours since Ky had seen her…kissed her, she drank her in as if they'd been apart for weeks.

Regan looked breathtaking in her favorite pair of blue jeans and her T-shirt with the *We've got great chemistry* slogan.

Ky smiled. *Yes, we do.* After years of denying it, it felt freeing to finally admit it. She walked over to kiss her hello. That she was allowed to do so still made her heart pound with joy. "Hey, you're early." She brushed her lips against Regan's, then lingered for a moment. God, she smelled good, like apricot and some kind of lotion. "And you used your key! You haven't done that in a while."

Regan jiggled her key ring. "It didn't feel right to let myself in when I picked you up for a date. But I figured after last night, we're not just dating anymore so…"

"Ooh, what happened last night?" Lilia asked as she joined them in the living room with Ky's sneaker.

Ky snatched it out of her hands and whacked her shoulder with it before putting it on. "None of your business." The first time they had said "I love you" was too private to share, even with someone she considered a friend.

Once they had waved goodbye to Lilia and had gotten in the car, Regan reached across the middle console and took Ky's hand. "Thank you for last night."

"No, thank *you*—for having the courage to say it."

"Say what?" Regan gave her a blank stare.

Ky stared back. What on earth...? Then she caught on and couldn't help smiling. "Ah. You just want to hear me say it again."

The corners of Regan's mouth curled into an impish grin. "I really wouldn't mind."

Ky pulled Regan closer by their joined hands. "I love you."

A soft light shone in Regan's dark eyes. "I love you too."

Their lips met for a quick kiss, which then turned into a not-so-quick kiss.

Finally, Regan pulled back with obvious reluctance. "We'd better get going before they burn our pizza. I called the Pizza Lounge before I came over."

Unless Ky cooked or Regan made sandwiches, that was their usual routine for Netflix night, but Ky hadn't been sure if that was what Regan had planned for tonight. *What else? It's just Netflix. Not Netflix and chill.*

That thought should have been comforting—after all, she was the one who had requested going slow. But now Ky found that she was actually a little disappointed. She laughed at herself.

"What?" Regan asked as she started the car.

"Uh, nothing."

An hour later, they sat on Regan's couch, the empty pizza box discarded on the floor because they needed the space on the coffee table for the motivational posters they were making for Regan's students.

They had broken with tradition and were watching *Central Precinct* instead of *Rizzoli and Isles*—a show in which the hot female detective and the cute medical examiner actually got together.

Ky smiled. Interesting how their choice of TV shows reflected their lives. She definitely looked at Regan the way the detective looked at the medical examiner—especially because Regan's T-shirt was a little too big and too loose at the neck, so it kept sliding off one shoulder, revealing smooth skin.

Not that their choice of shows mattered. Ky barely paid it any attention since she was busy watching Regan.

Muttering something, Regan clamped the pen she'd been using between her teeth so she could push the shirt back up.

Ky pointed at Regan's poster. "Is that supposed to rhyme, like the others?"

"Of course," Regan mumbled around the pen.

"Um, I don't know how to tell you this, but *breath* and *best* don't rhyme."

Regan took the pen from her mouth and poked Ky with its end. "But they sound very poetic. And motivational."

"Oh, they do?"

"Very." Regan's husky voice made Ky's pulse speed up. "Want me to demonstrate?"

The air between them seemed to hum with electricity.

Ky's mouth went dry, so she just nodded.

Regan dropped her pen onto the coffee table, took Ky's from her hand, and put both of their posters safely out of the way. Like a lithe panther, she crawled toward Ky, then knelt next to her and steadied herself with one hand on Ky's jean-clad thigh.

Heat swept up Ky's body.

"These very poetic words can be used to form a sentence like…" Regan leaned down and lowered her voice to a sensual whisper. "Regan leaves Ky breathless because she totally kisses the best."

Breathless indeed. Ky could barely think, much less breathe. "You're right," she got out. "That's very motivational. But the only thing it motivates me to do is this." She cradled Regan's face in both hands and guided her down until their lips met.

Regan's moan reverberated against Ky's lips. Eagerly, she deepened the kiss.

Their tongues touched and tasted, circled and stroked.

Regan dug her hand into Ky's thigh as if struggling to stay upright, then slid her leg across Ky's lap and straddled her without breaking the kiss.

*Oh God!* Fire leaped through Ky. She clutched Regan's hips with both hands.

Something urgent flared to life between them.

The back-and-forth of lips and tongues grew more demanding with every pass.

Regan fisted Ky's shirt, then tugged it out of her jeans and slipped her hands beneath.

The slide of her fingers up her bare sides made Ky gasp.

Regan pressed closer, softly rocking against her. As she trailed her fingers back down, she grazed the outer curve of Ky's breasts.

A current skittered through Ky's body.

Then, on the next stroke up, Regan paused and cupped one breast through her bra.

Ky felt as if she would come undone right then and there. She arched against Regan and dug her fingers into her tight butt to pull her closer.

Regan made a little sound in the back of her throat, jolting Ky's senses.

Holy shit! This was possibly the hottest moment of her life—and it was happening with Regan!

Gasping, Ky tore her lips away.

Regan stared down at her with a hunger Ky had never expected to see in her eyes. Then Regan blinked, and her pupils widened even more in what looked like a mix of shock and desire. "Oh God. I'm touching your breast." She pulled her hands out from beneath Ky's shirt and looked at one of them as if she barely recognized it as her own.

The almost comical look on her face made Ky laugh, finally breaking her tension.

Regan stared for a few seconds longer, then her booming laughter vibrated through Ky. She slumped forward and rested her forehead against Ky's shoulder.

The intimate press of her thighs against Ky's hips sent a renewed wave of heat through Ky. "God, what you are doing to me. And, to be honest, the fact that this is you doing this to me is freaking me out a little."

"Me too," Regan whispered against her shoulder. Her warm breath grazed Ky's neck, raising a trail of goose bumps. "My mind is kinda caught between 'What the hell are we doing?' and 'Why aren't we doing more of it?'"

"Which one is winning?"

Regan kissed a sensitive spot beneath Ky's ear. "What do you think?"

"I think…" Ky shivered beneath Regan's lips. She slid her fingers into Regan's curly hair, caressed her for a moment, then gently pulled Regan's mouth away from her skin so she could think. This was a big step for them, and she wanted to take it fully conscious of what it meant, not in a daze of desire. She looked into Regan's eyes and said, "I think I'd like it to be the 'doing more of it.' But not here. Take me to bed."

Regan's sharp inhale echoed through the room. She touched her fingertips to Ky's cheek. "Are you sure?"

"You've always been the one sure thing in my life, and while a lot between us has changed, that hasn't." Ky caressed the small of Regan's back. "I want this with you. I want you."

With a low moan, Regan pressed her lips to Ky's once more, then slid off her lap and held out her hand.

Ky's body instantly protested the loss of contact so she locked their fingers together and followed her on shaky legs.

Hand in hand, they stumbled to the bedroom.

A hazy fog filled Regan's mind as she stood next to her bed. Her body ached where she had straddled Ky and rocked against her. God, had she really just done that?

*Yes, and we're about to do so much more. This is happening. We're about to make love.*

She wanted that—wanted it desperately, but she wasn't sure where to start, afraid the wrong move or wrong word would break the mood. Earlier, on the couch, it had been easy because she hadn't been thinking, only feeling.

*Then do that again. Don't think. Feel.*

She grasped the hem of her T-shirt and peeked at Ky, who was fiddling with the hem of hers and peering at Regan.

Both laughed nervously.

The air in the bedroom seemed thick with a mix of nerves and desire.

Regan decided to take the initiative. Ky already knew what parts of her body she was self-conscious about, just as Regan knew Ky didn't like her own thighs, so Regan wasn't shy about baring herself to Ky. She was safe with Ky, and yet her hands shook as she stripped off her T-shirt and let it drop to the floor.

Her bra wasn't exactly sexy—just simple white cotton since she hadn't been prepared for this kind of sleepover—but it didn't matter. Not when Ky looked at her as if she wanted to worship every inch of her…if she found the courage to give in to that urge.

Regan unbuttoned her jeans and eased them down her hips and legs.

Ky stood very, very still, the hem of her shirt bunched in both fists, her gaze following the path of the jeans down.

When they pooled around Regan's ankles, she kicked them aside.

Her heart picked up its already rapid pace as Ky pulled up her own shirt, revealing inch after inch of smooth-looking skin.

With awe, Regan took in the sexy flare of Ky's broad hips, her slender waist, long, elegant torso, and strong shoulders. Of course, she had seen Ky half-naked before, but never when she'd been about to touch her.

Ky dropped the shirt and stood in front of Regan in just her jeans and a black bra that was as simple as Regan's. Her short hair was deliciously disheveled since she'd pulled the shirt over her head, making her bold features look softer.

Regan ached to touch her and had to remind herself it was all right to want that—and to do it. She bridged the remaining space between them and ran her fingertips along one bra strap, then down Ky's back until she reached the waistband of her pants. "I always thought you look great in jeans, but you look even better in *just* jeans."

Ky's lashes fluttered at that barely there touch. "It isn't just jeans yet," she said, her voice hoarse.

"Mmm, right. Let's remedy that." Regan traced a path back up along Ky's spine until she reached the catch of her bra, where she paused and waited for Ky's nod of approval. When it came, she undid the hooks, taking the opportunity when she was already close to press her lips to Ky's collarbone, then trace the edge of her bra before placing a line of kisses up her neck.

A noticeable shudder went through Ky. She wrapped her arms around Regan and brought their bodies together. Their nearly bare chests pressed against each other, with Regan's bra-clad breasts nestled beneath Ky's, instantly generating heat.

A low moan escaped Regan. Ky was doing a great job at helping her feel, not think. Regan couldn't get enough of having her this close. She touched her lips to the spot where Ky's pulse pounded urgently.

Groaning, Ky slid one hand into Regan's hair and gently pulled her head up until their mouths met.

Ky's bare skin on her own, her tongue against hers sent tiny electrical pulses through Regan's body. Finally, she couldn't stand it anymore. She had to feel all of her. She pulled back and slid the straps down Ky's shoulders.

The bra tumbled to the floor—along with her own.

Apparently, Ky had somehow managed to open her bra without Regan noticing.

Regan grinned at her. "And here I thought I knew all of your skills." Then she stopped joking and took her in: the line where the lightly tanned skin of Ky's upper chest met the creamy swell of her breasts; the pleasing curve; her pink nipples, lighter than her own.

She wanted to tell Ky that she *did* look even better in just her jeans, but her vocal cords didn't cooperate, allowing only a moan of appreciation, so she decided to show her instead. Slowly, she cupped one breast in her palm.

For a second, it felt surreal to touch Ky like this, but it also felt so very right, and as she stroked its outer curve with her thumb, drawing a gasp from Ky, that surreal feeling faded away and left only passion behind.

When Regan's thumb grazed her nipple, Ky let out a tortured groan. She slid her hands down Regan's bare back, grasped her hips, and kissed her, deep and demanding.

Regan's head spun as Ky directed her backward, onto the bed. She moved to the middle and waited for Ky to follow her down, but instead, Ky braced herself on one knee and studied her. Her eyes looked gray now, with sparks of greenish amber, as if they were smoldering.

Their entire lives, Regan had always taken the lead in all their adventures, and this role reversal was unexpected—and totally hot.

Too hot for Regan to wait. She hooked her fingers through the belt loops of Ky's jeans and tugged her down.

Still in her jeans, Ky covered Regan with her body, perfectly evening out their height difference.

A shiver went through Regan as Ky settled in the V of her thighs. The skin-on-skin contact, Ky's gentle weight on top of her, and the light pressure of Ky's pelvis against her center left Regan flushed.

Ky braced herself on her elbows and tenderly kissed the racing pulse in Regan's neck, then followed the path of Regan's freckles across her shoulders and down one arm.

Ky's lips found the inside of Regan's forearm. Wow. When had that spot become an erogenous zone? Regan shivered and clutched her closer.

With leisurely caresses that made Regan quiver and sigh, Ky explored her body. She kissed a mole on Regan's arm, then the scar on her elbow from when Regan had fallen off her bike as a kid. With her hands and lips, Ky charted a blazing path down her body, pausing at each and every little mark to lavish attention on it.

Finally, she trailed her tongue over the first of the three tiny appendix scars, this one barely visible on Regan's upper belly.

A gasp escaped Regan. She buried her finger in Ky's silky hair and squirmed against her as Ky's lips moved lower.

Ky trailed a line of licks down Regan's belly, then kissed the edge of the second scar, hidden in Regan's belly button, before moving on.

The slow glide of her mouth across her skin sent Regan's senses reeling. It took her dazed brain a few moments to grasp where Ky was heading: to the third tiny appendix scar, right beneath the edge of her panties.

Desire crashed through her. She bucked against Ky and clutched at her head, not knowing if she wanted to push her down or pull her up. Ky already had her slick with need, and if she slid any farther down, she'd discover how wet the cotton between her legs was. Regan's cheeks burned.

Ky paused, her lips hovering over the edge of Regan's panties. She sent a questioning gaze up, into Regan's eyes.

The look on Ky's face, reverent and hungry, stilled the nervous flutter in Regan's belly. Ky wanted her, wanted this as much as she did.

Whatever Ky saw in Regan's own expression seemed to be encouragement enough for her to slide down the elastic and kiss the little scar. Her chin brushed Regan's damp curls, and her nostrils flared as she breathed in her scent.

Regan couldn't stand it any longer. She arched up her hips and shoved at her panties. "Off. Now. Yours too."

Ky slid them down Regan's hips and legs, then tossed them aside, followed by her own jeans and underwear.

Regan barely had time to take in her dark curls and curvy thighs before Ky was back on the bed. She slid her lips up one leg, to the roller-skating scar on Regan's knee.

*Oh God.* If Ky kissed a path up her thigh to where Regan needed her most, this would all be over in ten point two seconds, and Regan didn't want that. "Come up here."

Ky brushed openmouthed kisses across the top of Regan's thighs and over her hipbones, then moved up her body. Her hard nipples traced a path along Regan's skin, making Regan's breath hitch.

When their naked bodies finally came into full contact for the first time, they both moaned.

Regan felt as if she was catching on fire. She threaded her fingers through Ky's hair again and pulled her down.

As their lips met in a long kiss, their legs intertwined.

Regan gasped into her mouth and pressed her wetness against Ky.

Breathing heavily, Ky broke the kiss. Her arousal painted Regan's skin as she moved down, nipping and kissing Regan's throat, the hollow between her collarbones, and down the slope of one breast.

The first touch of Ky's tongue on her nipple sent Regan's brain into a tailspin.

Ky looked up, and the passion in her eyes made Regan as breathless as what she was doing with her tongue. Then Ky gently closed her lips around her nipple.

The pull of her mouth sent a jolt straight to Regan's core.

"God, Ky, you..." Regan's words were lost when Ky brought up her hand and started to caress the other breast at the same time.

She clutched Ky's head with both hands and writhed against her with no inhibitions, no insecurities. She wasn't embarrassed by the sounds that came from her throat. This was Ky. She was safe with her. "Ky. Please. I need you." It was too much and not enough at the same time.

Ky stroked her thumb across Regan's nipple one last time, then rolled to the side a little to give herself more access to Regan's body. Braced on one elbow, she slid her hand down Regan's quivering belly. Her palm was hot against Regan's skin as she caressed the sensitive spot at the bend of her leg.

Regan lightly scraped her nails down the back of Ky's neck.

A guttural groan escaped Ky.

Apparently, she liked that. Regan tried to file it away, but then Ky trailed her fingertips down, through her damp curls, and between her thighs, and all thoughts fled.

Ky stroked her softly at first. Her mouth still hovered an inch above Regan's breast, and her rapid breath washed over Regan's nipple, adding to the sensations coursing through her.

Regan's eyes, heavy with pleasure, fluttered shut. She slid her hands up and down Ky's back in a restless caress.

"Regan." Ky's voice was urgent with need. "Look at me."

When Regan opened her eyes and looked into Ky's, Ky trailed her fingers down and circled her entrance. "Do you—?"

"Yes. God, yes!" Regan arched up, into her touch.

Ky filled her, first with one finger, then two.

Pleasure jolted through Regan. A throaty sound, half cry, half moan, escaped her.

Ky stilled against her for a moment, a look of dazed awe on her face. She dug her teeth into her own bottom lip as if trying to restrain herself.

But Regan didn't want restraint. She canted her hips against Ky to press her deeper and urged Ky's mouth to hers.

They kissed with growing passion as they began to rock against each other. The way they moved together was intoxicating. Their bodies effortlessly found the perfect rhythm.

Finally, Regan had to break the kiss to draw a ragged breath.

Ky was panting too.

Regan saw every sensation, every emotion she experienced mirrored on Ky's flushed face.

A clenching sensation started low in Regan's belly. Her body tightened, strained against Ky's at a faster pace, which Ky immediately picked up.

Every clear thought disintegrated except for *yes*, *more,* and *faster!*

Her pleasure built and built, then, when Ky slid her thumb over her clit, it finally spiked. A kaleidoscope of colors burst behind her eyelids, and a scream slipped free.

She groaned Ky's name into her shoulder as she arched up one last time, then collapsed back onto the bed.

Ky stilled her fingers but placed light kisses on her shoulders, her breasts, her cheeks, her lips.

Slowly, the last delicious little shivers faded away, but Regan still couldn't form even a single word. She blinked until Ky's face swam into focus.

Ky stared down at her, pupils blown wide. "Regan," she whispered, her voice rough with awe and need.

The sound of her name had never made Regan feel so much.

Ky kissed the rim of her ear. "You okay?"

Regan shivered at the tickling breath. Her muscles felt sluggish, as if she'd spent an hour in a hot bubble bath, as she lifted her hand and trailed her fingertips through Ky's hair and down the nape of her neck. Finally, she rested her palm on her sweat-dampened back, keeping Ky close. "Mm-hmm. If I felt any better, I'd float away."

"Can't have that." Ky carefully withdrew her fingers, causing one last quiver, then eased one thigh between Regan's and pressed her hips against Regan as if anchoring her to the bed.

The slide of Ky's wetness against her skin made them both moan.

Ky's arm, which braced her weight half next to Regan, half on top of her, trembled.

A different kind of urgency swept through Regan, and she surged up to capture Ky's mouth in an intense kiss. When it ended, she whispered against Ky's lips: "Let's see if we can make *you* float." She hooked one leg over the back of Ky's, placed one hand on her shoulder, and tried to tip her onto her back with a tilt of her hips, even though Ky was taller and heavier.

Ky rolled with her, melting and eager beneath her hands.

With their legs still intertwined, Regan looked down at her. She had always thought of Ky as striking, but she'd never seen her as beautiful and vulnerable as this. Ky's heartbeat drummed against Regan's chest, echoed by the rapid rhythm of her own. She stroked Ky's overheated cheeks, caressed her strong chin and wide forehead with her fingertips, then traced the arc of one eyebrow. Gently, she touched her lips to the scar.

Ky gently nipped the sensitive skin of Regan's neck. "I don't have any other scars for you to kiss."

"Right. Hmm, that's a problem."

"Nah. You're a scientist. I'm sure you'll find a solution." Ky's words were light, but she peered at Regan through heavy-lidded eyes, as if the ability to banter was quickly slipping away from her.

"True. I'm always up for a little research. Let's see… Where else could I kiss you instead? Maybe here?" She kissed Ky's jaw, her throat, her collarbone. "Or here?" She trailed her lips down to the valley between her breasts, tasting her salty skin, then glanced back up.

"Anywhere you want." Raw need flashed across Ky's face. Need for her.

Regan gave up on her playful teasing and began to explore in earnest, using her hands, her mouth, her entire body to find every place that made Ky moan, every spot that made her tremble.

Goose bumps rippled across Ky's skin everywhere she touched. Her groans intensified as Regan ran her finger along the satiny skin right beneath one nipple.

Regan dipped her head, swirled her tongue around Ky's nipple, then grazed it with a light kiss. It instantly hardened as she took it into her mouth.

A low, desperate sound tore from Ky's throat. She tangled her fingers in Regan's hair.

Pleasure twisted down Regan's spine as if it were Ky's mouth on her, not the other way around. It was surprisingly arousing that she could undo Ky so easily. She cupped one hand around Ky's breast, holding it to her lips as she rolled her tongue over the tight nipple.

"Regan," Ky choked out. "Please." She put her hand on top of Regan's, laced her fingers though hers, and pressed their joined hands against her breast before sliding them down her body.

God. So sexy. Regan squeezed her legs together. Never before had she experienced so much pleasure from touching someone. She skated her fingertips along the long line of Ky's belly, then over the curve of her hip and, finally, to her inner thigh. The skin there was incredibly soft and already damp with arousal.

Ky's fingers clenched around her hand, then let go. Instead, she dug her fingers into the sheets, giving Regan full control.

The trust and open need in Ky's eyes made Regan's breath catch. She dipped her fingers lower, into Ky's wetness.

They both moaned at the contact.

Ky rocked her hips forward, pressed herself into Regan's hand. Her eyes went hazy, but she didn't look away.

Regan kept her gaze on Ky's face too as she moved her fingers, circling, then stroking in long swipes, learning what kind of touch Ky needed. "Like this?"

"Mm. Just...God...a little..."

"Here?"

"Yes!"

She was so attuned to Ky, she felt every shudder, every groan, every hitch of her breath. The sounds Ky made as she started to lose control were so incredibly hot.

Their breaths, fast and shallow, mingled as Ky arched up and captured her mouth in an urgent kiss.

Regan's own excitement built along with Ky's as she stroked her faster. She had to feel more of Ky, to claim her and give her as much as Ky had given her, so she slid one finger lower, into her heat.

Ky tore her mouth away and arched her head back against the pillow.

The sight of Ky stretched out beneath her, with passion-flushed cheeks, sent a thrill through her.

One of Ky's hands found Regan's free one and threaded their fingers together. She rocked against Regan.

"More?"

Ky made a sound that might have been a yes, but the pleading, desperate look in her eyes gave a more unmistakable answer.

When Ky rolled her hips against her once more, Regan slid into her with a second finger. She held eye contact as she drove her higher with deep strokes, following the rhythm Ky set, then pressed the heel of her palm against Ky's clit.

A tremor ran through Ky's thighs. Her body went taut beneath Regan, and her neck arched back.

Regan couldn't resist putting her mouth to her throat and gently rasping her teeth over the tender skin.

A long moan rose up Ky's chest, ending in a shout. "Regan!" She tightened around Regan's fingers.

Regan lifted her mouth away and watched her come. God, so beautiful.

With a breathy whisper of Regan's name, Ky finally stilled.

When Regan withdrew her fingers and settled next to her, Ky pulled her close.

Regan curled up in her arms and luxuriated in the feeling of Ky's sweat-dampened skin on her own. She kissed the spot between Ky's breasts, then laid her head onto her chest to listen to the thudding of her heart as it slowed. A peaceful feeling filled her. Every remaining doubt and fear had completely evaporated. This was where she belonged. This was what she and Ky were supposed to be.

Ky trailed one finger along her cheekbone and swiped a strand of hair behind Regan's ear with a tenderness that made Regan ache in a different way. "That was…"

Regan loved that breathless note in Ky's voice. She grinned at her. "The ultimate chemical reaction?"

A chuckle vibrated beneath Regan's ear. "Something like that." Ky peeked at her. "What? No smart-ass remark about how you scientists are always after repeating experiments to see if the result can be replicated?" She swept her fingertips down Regan's back, then ran her nails over her butt.

Regan shivered. New heat gathered deep inside of her. How could Ky have her so aroused again so soon, with only one touch? Forming words to banter back was already taking a lot of effort. "Personally, I'm not into replicating."

Ky rolled them over so she was on top. "No?" she asked, her lips only inches from Regan's. "Then I'll have to find another way to cause a combustion."

A hoarse laugh escaped Regan. "And here I thought you didn't pay attention in chem class."

"I paid attention to you." Tenderness and passion mingled in Ky's voice. "Let's see if I can apply what I learned…" She kissed, nibbled, and licked a path down Regan's body, not stopping until all thoughts of chemistry fled from Regan's mind.

# Chapter 16

Ky had woken up with Regan in her arms before, but never when they were naked. The feeling of Regan's soft skin against her own was the best thing she had experienced since…okay, since last night.

Or rather this morning.

They had made love until sometime after three, exploring each other's bodies over and over again. Ky hadn't been able to get enough of Regan, and Regan had been just as insatiable. It was fascinating getting to experience a whole new side of her.

Ky had marveled at each new discovery—what made Regan sigh with pleasure, what made her shout out her name, and what made her growl and take control, leaving Ky as weak with need as she left Regan.

In between rounds of lovemaking, they had bantered and teased as they had in the past, proving that this part of their relationship wasn't lost. Now their playful exchanges held a deeper meaning and were interspersed with whispered "I love yous."

It was everything Ky had ever wanted in a relationship and never thought she would have. After decades of assuming it was impossible and burying that yearning deep inside of her, she now had what she'd always longed for, and it was even better than she could have imagined. For the first time in fourteen years—or maybe for the first time in her life—everything was in perfect balance, exactly the way it was supposed to be.

She felt as if she could do anything she wanted to do, *be* who she wanted to be. At the moment, that was only one thing: the person Regan loved and who got to love her in return.

They were lying face-to-face, cuddled up, with Regan's head pillowed on Ky's arm. Her disheveled curls spilled across the pillow and Ky's skin, tickling softly. A golden stripe of sunlight fell through the blinds and across Regan's face. She looked so beautiful that Ky's breath caught.

Regan scrunched up her nose and stirred against her.

Ky's heart melted into a puddle at so much adorableness. Was that even a word? Well, it was now because it described Regan to perfection.

Regan's toes slid along Ky's leg as she stretched. She opened one eye and squinted at Ky, then closed it and buried her face against Ky's shoulder with a mewl of protest. "It's not morning yet," she mumbled against her skin.

Grumpy-in-the-morning Regan was the cutest thing ever. Ky had always thought so, but now she had a new way to help ease her into the day. She brushed Regan's tousled hair aside and kissed her neck.

Another mewl escaped Regan, but this one sounded a lot more sensual. She ran one hand up Ky's back and into her hair as she pressed into the touch.

Ky let her lips wander up her neck, along her jaw, across her chin, to her lips, where she paused, inches from Regan's mouth.

Both of Regan's eyes were now open, but still bleary with sleep.

Ky leaned forward to kiss her fully awake.

"Morning breath," Regan mumbled, one hand braced against Ky's chest.

"I couldn't care less." When Regan's arm lost its tension, Ky dipped her head and kissed her tenderly, but left it at a short, gentle caress of their lips, not yet sure what Regan would be comfortable with. She looked forward to finding out and learning all the new things about her.

When the kiss ended, Regan snuggled closer. When Ky rolled onto her back, she settled her head on Ky's shoulder and tucked one foot between her calves.

The intimate slide of skin on skin sent a tingle up Ky's legs and made her wonder what Regan thought of morning sex.

Before she could find out, Regan lifted her head and studied her with an expression so vulnerable that Ky's heart ached. "I'm so glad you're still here." Her voice was quiet, yet it still seemed to echo through the bedroom.

"Still here?" Ky repeated to give her brain time to understand. "Where else would I be?" If it were up to her, they would never leave this bed again.

Regan's fingers restlessly played across a sun-warmed stripe of golden light along Ky's upper chest. "Last week, you ran from this. From us. And just yesterday, you said you wanted to take things slow. I was fine with that, and I didn't mean to ambush or rush you in any way, but then you kissed me on the couch, and you were so damn sexy, and next thing I know…" She waved her hand back and forth between their naked bodies.

Ky soothingly trailed her hand down Regan's back and circled her delicate shoulder blades. "Hey, it's not like I wasn't a willing participant." Images from last night flashed through her mind. "A very, very willing participant."

"Yeah, I know." Regan's voice dipped low. She paused to clear her throat. "But in the heat of the moment, things often—"

"That wasn't it. I mean, yeah, there were plenty of heated moments last night, but I made a conscious decision not to let my fears stop me from being happy. Besides, sex…making love with you wasn't really what scared me. It was wanting more…and then losing it all."

Her explanation might have been confusing to anyone else, but Regan nodded. "The way your parents lost everything…you lost everything… because they kept wanting more." Her gaze seemed to reach deep within Ky and caress her battered heart.

"Yeah," Ky croaked out. Being understood on such a fundamental level was the most incredible experience of Ky's life, rivaling even their lovemaking. "Although…" She forced a grin to lighten the mood. "While I definitely wasn't scared of sex with you, knowing bits and pieces about what you and a certain ex of yours did in that hotel room in Florida…"

Regan groaned and hid her face against Ky's shoulder, then peeked at her. "That's the one disadvantage of starting a relationship with your best friend." She poked her playfully. "You know too much."

Ky firmly shook her head. "There's no such thing as knowing too much about you. But I admit that particular piece of knowledge did make me wonder how I'd compare."

Regan gave her an incredulous look. "You're kidding, right? There's no comparison."

"No?"

"No!" Regan indicated the two of them and the rumpled sheets. "This was a clear 100 on the pH scale."

"I have it on good authority that the pH scale only goes to 14."

Regan shrugged. "They should extend the scale. It was a 100 out of 14."

"So…I'm better than drain cleaner?"

Regan burst out laughing and stroked Ky's shoulder.

The sound warmed Ky almost as much as Regan's hand on her skin. "God, I love that sound." She touched her fingertip to the corner of Regan's mouth.

Regan kissed the pad of her finger. "And I love you."

"I love you too." Ky rolled them over so she was on top, eliciting simultaneous moans as her thigh slid between Regan's legs. She captured her mouth in a passionate kiss, morning breath be damned. "Let's see if we can extend that scale some more."

When Regan woke up for the second time, the sun had risen higher in the sky.

Ky was spooning her from behind, tenderly cradling Regan's breast in one palm while she slept. Regan's arm rested over Ky's to keep her hand in place. She stayed still, relished the feeling of Ky's bare skin against her own, and let the sense of peace and happiness fill her until she thought she might burst.

*Mmm, I could really come to love mornings.* Was it even still morning? She had no idea how late it had been when they had fallen asleep again.

Careful not to dislodge Ky's arm, Regan lifted her head and peered at the alarm clock on her bedside table.

Nearly eleven o'clock.

*Shit.* She had to wake Ky up because they were meeting their friends for lunch at The Observatory in an hour. Reluctantly, she turned in Ky's arms.

Ky cuddled closer, pressing her breasts against Regan's.

Arousal flared through Regan. She bit back a moan. That so wasn't motivating her to get out of bed. Would it be too conspicuous if both of them texted to say they couldn't make it to lunch?

"Ky?" Regan traced her fingertips up and down Ky's spine to wake her up as gently as she could.

"Again?" Ky mumbled sleepily.

A giggle rose up Regan's chest. One night and Ky already thought she was insatiable? Okay, maybe she was, at least where Ky was concerned. "Nope. I'm not waking you for that. But we have to get ready, or we'll be late for lunch with Eliza, Denny, and the others."

Ky opened her eyes and lifted her head off the pillow. Her bangs flopped forward, tickling Regan's nose. "Oh." She actually sounded disappointed.

Apparently, Regan wasn't the only insatiable one.

"How long do we have?" Ky asked, now fully awake.

"Not long enough for that. Unfortunately."

Ky chuckled. "That's not why I was asking. I just want to lie here with you for a few more minutes and bask."

The way she said it made Regan smile. "Bask?"

"Yeah. I..." Ky reached up and cradled Regan's face in one hand. She lightly traced the rim of Regan's ear with her index finger. "I'm happy, Regan. It might just be endorphins or some other chemistry thing, but...I'm so incredibly happy that it's almost unreal." Her eyes were alight with so much joy that Regan could barely believe she'd caused it.

Her own eyes filled with tears as her emotions spilled over. She pressed her hand over Ky's. "I'm incredibly happy too. You make me happy."

Their lips met in a tender kiss.

"And it's so much more than just a chemistry thing," Regan added in a whisper.

"More than chemistry?" Ky widened her eyes. "I never thought I'd hear you say that."

"I didn't either."

They kissed again, and this time, the kiss quickly heated up.

"Are you sure we don't have time?" Ky asked breathlessly.

"Yeah. It's eleven, and we really need to shower before we leave."

"Eleven?" Ky wasn't normally one to sleep that late. "How did that happen?"

Regan grinned. "I could explain...or show you, but that would make us late." She kissed her again and murmured against her lips, "Very, very late."

Ky let out a frustrated growl. "Damn. I'd like to pay for Eliza's and Denny's lunch to say thanks for driving me to Lake O last weekend, so I guess we have to show up." She slid out from under the covers and sat up, but Regan pulled her back, not ready to share her with anyone, even their friends.

"Basking," she said firmly. "Two minutes."

Ky sank against her with a happy sigh.

Despite their best intentions, basking had made them ten minutes late. Not that Ky cared. Their friends would probably assume Regan's infamous dislike of mornings was what had made them late.

All the parking spots in front of The Observatory were taken, so they had to park a few blocks away.

Hand in hand, they rushed down Stark Street.

As they approached the sidewalk tables, Regan pulled her to a sudden stop. "Wait!"

Ky sent her a questioning look. "Did you forget something?"

"Yes. We both did. Our friends don't know about us yet, and this"—Regan held up their joined hands—"is a dead giveaway."

"Oops." Ky stared down at their hands. Amazing how natural it felt already, as if it had never been any other way, yet it had been barely more than four weeks since they had first gone on a date to prove they didn't have any chemistry. "Should we just tell them?"

"Your call," Regan said.

Ky shook her head. "Our call. That's a decision we should make together. What do you think?"

"Hey, you two! Wait up," a familiar voice behind them interrupted before Regan could say anything.

They traded a long look, then squeezed each other's hand once before letting go. Their friends would have a heart attack if they walked up holding hands. They'd have to find the right moment to tell them.

When they turned, Denny and Eliza hurried toward them hand in hand.

*Damn.* The sight instantly made Ky regret letting go of Regan's.

Regan brushed the back of her fingers with her own as if sensing her thoughts. She flashed a grin at their friends. "And here I thought we were the only late ones."

A deep blush rose up Denny's neck. Her short hair was still damp. "Um, we…"

"…had a problem with the shower at our place," Eliza smoothly finished her sentence. She practically glowed at the *our place* statement, as if the newness of living together still hadn't worn off.

Regan laughed her booming laugh that made Ky grin reflexively. "Oh yeah, I can see that." She nodded at Denny's hair.

Eliza gave an unrepentant shrug and leaned into Denny. "So what made the two of you late? Can't be a shower problem."

A mischievous twinkle entered Regan's dark eyes. "Bask—"

Ky pinched her hip. "Oh, you know Regan. It's hard to get her out of bed in the morning."

"Me?" Regan pinched her back.

Heather stuck her head out of the restaurant. "Are we having lunch on the sidewalk?"

Together, they trooped inside, where Miranda was already waiting at their usual table.

Regan slid onto her favorite seat at the window, and Ky quickly sat next to her. Not that anyone else would have taken that spot anyway. It had always been hers.

The waitress took their drink orders. It was the blonde woman who had tried to slip Ky her phone number, and she avoided looking at Regan as she held out a stack of menus.

"I don't think we need them," Heather said. "We all know exactly what we want, right?"

Ky pressed her knee to Regan's and smiled. "I do."

"Me too." Regan swiped her thumb over Ky's hand beneath the table.

It took considerable self-control not to take Regan's hand, pull it to her lips, and kiss it. God, this pretending to have nothing but platonic feelings was harder than expected. How on earth had she done it for so many years? Now that she had experienced how wonderful it was to love Regan with everything she had, there was no going back.

"So everyone wants their usual?" The waitress looked at Ky. "The pulled-pork sandwich and… I'm sorry, I forgot what everyone else usually orders." A blush stained her fair cheeks as she peeked over at Regan. More quietly, she added, "And I'm also sorry about last time. I really had no idea the two of you…"

"It's okay." Regan's kind smile crinkled the skin around her eyes. "Neither did we."

"Oh," the waitress said, but Ky could tell that she didn't get it.

It didn't matter—as long as she got that Ky was with Regan and wasn't interested in anyone else.

Once the waitress had taken their orders and walked away, their friends gave each other puzzled looks.

"What was that all about?" Eliza waved her hand toward the waitress's retreating back. "And what did you mean by 'neither did we'?"

Ky looked at Regan. Not telling their friends right away was one thing, but actively lying about their relationship…

Regan nodded her agreement.

"Wait a min!" Wide-eyed, Heather stared back and forth between them. "You didn't mean…?"

Miranda leaned across the table as if afraid she would miss something. "What, what, what?"

"Turns out I didn't know as much about chemistry as I thought I did. At least not about the chemistry between Ky and me." Regan tangled her fingers with Ky's, lifted their joined hands to her lips, and kissed Ky's knuckles.

Silence settled over the group for a moment as everyone stared at them. Then they all shouted something at the same time, and chaos broke out.

"I knew it!"

"No chemistry, my ass!"

"It's about time!"

"You owe me fifty bucks!"

Then came the questions, but Ky didn't fully understand any of them because everyone was talking over each other.

"Settle down, everyone." Regan used her teacher voice on them, then pointed at Eliza as if calling on one of her students.

It worked. Everyone else fell quiet.

Ky gave her an impressed nod. If they ever had children, that voice would come in handy. Then Ky froze. *Whoa, kids? Slow down!* That was a topic for down the road. Way down the road.

"When…? How…?" was all Eliza got out, pulling Ky's attention back to the conversation.

"It's all Jenna Blake's fault," Ky said with a big grin.

Regan laughed. "That's not really how it all started."

"I know, but it made you laugh, and that's my favorite sound." *Well, except for the little gasp you make when I touch you. As if nothing has ever felt so good.*

Fire sparked in Regan's eyes, as if she knew exactly what Ky was thinking.

"Is that what we're in for now?" Heather asked. "Mutual adoration and lovesick looks?"

"Not that different from before," Miranda muttered.

"Um, Heather," Eliza said quietly. "We don't know that they're ready to call it love."

Heather's eyes widened. "Shit. You're right. I shouldn't jump to conclusions. So, you two… This isn't just a friends-with-benefits thing, right? I mean, I'm cool with it if it is, but—"

"No," Regan said firmly. "It's not. I know it's pretty fast, but…" She looked at Ky, who held her hand more tightly and finished the sentence with her. "…we're head over heels in love."

"Aww." Eliza sighed happily.

Heather snorted. "After twenty-something years, I wouldn't exactly call it fast. More like crawling to the finish line in reverse. But congratulations. What made you finally figure it out?"

"Actually…you did."

"Me?"

"Well, all of you. You just wouldn't stop with all these remarks about how perfect we would be for each other, and when we went on a date—or three—to prove that there was no chemistry between us, we started to see each other in a new light." Regan's words addressed their friends, but her gaze was on Ky.

"So it's been going on since last month?" Miranda asked. "Why didn't you tell us?"

"There wasn't anything to tell at first," Regan said. "At least that's what I had convinced myself of. I told myself it was only a fluke. Until I kissed her."

Denny lifted one hand. "Wait. *You* kissed *her*?"

"Oh, as if you got up the courage to kiss Eliza first," Ky muttered.

Miranda shook her head as if to clear it. "I feel like I've missed a few steps here. Tell us everything from the beginning."

Regan stole the pickle garnish from the plate the waitress slid in front of Ky. "Well," she said with a grin, "it all started with a family-size bag of M&Ms…"

# Chapter 17

Ky HAD SPENT MOST OF the following week fantasizing about Regan and their weekend plans, which involved only the two of them and Regan's queen-sized bed.

But then Regan's father had called, asking for help with the restaurant opening, and now they were on their way to the Vancouver Waterfront, where the second location was.

Ky tried hard not to be disappointed. *Come on. You love spending time with the Romanos.* Her pep talk was less than successful because right now, there was only one Romano she wanted to spend time with. *God, you're so smitten.*

Regan took the City Center exit and continued west. She glanced over at Ky for a moment. "I'm really sorry."

Ky reached across the middle console and slid one hand onto Regan's thigh, marveling at how good it felt to no longer have to restrict how often and how long she touched her. Finally, she could truly be herself, keeping no barriers between them at all. "Stop apologizing. It's not your fault Vanessa got sick on opening day."

"I know, but you work in a kitchen all week. You shouldn't have to fill in for my cousin on the weekend."

"Hey, your family is my family. That has always been true, and it's especially true now that we..."

"...are doing the no-pants dance?" Regan stopped at a red light and grinned at Ky, eyes twinkling.

"Admitted we're in love," Ky said.

The teasing expression on Regan's face transformed into a blissful smile. "Aww. As much as I love doing the no-pants dance with you, I think your version of the sentence is even better."

Ky couldn't resist leaning over the middle console to kiss her.

Before their lips could meet, loud honking from behind startled them apart.

"Oops." Regan tore her gaze away from Ky's and steered the car across the intersection and toward the waterfront. "You really don't mind helping out at the restaurant, do you?"

"Not at all. Cooking is fun, and getting to do it with you and your dad is even better."

Regan chuckled. "It's better for customer satisfaction if I'm not doing any cooking. I'm just along as your driver and fan club."

"That's what you think. I'm sure your sister will take advantage of her role as the restaurant's business manager to boss you around."

"True. She already threatened to put me to work as a bartender."

"Ah, mixing stuff together. That should be right up your alley."

"Yeah, it should be fun." Regan sighed.

Ky studied her. "That was not the fun kind of sigh. Um, I mean…"

"There are a dozen different replies running through my mind right now," Regan said, her voice low and sultry, "none of them safe to mention five minutes before we'll see my family, so I'll resist…for now."

Ky squirmed in the passenger seat. God, the things Regan could do to her with just a few words… She tried to direct her thoughts back to the topic at hand. "So why the unfun kind of sigh?"

"I'm looking forward to seeing my dad and Mac and the new location, but if I'm being totally honest…" Regan let go of the wheel with one hand to rub her cheek. Was she blushing? "I admit I was more looking forward to having you all to myself tonight." Her voice dipped to a husky tone that made Ky flush along with her.

She cleared her throat. "I have to confess I was really looking forward to that too."

"Good to know it's not just me. I was starting to feel a little silly."

"It's not silly, and it's definitely not just you; believe me." Now it was Ky's voice that became husky.

A visible shiver went through Regan. "We'll have fun helping out my family," she said loudly, as if trying to convince herself. "It shouldn't be this hard to keep our hands off each other for a few hours, right? I mean, we spent the past twenty-five years without constantly fighting the urge to rip each other's clothes off."

Ky shoved away the images flashing through her mind at Regan's words. "Yeah, but we were just kids for most of those years, and we didn't know the two of us would be…better than drain cleaner together."

Regan's contagious laughter filled the car.

Ky chuckled along with her and caressed Regan's leg with her thumb. "Seriously, it took me a moment to adjust to the change of plans, but I really don't mind helping out your family. It's only three more weeks until summer break, and then it'll be just the two of us."

"Us and Rizzoli and Isles, at least on Saturdays." Regan playfully wrinkled her nose. "Or would that be considered a double date?"

"I'd be willing to risk it," Ky said. "Because this time, I'll finally have the right woman as my date."

"Mm-hmm, me too." Regan made a left onto Grant Street and found a free space in the parking lot just a few steps from the restaurant. She turned off the engine, unbuckled her seat belt, and leaned across the middle console. "Now, where were we when that rude honking interrupted us?"

Ky lowered her mouth toward those tempting lips. "Here?" She placed a soft kiss on Regan's upper lip. "Or maybe here?" She gently nipped the bottom one. "Or—"

Regan surged forward, slid one hand into Ky's hair, and captured her lips in a demanding kiss that made Ky forget her teasing game.

She had no idea how much time had passed when they each finally sank back into their own seats, breathing hard.

"Wow," Ky whispered. "If that's my reward for helping out at a Romano restaurant, maybe I really should consider working for your dad."

Regan placed another kiss on her lips but kept it chaste. "Maybe you should." She opened the driver's side door without waiting for a reply. "Come on. Let's go rescue Dad and Mac."

Ky followed her and looked around. Her disappointment at not getting to spend the evening alone with Regan had distracted her from any nervousness, but one glance at the new restaurant brought it back in full force.

The floor-to-ceiling windows revealed a sleek, modern dining room with a long bar. One thing was the same as at La Casa Nostra: The pizza oven and the counter around it were clearly the focal points of the restaurant. Everyone's attention would be on the pizza chefs while they worked. Each misstep would be on display.

Sweat broke out along Ky's back. Was she ready for this?

As if sensing her thoughts, Regan paused a few steps from the front door and captured Ky's hand. "Before we go in, I have to tell you something."

Ky swallowed. Maybe she was worrying about the wrong thing. "You haven't told your sister about us yet, and you think she won't like it?"

"Are you kidding me? The entire family, including a few dozen distant cousins, knew within an hour of my parents finding out, and Mac was ecstatic."

"Phew. What is it, then?"

"Remember how we all tell my dad his pizza is the best every time we have it?"

Ky nodded. "Of course." Where was Regan going with this?

"Don't tell him, but that's actually a tiny bit of a lie. I mean, his pizza is great and all, but it's not my favorite."

The lightbulb came on. Ky couldn't help grinning. "You're seriously telling me you like my pizza better than your dad's?"

Regan affected a look of confusion. "Yours? No, I was talking about that frozen pizza I had for dinner yesterday." She trailed her thumb along Ky's wrist, setting off pleasant shivers. "Of course I meant yours. If there's one thing you don't have to worry about tonight, it's your pizza not measuring up."

"How do you know I'm worried?"

Regan gave her a tender smile. "Because I know you annoyingly well. Honestly, Ky, you've got no reason to worry. Your pizza will blow their socks off."

Ky lifted their joined hands to her lips and kissed Regan's knuckles. "Thank you."

They lowered their hands, but neither let go.

"Ready?" Regan asked.

Ky squared her shoulders and tightened her grasp on Regan's fingers. "Ready."

Cooking would probably never be Regan's thing, but she had missed spending time with her family and in a restaurant setting.

The hustle and bustle on a busy Saturday evening transported her back to her childhood—only now she had found a way to contribute.

Making cocktails was so much like mixing together the chemicals in an experiment that not wearing goggles, gloves, and a lab coat felt strange. She carefully measured lemon juice into a jigger, then poured it into a cocktail shaker filled with ice before adding rhubarb syrup, gin, and sherry.

The shaking was her favorite part—because it afforded her a full minute of staring over at Ky.

From her place behind the long bar, Regan had a perfect view of the counter and the pizza oven, where Ky was stretching the pizza dough and flipping it over until it had the perfect shape.

Most often, she and Ky timed it just right, and Regan started the shaking just as Ky slid the pizza into the oven.

Then they grinned at each other, and the bustling restaurant faded into the background as they held an entire conversation with only one look.

Other times, she watched Ky spoon tomato sauce onto the pizza, add fresh basil and mozzarella, and drizzle her creation with olive oil. Her cheeks were flushed from the heat of the oven, and she laughed at something Regan's dad said as they worked side by side.

Regan's heart expanded with joy. This was where Ky belonged. Well, not necessarily here, in Vancouver, but in a kitchen with fewer rules and regulations that constrained her creativity—preferably one where she got to work with family.

Mac cleared her throat next to Regan. "Hey, did you come here to help or to ogle your girlfriend?"

Regan flashed her an unrepentant grin. "Ogle my girlfriend." But she reluctantly looked away from Ky, poured the Rhubarb Fix through the strainer into a chilled cocktail glass, and slid it over to her sister.

Mac garnished the drink with a mint sprig and placed it on a waitress's tray. "I still can't believe I finally get to call Kylie that without running the risk of you throwing that drink in my face."

"Okay, okay, I admit you were right about us. But that doesn't make all that meddling any less annoying. It probably made me even more determined to keep Ky in that handy little friendship box."

"Yeah, you always were the stubborn one."

Regan rinsed the cocktail shaker and barely resisted the urge to flick some water at her. "Oh, while you are always perfectly reasonable."

"Of course," Mac answered with an almost straight face. "But seriously, I'm really happy for you two...even though seeing my baby sister have eye sex with her childhood friend will take some getting used to."

Regan's cheeks flamed. "We're not having"—she lowered her voice—"eye sex. I just love watching her cook."

Mac glanced toward the pizza oven too. "She looks right at home there, doesn't she? If Mom and Dad aren't careful, I'll steal her from under their noses and talk her into working for me and Vanessa. In fact, let me—"

When Mac tried to step out from behind the bar, Regan held on to her sleeve. "No."

Mac stared at her. "No? You don't want her to work for the family?"

"I want her to work *with* the family, and frankly, I'd rather she work in Lake O with Dad, taking some of the load off his shoulders, instead of working here. But it doesn't matter what I want. It needs to be Ky's decision. She needs to feel ready for it, and I'm not going to poke and prod her—and neither are you." Regan sent her sister a warning glare.

Mac smiled. "My baby sister in defensive girlfriend mode. Never thought I'd see the day."

"Hey, I was plenty defensive with Melissa, Justin, and Alex."

"Don't bother. You were never like this with any of them." With a wave of her hand, Mac walked away and tossed over her shoulder. "I like it."

Regan stared after her, then whispered to herself, "I really like it too."

It was long past midnight by the time the last guest left and they had cleaned the kitchen.

Once everything was squared away, they sat on the heated outdoor patio, their backs to the floor-to-ceiling windows of the restaurant so they could take in the view of the lights reflecting off the Columbia River.

Ky slid her chair closer to Regan's, tucked a blanket over their laps, and raised the tall glass with the cocktail Regan had made for her. "Congratulations, you two," she said to Joe and Mac. "I think the opening couldn't have gone any better."

Joe nodded. "In large part because of you. Thanks again for stepping in for Vanessa and saving the day."

"My pleasure," Ky said, meaning it. Her initial disappointment about not getting to spend the evening alone with Regan had quickly turned into the joy of being part of a team...part of a family.

Regan squeezed her leg under the blanket. The pride she radiated warmed Ky just as much as the heaters behind them.

They all clinked glasses.

Ky took a sip of her cocktail. A refreshing mix of sweetness and spice hit her taste buds. "Yum. What's this?"

"A Dark 'n' Stormy," Regan answered. "Just ginger beer, dark rum, and a little lime juice to balance it out."

Ky sipped again. Of course Regan had put her chemistry skills to good use to create the perfect mix of flavors. "It's amazing. You should hire on as a bartender."

Regan smiled and kissed her cheek. "No, thanks. I had fun, but I already have a job I love."

Could she say the same about herself? Ky was proud of her contribution toward feeding so many kids every day, but if she was honest, she didn't enjoy it the same way she had enjoyed helping out in the restaurant tonight.

Joe handled every ingredient he added to his dishes with a loving care that Ky rarely had time for in the cafeteria. He treated all members of his team, from the busboy to the waitresses, more like family than employees. And not once had he double-checked her work tonight. At first, she had wished he would since the quantities were very different from what she was used to.

But luckily, she had adapted much faster than she had expected, and now she could barely remember why she'd been so worried about not being able to keep up.

Ky let her gaze trail over the beautiful patio, with twinkling lights strung above them, then looked at Joe. "Could you have ever imagined this"—she waved her free hand—"when you first opened the little family restaurant you had when we were kids?"

Joe laughed. "Never. My father-in-law was sure I'd run it into the ground my first year." He took a swig of beer. "And he was right. I probably would have."

Ky gave him a puzzled look. "Why would you say that? The Lake O restaurant is a big success, and if tonight is any indication, this one will be too."

"Not because of me. I just bake the pizza."

"Just?" Ky, Regan, and Mac echoed.

Joe shrugged. "As much as it pains me to admit, pizza is a dime a dozen."

"Not good Neapolitan pizza baked to perfection in a wood oven," Regan said. In the dim light, her dark eyes held a passionate glint that made Ky smile.

Chuckling, Joe raised his beer bottle and toasted her. "Looks like I raised you well. Of course, great pizza is a must, but Tammy is the real secret to our success. I was a busboy when we met. She's the one who brought the money into our marriage—and the one with the business sense. She suggested moving us to Lake View Village just as it opened and switched us to using only regionally sourced produce long before it became a trend."

Regan's parents had always seemed like a team to Ky, and she had never stopped to ponder who contributed what. Maybe that was the true secret of the Romanos' success: they all contributed something, so no one had to be good at everything.

Could that work for her too? Maybe she could consider Joe's job offer and "just bake the pizza" too, while Tammy or Mac took care of the business side.

In the past, she would have shoved that thought away, afraid of letting herself dream, but now she allowed those images to take root. For the first time in her life, she was starting to allow herself to want more, not only in her private life but in her professional one too.

She wouldn't move to Lake Oswego without Regan, and it was much too soon in their relationship for a conversation like that, yet now that they were together as a couple, everything seemed possible for the future.

Joe's phone buzzed. He quickly picked up, as if he had been waiting for it. "Hi, love. Yeah, of course. Without a hitch. Give me a second, and I'll call you back from the car." He put his only half-empty beer down but kept his phone in his hand as he got up. "I'd better get myself home now. I want to hear how Tammy and the team managed without me."

He hugged first Mac, then Regan and Ky, and Ky's embrace lasted as long and was just as tight as the ones he gave his daughters. "Thanks again," he said quietly. "I'd love to have you join our team for good—or even just as a summer job for now. Think about it, okay?"

She swallowed down the lump in her throat and nodded.

Mac walked him out while Regan and Ky stayed back to finish their drinks.

Regan cuddled closer, warming her against the cool breeze from the river. They leaned their heads together and looked toward the illuminated triangle of Grant Street Pier, which jutted out over the water.

Without turning her head, Ky pointed behind them. "My dad now lives somewhere around here. Well, I don't actually know where he lives, but he works for a small nonprofit nearby."

Regan straightened and stared at her. "A nonprofit? Your dad?"

"Yeah. That was my reaction too. But apparently, he does."

"How do you know?"

Ky looked away. "I googled him last night. Sorry I didn't tell you. I wanted to but then forgot when your dad called and—"

"It's okay. I know you like to process stuff first before talking about it."

It was wonderful to be in a relationship where she didn't have to explain, because Regan already knew all her quirks and habits. Ky exhaled and rested her head against Regan's shoulder.

Regan smoothed her fingers over Ky's forehead as if trying to calm her turbulent thoughts. "Are you thinking about meeting with him?"

"I don't know." As Regan continued her soothing caresses, Ky's stomach stopped churning. "Maybe I should. I think I was a bit too hard on him the last time we talked on the phone." She looked out over the dark waters of the Columbia. "I basically accused him of making my mom kill herself. Not that he didn't contribute to it. He made a mistake. Lots of mistakes. But I don't think he wanted that to happen."

"No, of course he didn't." Regan slid her hand down to Ky's cheek and cupped it. "You know my offer still stands, right? To go with you should you decide to meet with him."

Ky leaned into her touch and closed her eyes for a moment. Regan wasn't just good at balancing the different flavors in a drink; she also provided the perfect balance for Ky's life. Never before had she felt so grounded or so loved. Maybe with Regan by her side, she was ready to take the risk and give him a second chance. "I think I will. But not right now. Maybe during summer break. For now, I'd like to focus on us."

"I'd like that too."

They shared a soft kiss that only ended when Mac cleared her throat from the open glass door. "Um, can I come back now?"

Ky laughed. "Get out here, you goof."

# Epilogue

**One year later**

"HEY, HON?" REGAN CALLED FROM their bedroom. "Could you come here for a second?"

Ky dropped her phone onto their brand-new couch and strode over to see what she could help her with. Tomorrow would be Regan's first day of teaching at her new school, and she was just as nervous as she was excited. The fact that she would be teaching at their old high school added to both the nervousness and the excitement.

"That was fast," Regan said as Ky walked through the doorway. Her eyes sparkled in the sunlight filtering in through the window. "Is it just me, or do you always react way faster when I'm calling you from the bedroom, compared to any other room?"

"Hmm, I really didn't notice. Maybe it's the kind of motivation that makes the difference. Some talented scientist should do a study on that."

"I think I know a scientist who'd be interested in that field of research, but first, she has to figure out another problem. Which one looks better? This?" Regan held up a wrap skirt and a white blouse. "Or that?" She pointed at a pair of linen pants and a light sweater on the bed.

Ky didn't even have to think about it. "Skirt and blouse."

Regan laughed—which still made Ky flush with pleasure. "How did I know you'd say that?"

"Because you know me annoyingly well." Ky walked over and kissed her, careful not to wrinkle the skirt and blouse in the process. "But seriously, you look incredibly sexy in either."

Regan eyed both outfits. "I wasn't going for sexy. I was going for professional yet fun teacher."

"I know. And you've achieved that too. The sexiness isn't about the clothes. It's about the woman wearing them."

This time, it was Regan who kissed her.

"But if you want to tone down the sexiness, I've got just the thing." Ky pulled open the drawer of her nightstand, where she had hid her first-day-of-school present. "I didn't have time to wrap it, but..." She spread the T-shirt out on her own chest so Regan could see it.

At the bottom of the shirt, a heart encircled two squares representing the elements uranium and iodine. The text above it said, *If I could rearrange the periodic table, I'd put U and I together.*

"Aww. That's really cute. *You're* really cute. Thank you." Regan kissed her again. "I actually got you a new T-shirt for your first day too." She put her outfit down on the bed and dug through her own nightstand.

When she returned, she held out a T-shirt that said, *Not all superheroes wear a cape. Some wear an apron and are hot pizza chefs.*

Ky trailed her fingers over the shirt. "I love it...but I'm not sure I should wear it tomorrow. After all, I'll be working for your parents, and I'm not sure they'll want to be reminded of how hot their daughter thinks I am every time they look at me."

Regan firmly shook her head. "You're not working *for* them. You're working *with* them. If they get their wish, they'll retire in a couple of years, and you'll take over."

"They keep saying that, but..."

"What?" Regan put her hand on Ky's chest as if trying to feel her heartbeat. "You're not still convinced you aren't good enough or shouldn't strive for more, are you?"

"No, that's not it." It had been months since she had last thought about herself that way. "It's not like I'd take over anytime soon, so I could learn whatever I don't already know, as long as your sister deals with the paperwork for both restaurants."

"But?" Regan prompted.

"I'm not sure I want to be the boss just because I...um..."

"Have mind-blowing sex with the bosses' daughter on a regular basis?"

"Uh, not exactly how I would have phrased it, but...yeah."

Regan took the T-shirt from her and tossed both of them on the growing pile of clothes on the bed. Then she took Ky's hands. "That's not the reason they want you to run the restaurant. My parents have wanted you to take over ever since you made your first pizza."

Ky couldn't help staring. "I wasn't even ten when your dad taught me!"

"Exactly. Way before he had any idea that you might one day be his daughter-in-law. They want you to take over because you make damn good pizza…and because you're family. Always have been. Always will be." Regan lifted Ky's hands to her lips and kissed her knuckles. "Even if you and your father never fully mend your relationship, despite the baby steps you've been taking, you'll always have a family, okay?"

"Okay," Ky answered around the lump in her throat. Then she mentally played back Regan's words. "Wait! Did you just say…daughter-in-law?"

Regan went wide-eyed. "Uh…yes? I mean, I don't expect either of us to get down on one knee and propose anytime soon, but eventually…yeah, that's what I want. There's not a single doubt in my mind that you're the right person for me."

Ky blinked against tears of happiness that blurred her vision. "Always have been, always will be?"

"Yes," Regan answered softly. "Even when we were deeply in denial, it was always you for me. So? What do you say?"

"I thought you weren't proposing?"

"I'm not. Not yet. But—"

Ky tackled her to the bed and captured her mouth in a deep kiss. "Does that answer your question?" she asked breathlessly.

Giddy laughter shook Regan's short frame. "Well, it answers the question who'll dig through the remainder of the moving boxes for the iron." She gestured at the outfits that had gotten trapped beneath their intertwined bodies.

"I'm not getting the iron out because of a wrinkle or two. Now, if your blouse and the skirt were wrinkled all over…" Ky grinned down at her, their lips only an inch apart. "Can you think of anything that would make that happen?"

"Hmm. That's a question that might need more research too. Including extensive experiments to control all other factors that might have caused the wrinkling." Regan rocked her hips up into Ky, and her voice went hoarse. "Very, very extensive experiments."

"Fine with me," Ky gasped out. After all, it had been a little chemistry experiment that had gotten them here.

If you enjoyed this book and want to find out more about Regan and Ky's friends, check out Jae's romance novel *Wrong Number, Right Woman*, the book in which Eliza and Denny meet and fall in love.

Denny, a shy butch who helps raise her niece, gets a wrong-number text from a stranger named Eliza. There's an instant connection, but Eliza is straight…or isn't she?

# Other Books from Ylva Publishing

www.ylva-publishing.com

## *Wrong Number, Right Woman*

**Jae**

ISBN: 978-3-96324-401-8
Length: 370 pages (116,000 words)

Shy Denny has a simple life as a cashier who helps raise her niece. Then she gets a wrong-number text from a stranger named Eliza, asking her for dating advice.

Eliza, the queen of disastrous first dates, finds an instant connection with Denny that makes her question everything…like just how straight she really is.

A slow-burn lesbian romance with likable characters and low angst.

## *Never Say Never*

**Rachael Sommers**

ISBN: 978-3-96324-429-2
Length: 220 pages (75,000 words)

Ambitious Camila might have lost her marriage but she doesn't need love to build a TV empire and raise her young son. What she does need is a nanny.

Enter Emily—bright, naive, and new to New York City. Emily is everything Camila is not and that's not all that's unsettling.

Surely she can't be falling for the nanny?

An age-gap, opposites-attract lesbian romance with a puddle of melted ice queen.

## *A Story of Now*
**Emily O'Beirne**

ISBN: 978-3-95533-345-4
Length: 367 pages (140,000 words)

Nineteen-year-old Claire knows she needs a life. And new friends. Too sassy for her own good, she doesn't make friends easily anymore. And she has no clue where to start on the whole life front. At first, Robbie and Mia seem the least likely people to help her find it. But in a turbulent time, Claire finds new friends, a new self, and, with the warm, brilliant Mia, a whole new set of feelings.

A young woman finds first love and finds herself in the city of Melbourne in this beautiful lesbian romance novel.

## *Food for Love*
**C. Fonseca**

ISBN: 978-3-96324-082-9
Length: 276 pages (96,000 words)

When injured elite cyclist Jess flies to Australia to sort her late brother's estate, the last thing she wants is his stake in a rural eatery. She'd rather settle up, move on, and sidestep the restaurant's beautiful owner, Lili, and her child. Given her traumatic life, Jess isn't sure she'd survive letting her guard down. A lesbian romance about how nourishment is much more than the food we eat.

A lesbian romance about how nourishment is so much more than the food we eat.

# About Jae

Jae grew up amidst the vineyards of southern Germany. She spent her childhood with her nose buried in a book, earning her the nickname "professor." The writing bug bit her at the age of eleven. Since 2006, she has been writing mostly in English.

She used to work as a psychologist but gave up her day job in December 2013 to become a full-time writer and a part-time editor. As far as she's concerned, it's the best job in the world.

When she's not writing, she likes to spend her time reading, indulging her ice cream and office supply addictions, and watching way too many crime shows.

**CONNECT WITH JAE**

Website: www.jae-fiction.com

E-Mail: jae@jae-fiction.com

*Chemistry Lessons*


ISBN: 978-3-96324-547-3

Available in e-book and paperback formats.

Published by Ylva Publishing, legal entity of Ylva Verlag, e.Kfr.

Ylva Verlag, e.Kfr.
Owner: Astrid Ohletz
Am Kirschgarten 2
65830 Kriftel
Germany

www.ylva-publishing.com

First edition: 2021



Credits
Edited by Helen de Beer
Cover Design and Print Layout by Streetlight Graphics

Printed in Great Britain
by Amazon